SNOWBOUND

ALSO BY HARLAN HAGUE

SNOWBOUND

HARLAN HAGUE

WOLFPACK
PUBLISHING
— EST 2013 —

Snowbound
Paperback Edition
Copyright © 2025 by Harlan Hague

Wolfpack Publishing
1707 E. Diana Street
Tampa, FL 33610

www.wolfpackpublishing.com

Paperback ISBN 979-8-89567-209-9
Ebook ISBN 979-8-89567-208-2
LCCN 2025938148

SNOWBOUND

CHAPTER 1

THE GATHERING

Stephany stood in the middle of the cabin sitting room, looking around. The room was most inviting, with a comfortable couch, cushions on the couch and others stacked on the floor in front of the stone fireplace, a stack of firewood in a wooden box alongside. Stephany had snacked for breakfast and built a fire. Now, gold and silver flames danced above the dry logs, crackling and popping. She looked over the dining table, set for seven. Smiling, she shivered. From excitement, not temperature.

She went to the front door, opened it, and walked out to the covered porch. Trees of the mixed cedar, oak, and pine forest towered above the cabin. The yard and gentle slope to the road were covered with dry leaves and needles. She always worried about the fire danger from the detritus but usually left it.

Pulling her coat tight, she shivered again, this time from the cold. November was usually mild, but a cold snap a few days ago dropped the temperature below freezing. A chance for snow was forecast, though when she checked in this morning at the resort in the valley below, the sun was bright and warm. She knew the weather could change quickly with little warning in California's high Sierra Nevada.

She drove from Berkeley yesterday and stayed the night at the resort. She knew the management from long association, so even when she decided spontaneously to drive up, they would find her a bed somewhere. She had a reservation this time. She had breakfast in the resort dining room this morning, then drove five miles up the steep, winding road through dense forest to her place. She didn't see a single vehicle on the drive. There were a few scattered cabins on the road, all holiday and getaway places, but no one seemed to be here at the moment. At least, there were no cars at the cabins.

Stephany owned her place, but there was a tenuous arrangement with the resort by which she was able to contract for road maintenance and security. They also held her mail for pickup, and she was able to buy groceries from the small store adjacent. The resort management, years ago, offered to run an electric wire to her cabin, but she declined. That is, David, her husband, declined since he decided their mountain retreat should be self-sufficient.

He had a water well sunk just behind the cabin, sending water to a tank in the attic. Solar panels on the roof and a wind generator on the knoll above the cabin charged batteries in the attic. He had half-seriously suggested an outhouse, but Stephany nixed that bright idea immediately. They had a local contractor construct a concrete septic tank that he said would not need servicing for a hundred years. He smiled when he said it.

They had not landscaped the property, leaving the five wooded acres exactly as they had been from the beginning, except for the rustic three-bedroom stone and log cabin, which was built from their design. They had expected to fill the bedrooms with children, but alas, they had been unlucky. The cabin was on a flat, but the land behind the cabin sloped up sharply. A trail led up to a viewpoint where one had a stunning view of the valley and resort below.

Stephany was devastated when David was killed in an auto accident less than a year after they built the cabin. She considered selling but decided to keep it for a time and think about it. Now, she wouldn't dream of selling it. It was her refuge, her quiet place, and she came up often. When she tired of the quiet, she worked longer hours on her current novel manuscript. More than one visitor was skeptical that the arrangement encouraged concentration. The placement of the computer at the large window gave her an unobstructed view of the lovely sky and scattered woods and the occasional deer or bear that wandered by. And there were no blinds to shut out the view.

Stephany walked back inside, closed the door slowly, stood just inside, pondering. Her guests would begin arriving any moment. They were scheduled to check in this morning at the resort below, drop a few things in their rooms, and drive up to the cabin. She had sent detailed instructions to each on how to navigate the narrow winding road through dense forest from the resort to her place. No internet access or GPS on this road. When you reach the end of the road, she told them, you have arrived. Park behind my car or anywhere on the road in front. She assured them they would not block traffic since the road ended at her place.

She smiled to herself. She had not seen these friends together since the seven graduated in the same class from UC Berkeley. Had it really been ten years? This bunch had been the best of friends, spending time together, sometimes including boyfriends or girlfriends, who came and went, but these seven remained constant.

Why had they drifted apart after university? Some went to graduate school, they moved, they married, unmarried, moved again, married again, moved again. They kept in touch by telephone, email, social media, infrequent visits, one or two at a time. But time and distance and other attractions and obligations interfered. They were all still in California but scattered from Los Angeles to the Oregon border. They were within a year or two of the same age; she was thirty-two. She wondered, staring at the fireplace, what their lives had been in the ten years since graduation.

At an unusually down moment last summer at her Berkeley flat, Stephany pondered. She had sent her latest novel manuscript to the publisher a month before and had endured agonizing hours, days, weeks since then, searching for a new storyline, and she still hadn't settled on a topic. She had no other obligations pending, and her mind began to wander, thinking back. Looking from her window across the rooftops to placid San Francisco Bay, she remembered the good times at university and the good friends.

What then? *Well, why not? I've seen one or two of them from time to time since then, but it's time to see them all again! All of them, together!* Before she was enveloped in a new novel, she would revisit good times with her good friends. She would invite them to gather at her mountain place. *Yes!* She went immediately to her computer to write to these six people who had meant so much to her, not so long ago.

She smiled, remembering that these friends called her Steph at Berkeley. Nobody else then or since had called her Steph, only her BFFs, her Best Friends Forever.

Maybe one of my BFFs will suggest a topic for my next book.

Stephany's reverie was broken by the sound of a car engine climbing the last hill below the cabin. She rushed outside, absentmindedly leaving the front door open. She stood on the porch for the next hour, wrapped up in the chill November day, waving to each arriving car. A couple of cars pulled into the yard behind her car, the others parking on the road in front. Steph stepped off the porch to the yard, where she shared in hugs and kisses and laughs with the others.

A man who Steph had just greeted waved to a woman who was climbing from her car. "There's Jangee!" he said and went to her.

"You still can't pronounce it," the Chinese woman said and returned his hug. They walked hand in hand, joining the group that strolled to the porch, smiling and chattering and wiping the occasional tear from a cheek as they went inside.

Stephany pointed them to the table, already set for lunch. "Lunch is buffet style," she said. "Food dishes are on the kitchen counter. Get your plates and make your lunch. Wine is on the table, cold beer on the cold back porch. Filled coffee pot is in the kitchen, and I'll make tea on demand."

Lunch was lively, conversation warm and spirited as the seven old friends reconnected over good food and drink. By the time lunch was finished, they knew something of what had transpired in each life since they parted. They all expressed regrets and astonishment that they had not reconnected in this fashion since graduation, all seven together.

When lunch was finished, all carried dishes to the kitchen, where Stephany brushed aside offers to help further. She pointed them to the sitting room where couches, plush chairs, and floor cushions were arrayed before the fireplace. Jon picked up a couple of pieces of wood from the box beside the fireplace and laid them carefully on the flames. The logs ignited immediately, crackling and sending sparks up the chimney.

"Steph, I knew you were an author, I've read some of your books, but gracious!" Melissa, wide-eyed, stood before a tall three-foot wide bookcase against a wall. The seven shelves were filled, and a few books lay on the tops of rows.

Stephany had just walked from the kitchen. She stood at the fireplace, holding a coffee cup. "They're not all mine. Mine are just the top three shelves. I call those my Vanity Shelves. The other books are for research and pleasure when I need to escape from what I'm working on."

Mindy took one of Stephany's titles from the top shelf. Carmelita and Jon walked over, studied the shelves and each took one of Stephany's books. They went back to their chairs and cushions, opened the books.

Adam had not moved from his seat on the couch. He stared at Donna, seated on a cushion before the fireplace, studying the flames. He smiled thinly, remembering his intentional massacring of her Chinese name, Xiangxi, his usual practice at Berkeley. He called her Janzy or some other corruption, which usually earned him a punch on an arm. Oh, how he remembered. He looked at the flames, remembering.

The afternoon was spent before the fire, catching up, laughing, sipping coffee and tea, nibbling on cookies and slices of delicious banana bread that Stephany assured them she had not baked. Melissa and Jon went out front and strolled up a trail from the end of the road. On their return, they joined the others on the front porch. The walkers told of watching a doe and two fawns that seemed as interested in the two intruders as they were of the forest creatures.

Stephany listened to the two, smiling, her mind elsewhere, remembering the good times during their senior year when Jon and Melissa were an item. Most of her friends called her *M'lis*, which Jon altered to *My Lis*. He had adored her.

Then, there was Carmelita. She was called Carmel, especially by the boys, because she was so sweet they wanted to eat her up. She tolerated the name without complaint.

Steph looked up into the forest canopy, on the edge of tears. On occasions such as these, a passage from a book she read many, too many, years ago, always came to mind: *Where gone them days,* reminiscences of an American Indian leader who had witnessed the loss of a way of life.

Donna and Adam sat on the edge of the porch, the others standing behind them. The old friends talked softly, watching the forest dim at the end of day.

The spell was broken. "Okay, group!" said Stephany, "it's time for dinner! This is another do-it-yourself. Follow me!" All went inside and worked at setting the table, warming dishes of food from the refrigerator, making salads and coffee, pouring wine and coffee. Stephany and Donna opted for hot tea.

Dinner was less spirited than lunch, but still warm and revealing, with smiles, some touching hands, and impromptu hugs. And the question, repeated over and over: *why have we not done this before?*

Dinner finished and dishes stacked in the kitchen sink, Jon and Adam, coffee cups in hand, went outside to the front porch. They looked up at the dark silhouette of pines outlined against the moonlit skies. Then they saw snowflakes, just a few delicate flakes swirling in the light breeze. They went back inside and told Stephany about the snowflakes.

"Yeah, we get a few flakes most evenings this time of year. No worry. Nothing's forecast."

The group kicked back on sofas and cushions before the fire, filled wineglasses and talked about old times and prospects. Have you seen so-and-so? What in the world do you do in Alturas? Have you gone to any UC reunions? Amazing that we haven't reconnected in all these years, all of us together. You're working in AI now? Ooh, you'll have to tell us about that. AI is exciting. AI is scary.

Jon stood, said he needed some fresh air from the heady conversation. "C'mon, M'lis." He reached for her, and she offered her hand, smiling thinly. They walked to the front door and went outside.

The door had hardly closed when it flew open. Jon stood there, holding the door wide open. "Steph, come see this."

Stephany frowned, stood and walked to him. They went outside to the porch. "Whoa," she said softly. They looked at a curtain of white. Snow fell in heavy flakes, drifting in the gentle, frigid breeze, obliterating the view, the ground already covered. They went inside, shivering.

"What's going on?" said Mindy. Stephany raised a hand, palm outward, found her cell phone in the kitchen and called the resort desk. She asked for information about the storm, listened, nodded. She lowered the phone, saw the others silently watching her.

"Well, folks, make yourself at home. Nobody's leaving tonight. All roads are closed. They won't be able to clear roads until the storm ends. Tomorrow at the earliest, though the desk says the storm gods may not cooperate. You can't get to your resort rooms below. You may be my guests longer than you planned." The six looked at each other, frowning, puzzled.

"I mean, you are now my overnight guests." The group exchanged surprised frowns. "Don't worry. I've got three beds, a couple of couches, lots of cushions and plenty of blankets. Plenty of firewood and plenty of food. I come up here fairly often and I keep an oversupply of frozen and packaged food handy. Hell, we could stay up here a week and not run out!" The others relaxed, smiled nervously, glancing at each other, uneasy. "Kick back and be comfortable," said Steph. "I'm going to retreat to the kitchen a bit, then I'll join you for more good conversation."

As usual, she turned down offers to help with the cleanup. She wanted time to think. She stood at the counter, holding a soapy, dripping plate. *Disappointing as hell.* The six friends had planned to drive down to the resort for the night, where each had reserved a room. They would come back in the morning for breakfast and conversation, lunch and then be off for their homes in the afternoon.

Steph wiped the plate and was putting it in the cupboard, but she stopped, the plate hanging in midair. *On the other hand—we might make something of this snow-storm.* She put the plate on the stack in the cupboard.

She decided she hadn't had nearly enough conversa-tion today with the group to refresh their friendship. She still knew so little of who they were at this moment. In her last call to the resort desk, the clerk said the storm likely would continue tomorrow. *Hmm.* Now what? Maybe they could gather at the fireplace...maybe she could get each person to tell something unique about themselves, or their past, or something of an ancestor's past, something that the others did not know. The stories should be interesting, revealing. At the very least, they could fill the hours while marooned here.

She wiped her hands on a dishtowel, hung it on the rack, and went to the sitting room. The others were scattered about before the fireplace, four holding wineglasses, others holding beer cans.

The loungers looked up at Stephany, smiling. Jon was grinning ear to ear. "You better get in here, Steph," said Jon, "we're talking about you!"

She frowned, relaxed. "Well. I won't even ask what you were saying because I'm about to point the conversation in another direction." The group sobered, some frowned. "We're going to be here long enough to talk a lot more than we had anticipated. And here's what I'm thinking. You are my best friends anywhere, and I regret not having kept in touch all these years. So...I want to hear something I haven't heard about your past or something about an ancestor. Something you haven't mentioned here, maybe something you haven't mentioned to anyone ever."

"Ooooh," said M'lis, pulling a face, looking around at the others.

"Yeah," said Stephany, "maybe something like that." She looked around the room. "Okay?"

The group agreed: Okay, yeah, right on, grins and raised glasses.

Stephany went to the table, poured a glass of wine for

herself and found a place at the end of the couch. She took a sip, looked around, scanning the room. "Who's first?"

"You mean now?" said David. "Tonight?"

"Yeah, why not? Who's first? C'mon."

The group looked at each other. Some studied their shoes or the contents of their wineglasses, looking up and aside, staring at the fire, smiling nervously.

Stephany frowned, relaxed. "Well, think about it. Everybody gets a turn, or I stop feeding the lot of you. In the meantime, get your wine or coffee or tea or whatever."

Chapter 2

Mindy

The friends wandered about, pouring drinks in the kitchen, standing before the fireplace, warming hands or backs, chatting about anything and nothing and the upcoming story time, wondering who would be performing this evening. Adam and Mindy, holding coffee cups, walked to the front door and went outside. After a few minutes, Adam came in alone.

"How does it look?" said Stephany. "Where's Mindy?"

"Still, no wind, light snow, and it's *freezing*!" said Adam. "Heavy overcast, but pretty clear underneath. Beautiful landscape. The cars look like big clumps of snow. Mindy said she wanted to stay out a bit. Seems she has something on her mind."

Steph frowned. "Hope she's all right. I'll check." She turned to Jon and Carmel. "Have everything you need?"

"Yeah," said Carmelita. "Ready to go! Who's story-telling this evening?"

Stephany pulled a face and shrugged. "You?" Carmel cringed, cowered behind Jon, smiled sheepishly.

"I'll get Mindy," said Stephany. "She's out front. Adam said she was sorting out something on the front porch. Probably planning a route over the mountain to the valley to escape." Stephany wiped her hands on a napkin, dropped it on the table.

She went to the front door and outside. Mindy stood at the front of the porch. She turned to Steph, solemn. "Everything okay?" Stephany said.

"Yep." Mindy looked into the darkness.

Steph waited. Finally, she asked: "You okay?"

Mindy turned to her. "Unless somebody else wants their turn tonight, I'd like to tell my story."

Stephany cocked her head. "Fantastic! You got it. Thanks for volunteering." Stephany reached for her and hugged. "You'll get this storytelling off to a great start. Since I announced it, I've had second thoughts, thinking it's silly. But now I've had third thoughts. I'm looking forward to it. Should be great fun. Let's get on with it! Everybody else is going to be as excited as I am." Stephany put an arm around Mindy's waist, and they went inside.

The others, sitting and standing near the fireplace, glasses or cups in hand, looked up. "Okay, bunch, are you ready for this? Mindy is going to warm us up. Mindy's storytelling tonight!" Cheers and huzzahs all around. "So fill your cups and glasses and make yourselves comfortable."

Adam moved aside on the couch, making room for Mindy and Stephany. Jon handed Stephany a glass and poured wine. He extended the bottle toward Mindy. She smiled, shook her head. All looked at Mindy. She cringed at the sudden attention, then recovered, smiling.

"Right. I'm going to tell you about an ancestor that I

have become quite acquainted with this past year. She was a shadowy figure in my youth that I heard about, but as children do, didn't take much interest in. But lately, I have talked at length with an elderly aunt who is the family genealogist and have become fascinated with her. I have never talked about her outside the family." She smiled, looking around. "But this bunch here is family, and I'm glad to share her with you.

"She was a stray of sorts. Her name was Mindy."

———

Michael lounged against the fort's open gate, arms crossed against his chest. He exhaled deeply. He was bored. He arrived at the fort a week ago and still was not sure why he was here. He had arrived in Monterey by ship last month, intent on joining the hordes heading for the Sierra Nevada foothills, whose streams reportedly were filled with gold for the taking. Most of the male passengers and a majority of the crewmen immediately on landing bought horses, searched for a source of supplies, determined to waste no time in heading for the gold diggings.

Michael and three shipmates, all of whom had jumped ship, were not in such a hurry. They strolled in Monterey's dusty main street, unsure where to begin their odyssey. They had no fear of pursuit by the captain since he had lost half of his crew.

Whatever they decided to do, they would need some basic supplies. One of Michaels's compatriots knew a little Spanish. He spoke to passing locals who directed them to a store owned by an American, Thomas O. Larkin, who they were told was the leading merchant in Monterey. He was also the United States Consul, they said. *The American Consul, a storekeeper?*

While the others went inside the store, Michael stopped in the middle of the street, frowning. The house was a two-story frame building with adobe walls and a hip roof. A flat-roof porch on the second level ran around both sides and the front. It looked like fine homes he had seen in New England, but he had not expected the same in Mexican California.

Michael went inside and saw his companions talking with a man behind the counter. He looked around the room, impressed with the store offerings. The walls were lined with shelves that were filled with home and farm goods of all description. Tools and kitchen implements hung from ceiling hooks, requiring the tall shopper to duck to avoid the longer pieces. All manner of materials were stacked on the floor.

"May I help you with something, young man?" Michael turned to see a dapper gentleman, dressed in a suit, obviously an American from his speech.

"Thank you, I'm waiting for my friends over there," motioning toward his companions at the counter. "We... well, they anyway, are heading for the mountains where we hear gold is lying about for anybody to collect." He smiled. "Well, at least we hear that there are good prospects for getting rich quick. I suspect that's an exaggeration. I'm not sure what I'm going to do to earn my keep."

"You're not interested?"

"Oh yes, but if it's true, I doubt we'd see many people walking around in your town or any other town in California. Everybody would be in the gold country getting rich, seems to me."

"Hmm. You could be right." He extended his hand. "I'm Thomas Larkin, owner of this store. Do you have time for a coffee with me? I'd like to talk with you."

Michael frowned, then relaxed. *A coffee with the United States Consul? Why not?* "Yes, thank you, sir, I would like that."

"Let's go outside." Larkin pointed to an outside door behind the counter. He called to the man behind the counter who was talking with Michael's shipmates. "Talbot, would you bring us coffees to the garden, please?" Talbot waved and nodded.

Larkin opened the side door and held out an arm, inviting him outside. He pointed to the low table and wicker chairs on the covered porch, and they sat. Talbot presently brought the coffees. Larkin thanked him, and he returned to the store through the side door.

"I always have coffee ready. Never know when we'll need liquid support. Course, in the evening, the support comes from good aguardiente. Perhaps there will be an opportunity to introduce you to the local drink another time. I highly recommend it." He smiled.

Michael sipped his coffee, looked around. "Nice garden."

Larkin nodded. "Yes, I often sit here in the evenings, pondering what's coming and going, possibilities and prospects." He waved over the garden. "Most of the plantings, I don't know. I do know manzanita, grove clover, bush mallow there." He pointed, sipped his coffee. "The garden changes with the changing seasons. You'll see."

Michael frowned. *I'll see? What's going on?*

Larkin smiled, seemingly sensing Michael's unease. He leaned forward. "Okay! We're both busy, so let's get right to the point. You need employment, and I need an employee. You and your friends have heard about the streams filled with gold and are eager to get to the placers. Let me add some caution. Quite a number of men who have gone to the gold country planning to make their fortunes quickly have given it up and returned with empty pockets."

Larkin leaned back in his chair. "Now, I'm an entrepreneur. I'm happy to make money anywhere I can. Question is, how do I cash in on the gold rush that has attracted so many people to California since the discovery in 1848, just two years ago? Do I employ people to pan for gold? Or, do I sell goods and equipment to gold miners? If the latter, how and where do I do that?

"So. I'm offering you a job that is more certain than panning for gold. Go to the gold country and study the operation. Visit Sutter's Fort in Sacramento first. After you've visited the fort and the diggings and have drawn some conclusions, report back to me." He leaned back, waiting.

Michael frowned. "Why me? You don't know me."

"I'm a quick judge of character."

Michael frowned, looked aside silently at the garden, full of spring bloom. "I'll take it."

———

Michael had seen nothing like Sutter's Fort, in the East or in his short time in California. Located roughly halfway between San Francisco Bay and the Sierra Nevada, the fort's log and frame structures were enclosed by adobe walls, three feet thick, eighteen feet high. Towers at the southeast and northwest corners contained cannon in their upper levels, which protected walls and entrances, though, he learned, they had never been fired since installation decades ago. Rifle loopholes pierced the walls at intervals.

Within the walls, structures of adobe and wood lined the walls. These included quarters for workers and shops, a gristmill, bakery, blanket shop and workshops of all sorts necessary for essentially a self-contained enterprise. A three-story structure in the center of the courtyard was John Sutter's headquarters and personal apartment.

Michael was not at all confident he was going to be any help to Larkin in his quest to profit in some fashion from the gold rush. Frankly, he admitted to himself, he had taken the job to earn a little cash while he investigated the prospects for mining on his own.

On arrival, he had reported to fort management who were sufficiently impressed with an envoy of Consul Larkin that he was assigned a room in a line of rooms and shops that backed up against the fort wall. The room was simply furnished with a bed and blankets, a simple bureau with a pan on top for washing water. And nothing more. A few hooks on a wall provided for hanging coats and hats. He tried to talk with fort authorities about his mission, but they deferred to Sutter who was away at the moment. They had no idea when he would return.

In conversation with fort employees, Michael learned about the fort's transformation since the gold discovery in the Sierra foothills attracted thousands of anxious treasure seekers. Since the discovery, the fort had changed from an enterprise based on fur trading and agriculture to a community of merchants who set up their shops inside and outside the walls to service the hordes of gold-seekers. Michael had to shake his head at the chaos he had seen inside and outside the fort since his arrival.

———

Michael was becoming increasingly annoyed by inactivity. He was accustomed to occupation, and this waiting was intolerable. Since breakfast on this day, he had been standing here in the open gateway in the fort wall, leaning against the log gate, watching the line of wagons rolling by on the road toward the camping place on a meadow just past the fort. He had watched the arrival and passing of emigrant wagons every day since arriving at the fort.

He turned at a shout from the fort's interior. An employee was calling to a shopkeeper. *None of my business.* Michael looked back to the road. A wagon was stopped just below the gate. The four oxen stood in place, their heads hanging. The other wagons in the caravan pulled around the stationary wagon and rolled on.

The last wagon in the moving line passed, leaving the stationary wagon alone. The driver of this wagon, standing on the far side of the team beside the lead ox, looked back toward the offside, then turned to the front. He said something unintelligible to the team and gently tapped the lead ox's back with a switch. The team leaned into the yoke, and the wagon moved ahead.

Michael stood upright abruptly. When the wagon had moved on, there stood a woman, two loaded sacks at her feet. Her long dress was badly soiled, and her bonnet was askew. She appeared to be looking at the fort, but Michael felt she looked directly into his eyes. He was mesmerized. Then he watched her drop to her knees, and her hands went to her face.

What! He ran to her. Bending, he took her hands in his and helped her stand. She wiped her eyes with a sleeve. "Can I help?" he said.

She closed her eyes, inhaled deeply, exhaled. "I suppose you can, if you're God Almighty."

"Sorry?"

She looked aside. "Sorry, don't listen to me. I have just passed through hell." She looked around, distracted. "Any place around here I can sit down, maybe get a drink of water?'

"Yes, yes, sorry. Let's go inside." Shouldering her bags, he took her arm, guided her toward the open gates in the fort wall. Inside, he supported her as they walked in front of a line of shops and rooms. Stopping at a bench before a room, he set the bags on the ground and helped her sit down. She leaned against the wall, eyes closed. He went to a door nearby and inside. He came out carrying a cup, went to the pump in the center of the courtyard, filled it and hurried to her. She eagerly took the filled cup from him with both hands and drained it, her eyes closed as she drank.

Leaning against the wall behind the bench, she seemed exhausted. She turned to him. "Thank you. First water I've had since daybreak." She handed him the empty cup. "People I was with were gettin' tired of me. They were glad to see the end of me." She inhaled deeply, exhaled, closed her eyes.

Michael waited. He studied her. *She can't be older than early twenties. Pretty, in spite of being exhausted.* Her long dress was soiled almost black at the hem, her bonnet now hanging about her shoulders.

She opened her eyes, looked up at him, fatigue written on her face. "You saved my life, you know. The Potters—that's the people who dropped me out there—figured I had eaten my last meal with them."

"Why would they figure that if you were traveling with them?"

"I was traveling with my brother, Rob. At the beginning, anyway." She lowered her head, stared at her hands in her lap. "He was killed in a buffalo stampede. Wrecked our wagon and killed our team. And Rob. The Potters offered to let me ride to the first stopping place in California. So here I am. They said people at the fort would know what to do."

"Why were you and your brother traveling to California?"

She looked aside, then at her feet. "We were desperate, Rob and me. We needed to fill the emptiness with something new. We lost Mama three years ago. She was just used up. Lost Daddy last year to consumption. We heard about California gold. Rob decided we would start over in California and get rich doin' it." She looked up at the clear blue sky. "God. Now what?"

After a long moment, "I'm Michael. What's your name?"

"Mindy." She smiled thinly. "Now you know everything about me. How 'bout you?"

He sat down beside her and told her about his decision to come to California and become a rich man in the gold fields. And he told her about the change in plan with Larkin's offer. He leaned back, his head resting against the wall, staring at nothing in the courtyard. "As for what I'm doing, the answer is I'm doing nothing. I have no idea what to tell Larkin. No surprise there. I learned from talking to people here that I'm the second person he has sent here to investigate opportunities for him. The other man decided he couldn't help Larkin and went to the diggings himself. Larkin didn't mention the other man to me, probably thought it might give me ideas. Maybe it has."

He turned to her. "Enough of my problems. What about you? You might find a job here at one of the shops in the fort or around the walls. But I wouldn't recommend it. Since the gold rush, some bad characters have been attracted to the fort. You're too pretty to get involved with the fort's business. On that point, I wouldn't ask old

Sutter personally for employment. He has his bunch of Indian mistresses, but I wager he would be real happy to add a young, pretty white woman."

"Young and pretty? You're too kind. I feel old and used up." She closed her eyes, took a deep breath, paused. She opened her eyes, looked at him. "Never thought about the prospect of bein' a mistress. Probably a good way to make some quick money. Good security too, I s'pose." She smiled, just a hint of a smile, as if the effort were difficult.

He pointed at her face. "Well, don't start thinkin' about it now." He frowned,paused. "Unless you were working here, you wouldn't find a place to stay inside the fort. Even if you found a room, you shouldn't stay alone." He looked down, frowning, then looked at her. "How about this? Stay in my room. It'll be dark soon, and you need to rest."

She looked up sharply at him. He raised both hands, palms outward. "No funny business. You get the bed, and I won't look. It's either this or sleep on the ground outside the walls. I guarantee you wouldn't finish the night alone."

"Thank you for the offer." She looked sternly at him. "I want you to know that I can take care of myself." She relaxed, smiled. "You're probably the only person in California who would do this for me." Her smile vanished, and she bent forward, her face in her hands, and she sobbed. "I'm sorry, everything's happened so fast. I've lost everything, everybody." She rocked back and forth.

Michael put an arm around her shoulders and pulled her to him. She leaned against him.

"Sorry, sorry," she said.

He stood, took her hand and helped her stand. Shouldering her bags, he walked toward the door, opened it and stepped back. "Yeah, I bet you can take care of yourself." She bumped against him, wiped her eyes with a sleeve and walked inside.

She wavered, almost stumbled. Inside, she stopped, looked around. "This is your room?"

"Yes." He pointed to the bed. "That's yours. You need to go to bed right now. If you need the toilet during the night, wake me up, and I'll walk you down. It's just down the way in the corner."

"I'll find it."

"You probably could, it's hard to miss, but you shouldn't walk anywhere in the fort alone at night. You wake me up, hear?"

She nodded, lay on the bed , exhaled heavily. She rose abruptly on an elbow. "Where are you going to sleep?"

"I'll be right over there." He pointed at the floor at the wall. "I have blankets and a heavy coat. Wake me if you need anything. Lie down before you collapse."

She lay down, closed her eyes. "Thank you. You're a good man," she mumbled softly.

———

Next morning, they stood at a counter in front of a tent that backed up against an outside wall of the fort. Each held a plate containing a flatbread rolled around shredded chicken, beans and cheese. The concoction was covered with a red sauce. They ate silently with forks supplied by the vendor.

"Mmm," Mindy said, "that's good. What's it called?"

"Enchilada," said Michael. "He said he has two sauces. One he calls hot-make-your-hair-stand-up-straight, and another he calls not-so-hot. I opt for the not-so-hot. I ate here the first day at the fort and have come back each morning since." He waved to the smiling cook standing at the grill just outside the tent entrance. "Bueno! Gracias!" Michael said.

The cook grinned, spoke to Mindy. "He learn Spanish fast. I think I hire him sell my enchiladas inside fort. Maybe at diggings." He chuckled.

Michael smiled, waved to the cook. He turned to Mindy. "Let's go over and sit in the shade." He put their forks and empty plates on a barrel top, waving to the cook who smiled and returned the wave.

They walked to a large oak and sat under the low branches. She closed her eyes and raised her chin, smiling.

"You look a lot better than last evening," said Michael.

She smiled, touched his hand. "I simply cannot believe what happened and where I am right at this moment. If you hadn't taken me in, I'm not certain I would have lasted the night. I just cannot picture in what state I would be in this morning." She inhaled deeply, touched his hand again. "But here I am, smiling. I can never repay you for your kindness. I didn't know there were people like you about."

He grimaced. "My, my, who are you talking about? There are good people everywhere."

"Mmm. I haven't met many lately, till now." She looked past him to the fort, then at the caravan of wagons rolling toward the fort. She turned to him. "Now what?"

He pondered. "As for that...I stayed awake most of the night. I checked on you a couple of times, just to confirm that you were still breathing." He smiled. "And I thought about lots of things, including this employment of mine. I don't believe I'm going to be able to give Larkin any advice on how he might make money on the gold rush, so I'm going to write to him and beg off this job.

"That leaves me unemployed and unattached again.

I've just about decided to do what I had intended when I came to California, go to the gold diggings." He paused. "I also spent a good portion of the night thinking about... you."

She frowned, cocked her head. "And what did you decide?"

"Would you...would you consider going with me to the diggings? We have a lot in common, and I think we would get on real well."

She leaned toward him, a smile playing about her lips. "What do we have in common? Hmm?"

He frowned, pondered. "Well, I'm a man, and you're a woman. A mighty pretty woman at that. And...we're both unattached and alone. That's not a good situation for you, or any pretty woman around here, right now." He resisted the temptation to touch her. "We're both at loose ends, no obligations. If you go with me and want to end it, I'll do whatever you want."

She rocked back and forth, slowly. "That means I'm sorta in control, doesn't it." She smiled thinly.

"I suppose it does."

"You're very kind." She looked past him to the meadow. "I'll go with you. I don't...don't have any other options, do I?" She put a hand to her mouth. "Sorry, that didn't come out right. I'm...just not thinking straight. I want to go with you." She frowned, pointed a finger at his face. "As long as you're a good boy, and we'll see what happens." She smiled. "And we go fifty-fifty on the gold we find." She pulled a face.

He pulled a face as well. "Good on all counts. Now. I've talked with men who have been in the placers. We need to buy stuff since we'll be camping. I've done some camping on hunting trips, so I have an idea of what we'll need. Tent, blankets, utensils, other stuff. I carry a pistol—

hope I don't need that—but might come in handy. I have a rifle for game. I have some cash, but it won't last long. I expect to find gold early. How's that for confidence?"

"I have money. We sold the farm a few months before leaving. The money is in my saddlebags. I never told the Potters about the money. I've been terrified of being robbed, but I still have it. I'll need a horse."

"Glad you ride. You do ride?"

She smiled. "Probably better than you. We raised horses and sold them in the neighborhood. I also want to buy trousers."

He recoiled, frowning. "Trousers? Men's trousers?"

"If I'm going to be looking for gold in a stream, probably standing in water, this dress won't do." She fluffed up the long dress. "Working outside in dresses is a nuisance! I've heard about a new thing for women called bloomers. Kind of a blousy short pants, no long dress dragging on the ground. Look at this!" She showed him her dress hem that was almost black from trailing on the ground.

"Yeah." He looked up. "The bloomers sound interesting. I'll help hunt for 'em. Doubt you'll find any around here. Might be just as well, you couldn't wear them outside our camp. I'm afraid I couldn't control the horny miners. They probably haven't seen a white woman for months and surely haven't seen anything like bloomers except maybe in a...well, a—".

"Whorehouse. Yeah, I know. But it seems that women wear bloomers everywhere back East. Except maybe in church."

———

During the two days following, they strolled through the shops and stalls inside the fort and outside the walls. They bought all the gear they would need for an extended camping excursion, including a tent they purchased from a failed miner who was delighted to find a buyer. When they started buying provisions, they learned that some enterprising merchants had already built small shops in the placers, having decided that they saw more promise in mining the miners than mining on their own. So, the two partners bought only enough provisions to last a few days.

They carried their purchases to the fort livery where Mindy wasted no time. She informed Michael that she would select her riding horse and a packhorse, and the tack for both, and she would pay for the lot. He was content to watch. The grizzled old liveryman was a bit put off by this young woman who knew horses better than he did, but he was satisfied with the prices she offered.

Michael, leaning on a corral pole, had silently watched her negotiations with the liveryman.

"How's that?" she said.

"I bet you can cook too."

She raised her chin. "I can. But I'm used to cooking on a stove. You'll have to do your part in this cooking outdoors, or we don't eat."

He stared.

She smiled. "Okay?" she said softly, cocking her head.

"Okay." He slowly put his arms around her shoulders and hugged her. He leaned back, kissed her lips lightly, then again, lightly. She encircled his waist with her arms. He hugged her again. "We're gonna get on just fine," he said softly.

"C'mon," she said, "let's get this stuff to your room. It's gonna be dark before long. I'll load the packhorse, and you lead my horse." They walked to his room in a few sprinkles, unloaded the purchases and led the two horses back to the livery. During their return to his room, the light shower became a driving downpour, and they ran, hand in hand.

Inside, in the half-light, they undressed each other and climbed under the covers of the bed as the driving rain and wind rattled shutters, lightning flashed repeatedly, and thunder burst and rolled.

Then it was over, the rainfall reduced to a shower and the soft thunder rolling in the distance, like the gentle bubbling of water in a kettle. Then it was still, quiet.

———

At first light, Michael and Mindy walked through the front gate of the fort, glancing aside to be sure no one was looking, pausing for a quick kiss and a giggle from Mindy. Walking outside around the walls, they joined half a dozen others at the lean-to at the fort wall, all munching on enchiladas, all watching Mindy's every move. Juanito handed plates of enchiladas and rice to Mindy and Michael.

"Not-so-hot sauce?" said Mindy.

Juanito smiled. "Sí, not-so-hot."

"Juanito," said Michael, "my friend here wants you to move your shop to the placers so she can eat your enchiladas every day." The other customers smiled, nodded their agreement, one waving his fork, all the while all staring at Mindy.

Juanito smiled thinly, glancing aside briefly at Michael. He looked at the other customers who were now deep in conversation with each other. Juanito leaned toward Michael and Mind, spoke softly. "I cannot do that. You have just arrived here. You will find out that the Americano miners do not like Californios in the gold country. They chase Californios, Mexicans, from the streams."

Michael frowned. "But...but that makes no sense. You were here long before they came. They are the newcomers."

Juanito shook his head. "It doesn't matter. They have the numbers, and they have the guns. You will see." He stepped toward a new customer standing nearby, waiting for his enchilada, watching them, particularly Mindy.

Michael, frowning, watched Juanito. Mindy took Michael's arm, and they walked away. Almost immediately, a man who had stared at them at the enchilada shop walked up behind them. "Uh, say there." They stopped and turned to the speaker.

"Don't mean to bother you. Heard you back there saying you was goin' to the placers for the first time." Michaell nodded, frowning. *What's that to do with you?*

"You got a gun?"

"I do."

"Well, you better wear it. Hope you know how to use it. Most of the miners are fine fellas, but there's some who ain't. I 'spect you know that you're gonna attract a considerable amount of attention since you have this pretty lady beside you." He blinked at Mindy, embarrassed, it seemed. "Sorry, missy, but the fellas up there ain't seen a pretty lady like you, a *white* pretty lady, for a long time. Most of 'em will mind their manners, but after a few drinks, watch out." He smiled thinly. "By the way, my pard and I are headin' up that way tomorrow morning. Maybe we'll see you two on the trail." He touched his hat, turned to go, then turned back. "I'm Barney, by the way." He walked away, waving over his shoulder.

Mindy and Michael watched him go. "Well, that was interesting," said Mindy. "Welcome to California." They set out toward the livery. After a bit, she turned to him. "Where did you learn to use a gun?"

He looked aside at her a moment, then turned back to the front and said nothing. They walked silently toward the livery.

She frowned. "Are you still with me?"

"Sorry...I was a Texas Ranger."

She stopped. "A Texas Ranger? I've heard about them. Weren't they——"

"Let's get the animals. We need to get on the road." They had arrived at the livery. Michael went inside the barn while Mindy opened the gate and found their three horses. Michael came out, carrying saddles and bridles and halter for the packhorse and went to Mindy. They saddled their horses and Mindy readied the packhorse for the panniers, large canvas bags that hung on each side of the packsaddle frame. They mounted and rode to Michael's room, where they dismounted, tied reins to the rail and went inside.

They brought the bags of personal things, camping gear and supplies outside where Michael watched Mindy load the panniers. He smiled. "My, my, you are going to come in handy."

She patted the packhorse on the rump, turned to Michael. "You need to learn everything I know about horses, buddy. I may not always be around."

He frowned. "Meaning?"

She pursed her lips. "I heard lots in the wagon train about gold miners and more since coming here. Women seem to be in short supply in the mines, and the ladies can get just about anything they want from the lonesome miners." She cocked her head.

He didn't smile. "Don't even joke about that. I've heard the stories, too. The only women they've seen for months at a time are Indian women, and they abuse them something awful, I'm told. No telling what they will do with a white woman. You're gonna have to watch your step until we see how things go in the placers. You're going to be an oddity, especially if you wear those trousers where they can see you. Never mind the bloomers! Glad you didn't find them."

She tied the thongs on a packsaddle bag, slapped the bag and turned to him. She looked around, grasped his shirt front, pulled him to her. "Okay, I'll be careful. Just stay close." She kissed him lightly.

He touched the tip of her nose with a finger. "I intend to stay real close." He untied the packhorse lead, they mounted and rode toward the rising sun. They soon left Sutter's Fort behind, riding on a well-traveled road.

"I still want to hear about the Texas Rangers," she said.

He looked straight ahead, turned to her, and she saw a face she had not seen before. He turned back to the front. "I'll tell you. Catch me sometime when I've had a couple of drinks."

———

The road they followed ran alongside the broad Sacramento River. Reeds and scattered oaks bordered the stream. An occasional wagon and riders passed them going in both directions, mostly eastward, toward the gold country. Small sailboats passed in both directions. They were surprised to see an impressive paddlewheel steamboat cruising eastward in midstream. Passengers on the deck waved. Some shouted, but their voices were carried away in the light breeze. Now in late afternoon, the stream and road were empty and quiet but for the lilting song of an unseen meadowlark.

"I'm hungry," said Mindy. "Should have brought an extra enchilada for lunch."

Michael looked behind at the sun that sat atop a line of trees in the west. "We should reach the inn soon. If the old boy who mentioned it knew what he was talking about. Do you remember—"

"Uh oh," she said softly.

He turned around to see the two men who had stepped from roadside brush into their path. One held a pistol trained on them. He motioned the riders off the road. Michael reined up, staring at the bandit, and the man motioned again. Michael turned off the road toward a stand of oaks. Mindy, wide-eyed, followed.

They rode to the oaks where the man with the gun gestured them to dismount. His companion, fear written on his face, stood behind him. Michael slowly dismounted, his eyes on the gunman. Mindy dismounted and stood beside her mount.

The man waved the gun toward Michael. "Dinero," he said, "money."

Michael did not move. He simply stared. Then he nodded. "Sí," He looked aside at Mindy and handed her his reins. His back to the bandit, he spoke softly to her. "Stand behind your horse." She moved around her horse, keeping her eyes on the bandit's gun.

Michael reached slowly toward his right pants pocket, his eyes on the gunman. He pushed the tips of his fingers into the pocket, then in a lightning move, withdrew the fingers and grabbed his pistol grip, drew the pistol, brought it up and fired. The bandit was blown backward, firing his pistol wildly in the air, and collapsed to the ground. The man's companion shouted in fear and jerked aside, his hands stretched above his head.

Michael went to the gunman, lying on his back, his face contorted in pain. He bent and examined the man's shoulder where the shirt was wet with blood. Standing, he looked at the cringing companion who held his hands high above his head.

"¡Sin arma, señor, sin arma!" the companion said. Michael nodded, signaled to lower his arms.

"What did he say?" Mindy said, her eyes wide.

"He said he doesn't have a gun." Michael kneeled beside the injured gunman and touched his shoulder. The man grimaced, his face contorted, eyes tightly closed. Michael looked up at the wounded man's companion. "¿Medico, Sutter's Fort, medico. Entender?"

"Sí, señor, sí. Entiendo." He nodded rapidly.

"Caballos?" said Michael.

"Sí." He pointed to the oak grove.

"Bien. Irse medico Sutter's Fort."

The man looked at Michael, jaw hanging.

"Ahora!" Michael said.

"Sí, sí." The man ran to the thicket and returned quickly, holding the reins of two horses. Michael helped him raise the fallen gunman who groaned as they helped him mount. The companion then mounted. He sat dumbly, holding the wounded man's reins, looking down at Michael.

"Go, dammit, ahora, do I have to do it for you? Sutter's Fort!" Michael pointed toward the road in a westerly direction and slapped the horse's rump. The horse jerked aside as the rider regained control and gently kicked his horse to a walk, leading the gunman's horse.

After a long moment, Michael turned and saw Mindy, already mounted, watching him. He took his reins from her and mounted. They reined into the road. He looked at her. She cocked her head.

"Later," he said.

———

They sat at the corner table in the dining room of The Stopover Inn. Their empty dinner dishes were stacked on a corner of the table. Only one other table of the five tables was occupied. The two rough-dressed men at the table had silently watched them come in, then resumed their soft conversation and sipped their drinks after their curiosity was satisfied. Both occasionally looked aside at the unusual sight of a white woman sitting in a café whose usual patrons were almost entirely associated with mining in the foothills.

Michael and Mindy held coffee cups. She leaned toward him. "Okay?" she said.

"Sí. Okay." He sipped from his cup, leaned back, inhaled deeply, then leaned forward, exhaled, stared into his cup. He looked up, spoke softly. "I told you I was a Texas Ranger. I joined up after my mama and daddy and little sister were killed by Mexican bandits. They came across the Rio Grande, the border, in broad daylight. They killed my family, stole our cattle and burned the house and barn. I was out hunting, or I would have died as well. I vowed I would kill the bandits, all of them, or die trying.

"I joined up. I knew the Rangers were trying to clean up the border by killing the gangs that were operating in the area. In the next couple of years, we broke up three cross-border gangs. We killed about three dozen rustlers. I could only hope the dead included the men who killed my family.

"I decided I'd done enough killing and left the Rangers, drifted a while in central and South Texas and on Mississippi riverboats, gambling and gettin' drunk. Finally, in a sober moment, I decided to go to California to have a look at the gold country we were hearing so much about. I went to New Orleans and signed on as crew on the next ship."

He picked up his cup, drained it, replaced it gently on the table. He looked up at her. "And here I am."

She said nothing for a moment, just stared at him. "I'm so sorry for your loss. Coming to California probably saved your life. Your coming saved *my* life, that's for sure. I shudder every time I think about what would have come of me if you hadn't been standing at that fort gate when they dumped me." She put a hand to his cheek, slapped the cheek lightly. She stood and reached for him. "C'mon, let's go to bed."

———

They sat their horses on the trail, shaded by huge oak trees that ran alongside the stream. He held the lead of the packhorse. They looked down the gentle slope to a tent camp on the edge of a thin sand beach. A fire circle and gear of all sorts lying about the site suggested an established claim.

Two miners, probably in their forties, barefoot and pants rolled up to their knees, squatted in the shallows. They held pans, water dripping from the edge. Both looked up the slope at the two strangers.

"Howdy," Michael called. "We're new here. May we come down?"

The miners stood, looked at each other. "Sure. Come on down," said one. The other waved. The two stepped from the water to the beach, set their pans on the sand and wiped hands on their trousers. They watched Michael and Mindy rein up, dismount and tie reins to a low branch of a streamside maple. They stared silently at Mindy a long moment, ignoring Michael. She smiled, almost laughed. She would explain later to Michael that they appeared to be twins, two peas in a pod.

One of the miners blinked, shook his head, turned to Michael. "So you just arrived here, did you? I suppose you want to ask us some questions. Wish I could offer coffee, but you're too late."

"And too early," said the other miner, grinning. The first miner looked at him, frowning. "Too early for supper coffee, I mean."

The first miner frowned at his partner. "Okay." He turned back to the visitors. "So you just arrived, and you're looking for a claim."

Michael and Mindy looked at each other. "That's precisely what we're doing," Michael said. "We wanted to ask for your advice since you seem to have been here a while."

"Yep," said the first miner. "We were one of the first on this stretch of the stream. Come up here from San Francisco just the day after ole' Sam Brannon marched up and down the streets yelling 'gold on the American River'. Brannon was one of the men in on the gold discovery at Sutter's sawmill, you know. Or maybe you don't know. Anyway, we beat him back to the foothills and been here ever since. We've moved our claim a couple of times, but always been lucky."

"Sounds fantastic," said Michael. "Could you lend us some of that luck and recommend a spot for us to post a claim?"

"Figured that's what you had in mind. As a matter of

fact, got just the spot for you, right nearby." He pointed. "Go back up the path to the trail, turn right, go past two claims—one has a tent and the other a small log cabin—and you'll see an unclaimed place. At least, it was still unclaimed yesterday. If you don't see any evidence of possession, that's your spot. Scatter some stuff around to show it's occupied, and it's yours.

"It's a good producer. The last owner didn't leave because it wasn't producing. He got sick, and his pard decided they needed to live in town. I've had questions from a couple others about open spots and didn't mention this one. I didn't want those particular characters for neighbors. You two seem to fit the bill for good neighbors." He looked pointedly at Mindy. "'specially you, missy. I s'pose your pard is okay as well." He pulled a face.

She smiled. "Yeah, he's okay. I can keep him in line." She bumped Michael's shoulder.

Both miners looked at each other, smiling. "I'm Hal, by the way," said the first miner. He gestured with a nod of his head at his pard. "He's Sal. Yeah, we're twins."

"You better git up there and post your claim before somebody else wanders by," said Sal.

"Don't be strangers," said Hal. "We like to talk with good neighbors."

"What do you do about bad neighbors?" said Mindy.

"Mostly, we *shoot* 'em!" said Sal. He guffawed loudly.

Hal frowned, waving off Sal. "Don't pay him no mind. We git along with most people." He pointed upstream. "Now git up there! Come see us when you're all set up." He waved toward the trail.

Michael started to walk away, turned back. "By the way, how do you know the limits of a claim? How big is a claim?"

"Well, that's a good question. Up and down the

diggings, the size is different, depending on where you are, anywhere from ten to thirty feet square. Around here, it's understood that claims are on the bigger size, thirty feet square. But that's really just a guideline. The limits of a claim, more often than not, are fixed by natural boundaries, like a line of brush, or a rocky ledge."

Michael and Mindy thanked Hal and Sal for their help, untied their horses' reins and mounted. Waves were exchanged, and they rode up the path to the trail. Turning to the right, heading upstream, they rode slowly past the two claims Hal described. A miner at the first claim, standing in the shallows, waved to them. They saw no one at the second claim, the one with the rough log cabin.

Passing a line of shrubs that lay from the trail to the stream, they saw a sandy beach on the near side, shaded by scattered oaks. Across the slow-moving stream, about twenty feet wide, an oak grove rose from a mass of thick shrubs. They rode down the narrow path on the gentle slope to the sand beach. Dismounting, they looked around. Everything in view appeared to belong in the sylvan setting. There was nothing manmade in view.

"It's ours," said Mindy. "I love it."

They tied reins to a manzanita. She unloaded the packhorse, and they went to work setting up camp. They erected the tent and deposited goods inside. He dug a firepit and collected stones at streamside to ring it.

She watched him building the fire circle, hands on hips. "We're going to find out real quick what we have forgotten."

He stood beside the firepit, hands on hips. "I've already discovered something we forgot. Matches. Since I'm not too good at making fire rubbing two sticks together, we'll need to borrow some. It's gonna get late and cool real soon. I'm going back to Hal-Sal's for matches." He dusted his hands, wiped them on his trousers. "I'll be just a few minutes. Gold pans are just inside the tent. Give 'em a try."

He climbed the path to the trail, turned left and walked downstream. At Hal and Sal's camp, he explained his predicament.

Sal went to their tent, returned and offered a handful of matches. "Come back if you remember something else you forgot. You have food for supper?"

"I do have that. Thanks for the matches. I'll pay you back when I find a store."

"No problem there. There's a new little store 'bout a half mile upstream. You can't miss it."

"Many thanks for that. I'll go up tomorrow. Should know by then what we need." He waved and walked up the path.

————

Two rough-dressed men stood on the trail above Michael and Mindy's tent. Both wore soiled clothing and sweat-stained felt hats. They looked below at Mindy who stood barefoot at streamside holding a gold pan at her side. The pantlegs of her trousers were rolled up above her knees, exposing her legs. She seemed to be studying the slow-moving stream.

"My, my, my," said one of the men softly, "do you see what I see?"

"I do, Gerald, I do. I think we should investigate." Gerald nodded, and they walked slowly, silently, down the path. At the bottom, they stopped a few feet behind Mindy.

"Find some nuggets, did yuh?"

She jumped and turned around abruptly. "You scared

me!" She relaxed, but was suddenly aware of her predicament. "Are you miners?"

"We are, and right now, I'm looking at a purty little treasure that we need to collect." He smiled at his pard who snorted, grinning. He stepped to her and gripped her arm, reaching toward her chest with the other hand.

Suddenly, his eyes opened wide, and he stiffened. Mindy almost laughed, looking over his shoulder.

"Hold it, right there, my man," said Michael. The muzzle of his pistol touched the back of the man's head. Michael looked slightly aside at the man's companion. "You back off and put your hands in the air or your friend's brains are gonna feed the birds." The man gasped as he stepped backward with hands stretched high.

Michael turned back to the man at the end of his pistol. "Now you listen. You just came near dying. Don't want to brag, fellows, but you should know that I'm a killer, and I don't hesitate removing anybody that threatens me or mine. This lady is mine. If I decide not to shoot you right now and you see either of us again, if you don't reverse course, I may decide to finish what I didn't finish today. Not yet, anyway." He paused, pushed the muzzle firmly against the man's head. "Is all this clear?" The miner nodded vigorously.

Michael glanced aside at the companion. "And you? You understand all this?" The man nodded, jaw hanging, hands still high above his head.

Michael lowered the pistol and stepped aside. The man dropped his hands, stared at Michael, jaw hanging.

"Git!" said Michael.

The man grabbed his pard who was still rigid. They ran toward the path and up the incline. At the top of the path, they turned right without looking below and broke into a run up the trail.

Michael looked at Mindy. He smiled.

She giggled. "I almost laughed. My, you're good!" She sobered. "Were you serious?"

"Sort of. If they had turned belligerent, I probably would've shot somebody. But they were so scared, I figured they weren't really hard cases. Still, if you see them again, be careful. They may take out their embarrassment on you. If I'm around and they act up, watch out."

———

Michael bent and stepped from the tent, pulling up his suspenders, tucking shirttails into his pants. He looked across the stream at the line of oaks, canopies illuminated by the bright morning sunshine of the new day. He inhaled deeply. He saw Mindy, squatting in the shallows, pants rolled up to her knees. She scooped a pan of sand from the bottom. He walked down, bent over and kissed the top of her head.

She jerked away and looked up. "Don't *do* that! Whistle or yell or something. You scared me."

"Who else were you expecting?"

She did not respond, continuing to swirl water and sand in the pan she held. She put the pan down, picked up a small bottle at her feet and showed him. The bottom was covered with a thin layer of flakes. "You waste time sleeping late."

He took the bottle from her, eyes wide, turned it around shook it. "My, my, I am impressed. Hal-Sal are good teachers. And you are a natural. I'm going to have to watch you and imitate you." He handed her the bottle. "As for sleeping late, it's your fault. You exhausted me last night, and I had to recuperate." He knelt behind her and put his arms around her shoulders, lightly caressing a breast.

She turned around and kissed him. "That's sweet, but it's daylight, and you need to get to work."

He stood. "Actually, I'm going to work on the tent this morning. It needs better staking and some ditching around it. Hal-Sal said they're expecting rain. After lunch, I'm going to the store Sal told me about. We're just about out of everything. Want to go?"

She swirled the sand in the pan. "You go on. I'm busy making money to buy your stuff."

––––––––––––

Michael lifted the two filled canvas bags, thanked the store owner and said his goodbyes to a couple of miners he had befriended on entering the store. They worked a claim a few hundred yards north of his. He went outside and down the steps. He hefted the load again, sure the two bags were going to get heavier every step of the trail to his claim, only about a half mile downstream. Setting out, he looked to the west where the sun disk hovered just above the tops of a line of oaks.

He stopped, set the bags on the ground, puffing, inhaled deeply. Picking up the bags, he walked on the tree-lined trail, mostly in shade, though he welcomed the sunny intervals as the day had begun to cool.

Turning off the trail on the path that sloped down to their claim, he stopped and admired the work he had done that morning. The tent was nicely ditched all around, and the canvas was stretched with taut stake ropes. Then he continued down the path to the sandy streamside.

He stopped, frowning. Mindy was nowhere in sight. He assumed she would have stopped panning by now and built a fire, maybe even with coffee ready for his return. His irritation quickly gave way to alarm. She had never left the camp on her own.

He hurried to drop the bags inside the tent and checked the pistol on his hip. Running up the path to the trail, he looked both ways. Which way would she likely go? Or if she were taken, which way would that be? There were more working claims upstream than down and more walkers on the upstream trail than down. But he had walked that trail coming back from the store. Surely, she would not have walked past the store without coming in. He would try downstream first.

He strode downstream, stopping only briefly to look down paths to claims along the stream. He called to a miner squatting in the shallows, another farther on sitting on the stoop of his small cabin, still another sitting at his cooking fire, tending a skillet, smoking his pipe. No one had seen a solitary woman on the trail, nor any woman, for that matter. He walked on, almost running, concern turning to fear.

Then he stopped, frowning. There she was, sitting at a fire circle with five men. The men, their faces illuminated by the flames and the setting sun, leaned toward her, listening, speaking softly, gesturing with pipes or hands, smiling and nodding.

Michael walked down the path, relief giving way to annoyance. The men at the fire looked at him, suddenly alert to the stranger. Mindy smiled. "Michael, come down and meet some friends." The men relaxed. A couple smiled, another beckoned Michael to come down.

Mindy reached up and took Michael's hand. He sat down slowly beside her, looking around, still wary of the group, still wondering.

She held Michael's hand. "This is Michael, everybody.

He's thinking right now how he's going to punish me for walking away from camp when he was gone to the store. But he won't punish me because he is a good man, and he will believe me when I explain."

A smiling miner pointed at Mindy. "Your little lady said you're new in the diggings. She's a good listener. Sometimes we git thoughtful and homesick, and there's nobody to talk to. Miners don't much want to talk with miners about folks back home. They're too preoccupied with here and now. Your lady listened to us, and we like that. Now, if you was *unhappy* with her, I'd like to take her off your hands, but I don't think that's the case." The miners smiled, some chuckled.

Michael nodded, but did not smile, looking aside at Mindy.

"We appreciated her talkin' to us," said another. "She reminds us of our family back home. She reminds me of my little sister, my sweet little sis." He looked away, wiped his cheek with a sleeve. His companion put a hand on his back.

"We don't want to keep you," said another, gesturing with his pipe. "You'll have your supper to fix." He turned to Mindy. "I want to thank you for talkin' with us, missy. I can't say how much we 'preciate it. You reminded us of what's good in life." General mumbled agreement from the group.

She nodded. "Thanks to all of you. I heard miners were gruff old buzzards, and here you are, good fellas." She looked at Michael. He stood, took her proffered hand and helped her up. The miners immediately stood, said their smiling goodbyes and waved. Michael and Mindy moved up the path to the trail and turned upstream toward their claim.

"Well," said Michael.

Mindy took his arm. "I'm sorry, honey. I meant only to walk a couple of minutes, but kept on, kinda lost track of time and distance, till one of the fellows at the stream called to me and invited me down. He was polite, and I thought I would go down for a couple of minutes. I haven't had a chance to talk with anybody but you and Hal-Sal and the grocer since we arrived."

"You're lucky. These fellas could have been like most miners, with something on their minds other than talking."

"Yeah, I thought that too, once I got down there. The fella who invited me down did look me over and might have had something like that in mind. But when two others came over, one of them said he was shocked when he saw me. He said he thought his little sister had walked into camp. He said I looked just like her. Then the conversation took a friendly turn."

He looked sternly at her. "Okay, I'm glad it turned out well. You were lucky, we were lucky." He playfully squeezed her face in a fist, puckering her lips. "Don't do it again." He kissed the puckered lips.

She pushed his hand away, took his arm and accelerated the pace. "C'mon, I'm hungry. Let's see whether you bought anything tasty."

Late spring showers increased the stream's flow only slightly and did not interfere with the gold panning. Michael acknowledged that Mindy was the more successful miner, and she was content to leave the shopping and camp maintenance to him. He extracted a promise from her that if he were away and she was bothered by an intruder, she would scream loudly. He alerted the miners on claims on each side of theirs to listen for the screams. She thought the scenario a little bizarre but agreed to the plan.

———

Michael left camp just after breakfast on a bright spring morning, planning to walk upstream to have a look at some reported new shops. He passed the grocer where he had shopped, expecting to stop on his return. Adjacent was a small new café run by Californios. He decided he would stop here for a coffee on his return to learn what sort of fare they offered. *Hope they serve enchiladas.*

Then there was the new Jewish clothing store Hal had mentioned last time they were together at the grocery store. He said this was one of the few places one would encounter Jews in the placers. Some Jews early on had tried their luck in the diggings, but they were run off. They might be one hundred percent fourth-generation Americans, Hal said, but they were Jews.

Michael had to shake his head at the memory. He recalled he had replied "stupid" during that grocery store conversation loud enough for bystanders to hear.

"Stupid? Why stupid?" Michael had turned to see the miner who had listened to the conversation with Hal. He looked at the miner and his pard, both glaring at him. Michael ignored them, turned back to Hal.

Immediately, the miner grabbed his arm and pulled him around. "I'm talkin' to you, sumbitch. Why *stupid*?"

Michael slowly looked at the hand that held his arm, then looked the miner in the face. "Take your hand off me," he said softly.

"By god, I'll—"

Michael jerked backward, brushing the hand aside,

drew his pistol and brought the grip down hard on the miner's head, and he was thrown backward, crumpling to the floor. Michael whipped the pistol aside and brought it up in the face of the man's companion who had advanced a step toward him. The man's face fell, and he stepped back, his jaw hanging.

Michael glared. "By god, I'll put up with a lot, but stupidity that threatens me I won't tolerate!"

Michael shook his head, remembering. Happily, he had not seen these two again.

Now Michael walked on the trail with his head down, mulling over that unfortunate confrontation. He had hardly passed the café when he heard shouting on the trail ahead. Miners were running from their claims and up the trail. He joined the throng and soon came up to a mob of a few dozen crowded around five Californios, trussed and sitting back-to-back in a shaded clearing.

Michael asked a bystander what was going on. He replied that the five men had robbed a gambler and were caught with the loot on them. A judge and twelve-member jury, all miners, had been formed to try the men. He didn't know how the judge and jury were named.

"Anyway," the miner said, "the jury found them guilty and sentenced them to forty lashes. Actually, thirty-nine." Michael had heard about the "forty lashes save one", the usual punishment for thieves in the diggings. He had tried to learn the origin of the practice but was still ignorant.

Michael watched the flogging. The men were lined up on their knees and whipped brutally, thirty-nine lashes with a heavy rope. Stunned and gasping, the men were then untied and helped to their feet. The five began stumbling toward the trail.

"Wait a minute!" said a bystander. He pointed at three of the culprits. "Those three escaped after robbing and killing some miners on the Stanislaus. I recognize them! I was there and saw them before they escaped!"

The" judge" ordered the three suspects to be held and the other two released. He reconvened the "jury" and tried the three on murder charges. At the judge's request, the miner who had identified the three recounted what he knew of the charges. The three culprits were still reeling from the rope whipping and said nothing. They stared blankly at the judge, heads hanging. "Have you anything to say before I pronounce the judgment of the court?" said the judge. The suspects looked at each other, frowning, blinking, and said nothing.

"Maybe they don't understand the charges," said Michael. "They are Californios." Suddenly, the mob was silent. All stared at Michael. "Maybe they don't understand English. Shall I tell them in Spanish?"

The judge frowned silently a long moment at Michael, then turned to the mob. He shouted: "What shall I do with them?"

The response was a loud unanimous, "Hang 'em!" The three were dragged to a nearby oak and unceremoniously strung up.

Michael was stunned. As he stared at the three corpses swinging, twisting slowly in the light breeze, miners walked past, glancing aside at him, sullen, hostile.

He walked toward the trail behind a couple of men who had watched the proceedings with considerable interest. "First hangin' I've seen in the diggings," said one. "They gonna bury 'em or just dump 'em in the woods and let the coyotes take care of 'em?"

The other miner drew back and looked at his compatriot with a hint of a smile. "Oh, they'll have to bury 'em! Coyotes won't touch Mex corpses. Mex eat so much chili peppers, coyotes won't touch Mex bodies." He sobered. "Now, if they was *white*, they *could* dump 'em in the woods, and the coyotes would clean the bones, but they probably would bury the bodies, out of respect."

Michael shook his head, quickened his pace and walked around the two men.

The incident eventually gave the settlement a name. Hangtown.

Back in camp, sitting at the dinner campfire, Michael described the affair to Mindy and added his usual advice: any time you see a gathering of miners, don't ask what's going on. Just get away as quickly as possible. She agreed, then reminded him that she could take care of herself. He lunged at her, and they wrestled, laughing and squealing.

———

High noon. Michael and Mindy sat in the shade of the large oak that towered over their tent and fire circle. They leaned against a down log, munching on the dry enchiladas, no sauce, he bought at the new café. They watched a pair of mourning doves scratching in the leafy debris beside the tent.

"Interesting morning," he said. "Confirmed some impressions of the diggings that have been forming since we arrived. It's white man's country. White *American* man's country. Californios will be tolerated as long as they are making enchiladas for sale, not competing at the streams. Likewise, Jews, as long as they're behind the counter of their clothing store. Even white foreigners better be careful. I heard that some Frenchies and Australians were chased from claims up north. Goes without sayin' that black people aren't tolerated on the streams. I've seen three Blacks since we arrived, all working in somebody's store. I understand there are some working the streams, all working for white men."

"That's probably true all over California, now that it's American, don't you think?"

"Yeah, probably."

They looked up at Hal and Sal scrambling down the path, slippery from the night's light rain. "Hey, folks," called Hal.

"Hal-Sal, come on down," said Michael.

"Morning, afternoon," said Sal, waving. They rubbed their shoes on grass, removing trail mud.

"I see you've discovered the new café," said Hal, pointing at the enchiladas.

"Yep," said Michael, "most welcome," holding up his enchilada.

"The café owners worked a claim 'bout a mile north of here till they were run off. They left but come back just a couple months later with a woman and opened the café. Everybody likes the café, including the roughnecks that had run 'em off."

"I s'pose they'll be tolerated now since they have learned their place and make fine enchiladas," said Mindy.

"You boys want to sit a spell?" Michael said.

"Thanks," said Hal, "but we're going up the trail to see where they're having the party this evening. It's at the new place that's goin' up, a saloon, they say. About a mile north up the trail. It's just a bare building with a few chairs and a board over a couple of barrels for a bar, but they say it will be a regular saloon before long. They're having a dance and music tonight with cheap drink, sort of an announcement of the opening of the place. You going up?"

Michael and Mindy looked at each other. "First I've heard of it," Michael said. "Maybe we'll see you there."

Hal and Sal said their goodbyes and scrambled up the slippery path to the trail. Once on the trail, they waved and disappeared behind brush.

Michael put an arm around her shoulders and squeezed. "Want to go?"

She leaned up and kissed him. "Why not? Might be a good chance to have a look at the local two-legged wildlife."

———

Mindy and Michael walked on the dark trail, barely visible in the moonlight. They heard the faint sounds of music and laughter in the darkness ahead before coming up to the clearing in front of the beginnings of a stout frame building. Lanterns hanging on the porch illuminated the yard and the three musicians, two violins and a guitarist, who played vigorously, swaying and gyrating on the porch. A large bonfire in the yard further illuminated the scene. Scores of people, all men, crowded around the fire and stood below the players, sloshing their drinks, dancing jigs, singing loudly, more shouting than singing, stomping and circling.

"Oh, my," Mindy said softly. They stood at the edge of light. She looked at Michael who stared at the yard, frowning.

"Hey, neighbors!" said Hal and Sal together. They held up their glasses and walked toward them.

"Come on in," Hal said, taking Michael by an arm, pulling him. Michael looked at Mindy. She pulled a face, nodded. The four walked together toward the fire circle.

As they advanced into the yard, they were increasingly illuminated by the fire and lanterns. As the revelers became aware of the newcomers, the noise level lessened until only the music and scattered voices beyond the light were heard. All stared at Mindy, clearly a young, pretty woman in spite of the man's trousers.

The noise level suddenly increased as tipsy men advanced on Mindy, asking for a dance, ignoring Michael. Can I get you a drink, come sit with me, I want to talk with you, and more, the talk becoming an alcoholic frenzy. Michael pushed suitors away, right and left. He reached for Mindy to pull her away.

Then, a man pushed his way past the others and stood before her. He bowed, extended his hand. "Missy, Mindy, may I have this dance?" Michael stepped toward him, and Mindy put a hand lightly on his arm to stop him. Michael recognized the man at the claim near theirs who had said Mindy looked like his little sister. Michael looked at Mindy who smiled. He stepped back.

She took the man's hand and walked with him toward the porch. They stopped in the yard below the players. The revelers quieted, moved aside, watched as Mindy and the man danced slowly to soft music from the trio. The mob had become spectators, entranced, silently watching the pair dancing.

When the music ended, the man stepped back, bowed to Mindy. She smiled, mouthed a *thank you* and went to Michael as the mob cheered, shouted, patted the man and Michael on their backs. Some weaved, bowed theatrically to Mindy, crowding around her. She smiled and nodded to them.

Michael took her arm. "Time to go before this mob gets out of hand." He led her away, waving off the miners who called to her for a dance or conversation. She ducked her head, smiling, waving.

On the trail, beyond firelight and lantern light, Michael and Mindy stopped. She put hands to her cheeks and turned to Michael, wide-eyed. "I'll never forget that as long as I live."

"Nor should you." He put an arm around her shoulders, and they walked down the dark trail, only lightly illuminated by slivers of moonlight that penetrated the canopy of the tall oaks.

"Michael!" They stopped, turned to see a man running toward them. The man stopped, breathing heavily. It was Barney who had introduced himself at the enchilada vendor at Sutter's Fort. "Thought that was you up at the dance." He smiled at Mindy. "Mindy, isn't it?" She smiled and nodded.

Barney was excited. "Michael, got a proposition for you. Less than a mile upstream from our place, some boys found a pocket of gold by digging a hole just off the beach at their claim. I want to give this a try. Me and my pard this afternoon went across the stream from our claim to have a look. The spot is not claimed, and the water at the bank is too deep for panning. Out of curiosity, we dug around back from the bank and found color about a foot down! We're gonna sink some deeper holes tomorrow and see what we can find. We don't intend to go real deep, but we still want to have some hands available in case we have a problem.

"How about coming up to our place, only about a half mile upstream from you and chip in? We'll go fifty-fifty on whatever we find. Tomorrow. If it pans out, we'll continue as long as it pays. How about it?"

Michael frowned. "Hmm. Never thought about that. We don't have anyone across the stream from us, either. That bank there also is too deep for panning." He frowned, turned to Mindy. "What do you think? Likely just for a day or so. We could get Hal-Sal to watch our place."

"Fine with me. Might be good to get away a day or two. Okay."

"How do we find your place? You said a half mile?" Michael said.

"Yeah. You'll know our claim by the derelict cabin just back from the stream. It was built by the fellas who had the claim before us. The cabin leans to the side, looks like it's about to collapse, sorta like me." He grinned. "You can't miss it."

———

The sun had barely cleared the eastern horizon when Mindy and Michael began the walk up the trail. He carried a shovel and a bucket with a slender rope attached. Sunbeams filtered through the heavy oak canopy across the stream and sparkled on the leafy ground vegetation.

They had visited Hal-Sal the previous evening and the twins said they would be happy to watch their claim. "Hal and Sal are such nice fellas," said Mindy. "I really like them."

"You really like fellas too easily. Gonna get you in trouble one of these days."

She smiled, put both arms around his waist awkwardly as they walked and squeezed. "You know, I bet I could have my pick of any male in the mines. Not because it's me, but because there's no competition."

He looked aside at her. "Yeah, you probably could, and that means I would have to shoot a few of those males to keep you at my side and in my bed. You want me to do that?"

"I guess I'll just have to be satisfied with what I have." She squeezed her hold on his waist, then jumped aside laughing when he reached for her butt.

"There it is," said Mindy. She pointed at the dilapidated cabin, leaning so much it indeed looked ready to collapse if simply touched. Barney and his pard stood in the shallows, bailing out the ruins of what had been a boat. They straightened and waved.

Mindy and Michael walked to the water's edge eyed the boat, only a few inches of water in the bottom. Michael frowned. "I think what you're telling us, Barney, is that we'll likely have to swim to the other side."

"No, no," Barney said, "we had it bailed out yesterday and rowed to the other side before it filled. I'll get you there, one at a time. Just, uh, be ready to swim if that becomes necessary."

Michael turned to Mindy. "You swim?"

"Yes. You?"

"No."

Barney held up a hand. "It's okay. The water's not deep, probably not over five feet anywhere."

"Probably."

"Michael," said Barney, "this wooden boat ain't gonna sink. Even if it fills with water, it won't sink. If that happens, just relax and hold onto the boat. We'll pull you over. Look, Eddy's already across." While they talked, Eddy had walked across on the bottom, swimming only the last few feet. He now stood on the bank, grinning, holding a shovel overhead.

"Okay," said Michael. "I'm getting in. I want you two on each side of the boat." He stepped gingerly into the boat, sat slowly on the seat and gripped the gunwales tightly. Barney and Mindy, holding the gunwales, walked slowly from the bank. She watched Michael, stern, jaw clenched, as he looked over the sides at the blue-green water. She turned aside, struggling to avoid laughing.

After less than a minute of floating, Michael looking over the side at the stream, the boat nudged the far bank. Eddy extended a hand and helped Michael step up to the bank. He inhaled deeply, looked around, exhaled. "I don't know what you people are going on about. That was nothing."

Eddy and Barney looked at each other as Eddy pulled a face. They picked up shovels from the bank and went to the spot that Barney had selected for the first excavation. Michael picked up his shovel and walked after them, Mindy trailing. She leaned up and kissed his cheek. "Good job, sailor."

They proceeded to dig a circular hole, about four feet wide. Two men dug, back-to-back. The soil was moist from recent light rains, and the hole deepened. At about two feet deep, Barney held up a hand.

"Hold on," said Barney. He stooped and carefully collected a flake from the last shovelful. He showed the others the flake, then dropped it into a small bottle on the level above the hole. He gripped the shovel and pushed it into the soil.

"Whoa," said Michael. He reached past Barney, dug a finger into the wall above Barney's shovel, pulled out a tiny nugget and showed it to the others.

They continued digging, deepening the hole, finding a flake here and there, but not enough to generate any great enthusiasm for the task.

Michael continued to dig while Barney climbed from the hole and stood at the top, hauling up the filled buckets. "How deep did these people upstream go down?" Michael said.

"They didn't really hit pay dirt till about twenty feet."

Michael looked at the bottom of the hole. He figured he was standing about ten or twelve feet below the surface. He had found an occasional flake and tiny nugget in the wall and in his shovel. Those on the surface had similar success from the filled buckets. They declared they would sift through the soil more carefully later.

Michael looked at the soil at his feet. "I wouldn't call this a bonanza. Got to go deeper." As he spoke, looking up, a sifting of soil fell from the wall above onto his head. He shook his head, tousled his hair vigorously with a hand. "Throw down that heavy rope."

Barney stepped back, out of Michael's sight, then returned and dropped a coil into the hole. Michael fashioned a slip noose at the end and dropped it over his shoulders, tightening it slightly under his arms.

"Just in case," Michael said.

"Be careful," said Mindy. "Should you come up now?"

"We'll try it a bit deeper. If I call, everybody up there pull like hell."

He pushed the shovel into the soil at the bottom and filled the bucket. He gave the bucket line a few tugs, and Barney pulled the bucket up. Michael returned to his shovel.

"Whoa! Whoa!" Barney shouted. "You hit it, Michael! This bucket is loaded. It's full of flakes and—look!—three little nuggets. Four! And here's a bigger one!"

Michael heard, but he wasn't listening. He looked at his feet, watching the water seeping up, covering his shoes. He looked up and blinked when a shower of soil broke from the tunnel side and dropped to his face. He winced, blinking, then shook his head when a heavy layer of soil slipped from the side and fell on his head. At a gurgling sound below, he looked down and saw that the water seep had become a steady flow and now covered his ankles.

"Pull! Pull! Pull me up! Now! Pull me up!"

Barney dropped the bucket and all three men grabbed the rope and pulled. Michael slid up the side of the hole slowly, his back against the side, then his front on the side, pushing against the wall with his hands. Soil broke from the side and dribbled down.

Suddenly, the rope loosened, and he dropped to the bottom. The pullers on the surface had lost their grip, and he fell. He dropped to the bottom, splashing into the pool, now waist- deep. Soil from tunnel sides above crumbled from a dozen surfaces and rained down.

"Pull! Pull!" Immediately, the rope tightened, and he began to move up, inch by inch, sliding up the wet wall.

Then it was over. His head and shoulders emerged from the hole, and all three on the surface grabbed arms and pulled him from the hole. He lay on his back, gasping. His clothing was completely soaked, and his face and hair were covered with muddy soil. Barney loosened the coil and untied the rope. Mindy rubbed his face with a bandanna. She leaned down, kissed his cheek.

Michael, on his back, looked up at Mindy. "Well, that was no fun."

"Sorry, old man. Sorry." Barney bent down, frowned. He fingered Michael's hair and withdrew a small nugget. He showed it to the others. "I swear, Michael, you're the strangest miner I ever knew. Never saw anybody else mining with his head." He put an arm around Michael's shoulders. "Now, let's get you up." Barney and Mindy helped Michael stand, weaving. He shuddered.

"C'mon, let's get you over there to the fire," Barney said. "Eddy's got the breakfast fire kindled, and it'll warm you up for the walk back to your place. I suppose you're finished for the day."

Michael looked grimly at him. "No, I'm not finished for the day. I'm *finished*."

Barney smiled. "I'm with you on that point, my man." He and Mindy each took an arm, guided him to the boat and ferried him across the stream with no hesitation and no problem.

On the other side, they sat by the fire, Michael wrapped in the blanket Eddy had handed him. "Are we coming down to your place tomorrow and dig some holes across the stream?" said Eddy, grinning.

"Go to hell," Michael said. He looked up, frowning. Then he relaxed and smiled.

Any thought about the prospect of digging holes across the stream at their claim was dismissed when Michael waded over and examined the soil. It was soaked from recent showers. He and Mindy decided that they were not serious enough about mining to risk their lives in the process. They agreed that they were content to enjoy their modest success in their beloved sylvan setting.

They squatted side by side in the shallows, dipping their pans in the stream. They started at loud shouts from the trail above camp.

"Indians! Indians!" Half a dozen excited men ran up the trail behind Michael and Mindy's tent. Michael stood, holding the dripping pan at his side.

Michael stood. "What's happening?" he shouted.

"Indians are killing people up there!" He pointed ahead, upstream, and ran on.

Michael looked at Mindy who still squatted in the shallows, looking at him. He bent quickly, kissed the top of her head. "Stay here!" Running toward the tent, he checked the pistol on his hip. He stooped and went inside, came out holding his rifle and ran toward the path.

"Be careful!" she said. "Don't forget to come back!"

Michael caught up with the running men on the trail. "What's going on," he said, breathlessly.

"Indians attacked a couple of miners who were out hunting. They killed one man. The other man ran back to the camps and raised the alarm. The word went out up and down the river, and we're going up to the camp where they're forming up."

They ran around a turning in the trail and almost collided with a large gathering of angry, rifle-wielding miners crowded around a man who held a fist aloft, shouting. His bearded face was hard, and he twisted round and round to make contact with all around him.

"We knew this was coming someday! The savages have finally attacked! We must respond to their treachery! Unless we respond now, we'll never be safe! We must wipe them out, once and for all!"

The angry mob responded, raising fists and brandishing rifles and pistols. "Wipe 'em out! Kill 'em all!"

Michael looked around. He was shocked at the spectacle. He knew some of the men on sight. He had spoken to some of them. But they did not resemble any of the soft-spoken men he had talked with on the trail or at the store. Now, they were altered, bent on killing.

"They're not all guilty. Some are good people." The voice came from the back of the mob, firm and forceful, loud enough to be heard above the tumult.

The crowd was suddenly quiet. All heads turned toward the speaker. He was dressed in rough work clothes, like every miner. His demeanor was not unlike the others, until this moment. He had questioned a view that gripped everyone here. He raised his chin, ever so slightly.

"Say your piece, Ezra. Quick," said the speaker. The mob glared at Ezra.

"A number of us had Indians working for us. I had three working for me. They were good workers."

"Were? What happened to 'em?" said the speaker. He looked around at the mob, a hint of a smile playing about his lips.

"You know what happened to them. You and your cronies beat 'em up and run 'em off. I never saw them again."

"They were *Indians!*" the speaker said. "We ain't safe with *Indians* around. You never know when they're gonna come at us! The trouble today proves it!"

Michael could restrain himself no longer. "This isn't the first killing in the mines." Everyone turned to see this new speaker. "I haven't been here long, and I've already heard of four killings within a couple or so miles of me. Miners killing miners. Have you chased these killers from the placers?"

"Michael, ain't it?" Michael nodded. "Those killings were justified. Self-defense. Drunk hot-heads git outta hand. This has nothin' to do with what we gotta do now...and apparently nothin' to do with you." He pointed a finger at Michael.

The speaker turned back to the mob, raised his fist. "Are you with me! We need to be after 'em before they git away!" The miners responded with a loud collective shout, waving pistols and rifles. The leader set out for the forest, striding hard and holding his rifle aloft. The others surged after him, checking six-shooters in holsters and gripping rifle straps on shoulders.

Members of the mob ran into the woods and disappeared, their shouting and laughter diminishing. Then it was quiet.

Only Michael and the miner who had spoken against the mob action were left. "Well, we didn't convince anyone, but at least they didn't shoot us," said Michael. He walked to the man and extended a hand. "I'm Michael."

The other man took his hand and shook, smiling. "Andy. Michael, best we get outta here and keep out of sight till all this settles down. If they don't kill a bunch of Indians, they might blame us. So watch out. I'm serious. I know old Fred, the leader of the mob." Andy and Michael set out in different directions.

Back at the claim, Michael told Mindy about the incident. He said to avoid anybody talking about Indian problems, especially a hard case named Fred. And to deny she knows anybody named Michael.

———

At mid-morning, Mindy squatted in the shallows, trousers rolled to her knees, working with the shallow pan. Upstream, at the edge of their claim, Michael dug into a rocky ledge with a short knife, breaking off chips, dislodging the occasional tiny gold bit. He carefully collected the bits and dropped them into the small glass bottle at his feet.

He picked up the bottle, compared it at a distance with the bottle on the beach behind Mindy. Her bottle held twice as much gold as his. He shook his head. She habitually was more successful than he in collecting flakes. He probably found more nuggets than she since he worked rock formations, but her collections invariably were richer than his.

"Hey, neighbors!" said Sal-Hal. Mindy and Michael looked up and waved at the twins sliding down the path.

Mindy and Michael stood. "Are you off to scout out another party?" said Mindy, smiling.

"Good morning, folks," said Hal. "On the contrary. We're going up to a burial. After you left the party the other night, one of the old boys there, Jerry by name, I didn't know him, Jerry had a heart attack and keeled over. Must have been too much excitement for him. They're gonna bury him at noon up at the new cemetery behind the café.

"There's gonna be a preacher there. When we were crowded around the old boy that night on the ground, one of the fellas said he used to be a preacher, and he would say a few words. Some of us looked around at each other, this fella being pretty tipsy, but why not? Anyway, he should be sober by now, and nobody else offered to say any words."

Michael looked at Mindy, and she nodded. He turned to Hal-Sal. "We'll join you. Noon, you said?" The twins nodded, smiled, waved and climbed the path to the trail.

———

Three dozen miners crowded around an open grave, caps in hand, listening to the self-proclaimed ex-preacher. Michael and Mindy stood at the back of the group. The new cemetery lay in an oak grove just off the trail near the café. The new open grave lay among three others that were no older than a few weeks, with scattered grass shoots growing on the mounds. Another appeared to be no older than a few days, the mound clean of any green growth.

The preacher-miner read from the open Bible he held. "For I am convinced that neither death, nor life, nor angels, nor rulers, nor things present, nor things to come, nor powers, nor height, nor depth, nor anything else in all creation, will be able to separate us..." He stopped, looking at a miner across the open grave.

The preacher-miner was distracted by the miner who seemed to have stopped listening. The miner had leaned forward, looking into the excavation. He leaned so far forward that he went to his knees. The preacher smiled ever so slightly at this act of devotion. Then, he was shocked when the miner eased slowly down into the open grave to stand beside the corpse. Other bystanders frowned, staring down at him.

The miner standing in the pit reached across the body to the opposite wall and plucked something from the side. He held up a pea-size gold nugget, smiling. Bystanders above gasped. The miner in the grave reached again to the wall, dug his fingers into the soil and pulled out a grape-sized nugget. He held it high, grinning from ear to ear.

The worshippers above shouted, laughed, jumped down into the grave and began digging into the walls with fingers and pocketknives. Mindy looked at Michael, her look a question. He frowned, shrugged, nodded. She eased down the wall into the pit, looked around, found a shell at the bottom of the pit and commenced digging into the wall.

"Haul him out, boys!" shouted a miner beside Mindy. Half a dozen men hefted the corpse and gently laid it above. As those in the pit found nuggets and flakes, exclaiming with each find, the preacher-miner tossed the Bible over his shoulder and jumped down into the grave.

The scratching and digging continued until sunset. Shovels were borrowed from nearby claims and eager miners cut into the sides of the grave and dug new pits around the open grave. Michael joined the throng at these new excavations. At dusk, the lot decided that the site had been essentially emptied of its treasure. All agreed it had been great fun.

They gently lowered the body to its resting place, filled the grave and tamped the soil down. A miner who said he knew the deceased said he would put up a cross the next day. The miner-preacher found his Bible in the brush, dusted it off and pushed it into his coat pocket with a handful of small gold nuggets.

As they walked from the cemetery, Mindy showed Michael the tiny nuggets she had collected. She dropped the nuggets into a pocket, took his arm in both hands and leaned on his shoulder. The sun had just dipped below the horizon, coloring the thin layers of filmy clouds shades of blue-gray and magenta.

"Most fun I've had at a funeral in a long time," Michael said. He pulled a handful of small nuggets from a pocket and showed her. She smiled and cocked her head.

She looked around, still holding his arm. When they were alone on the trail, she pushed a hand inside her pants pocket, pulled out a plum-sized gleaming nugget and showed it to him.

He stopped, eyes wide. "Wha—"

She giggled, wriggling, then laughed. She pushed the nugget back into the pocket, grabbed handfuls of his shirt with both hands and pulled him roughly to her. "I love you," she said. He leaned down and kissed her.

———

"I'm stopping here," said Mindy, looking around at the group who stared at her, mesmerized. "You probably know what happened next, anyway."

"Whew," said Carmel, fanning herself with a hand.

"What a pair. I'll let you stop, but I want to hear the rest of the story."

"Next time," said Mindy, leaning back, smiling.

"Yeah," Adam said, "we need to find out the reasoning behind naming Mindy for that hot little number."

Mindy smiled. "Well, I suppose we could talk about that."

Adam grinned, cocked his head. "Out on the front porch?"

Mindy punched him on a shoulder and smiled. "I'm going to bed," she said to the group, then looked at Adam, "all by myself."

The group stood, collected dishes and glasses and took them to the kitchen. They said their good nights and made their way toward their beds.

Adam and Jon headed toward their assigned bedroom. "That tale exhausted me," said Adam. "That little Mindy is one hot number."

"Which one?"

"Hmm."

CHAPTER 3

JON

During breakfast, in spite of some good-natured groaning about the quality of the accommodation, the guests agreed that they slept well, they were enjoying a surprisingly sumptuous breakfast, and they had enjoyed yesterday's story enormously.

"You know," said Adam, "I've read bits and pieces about the Forty-Niners and the gold rush, but I never paid much attention to the miners as people. They were individuals, and they had lives before reaching the Sierra placers. In the diggings, seems to me, they had to learn stuff completely new to them, adjusting to a completely new way of living. Pretty challenging." He looked around the table. "Good story." He looked at Stephany. "I'm ready for another story, Steph." Some mumbled agreement from the group, some enthusiastic comments.

"Well, thanks, Adam," said Stephany. "If you bunch didn't appear willing to listen to another story this morning, I was going to send you outside to shovel snow."

"Story, story," chanted Mindy and M'lis. General laughter and table thumping.

The six looked around the table. Silence. "Well?" said Stephany.

"You know, it's interesting," said Jon, "this story-telling." He frowned, staring at the window. "Quite a coincidence."

Stephany crossed her arms and leaned back. She focused on Jon, waited, then: "Go on."

"In just the past month or so, I've been thinking about the bits and pieces I've heard over the years about a shadowy ancestor. I've talked with family in central California and emailed a few in Oregon, and this fellow becomes more and more interesting."

"Why interesting?" said Carmelita. "What brands him interesting?"

Jon stared a long moment at Carmelita. "He was a murderer. Or he wasn't."

Stephany's eyes opened wide. "Whoa," she said softly. "You're going to tell us about him?"

Jon nodded.

Stephany rose and ushered all at the table toward the fireplace. Some pointed at the dishes. "Later," said Stephany. "I got a date with a murderer."

———

Dugan sprawled on the settee in the sitting room, sipping his second cup of coffee. He had volunteered to help his mother clean up the breakfast dishes, but she smiled and shooed him from the kitchen. It was the same scenario on most mornings, and both knew the routine. His shift at the mine didn't begin until 2:00, and he was content each morning to relax with the town's new daily newspaper while he could.

Dugan was not especially happy with miner's work,

but if you lived in Black Hawk, Colorado, and were an able-bodied male—he was a strapping thirty-two-year-old —more than likely you worked at the hard rock gold mine.

He looked up suddenly at muffled shouts from outside. He lowered the newspaper and saw through the panes of the closed window a throng of people in the street running in the same direction, shouting and waving. He threw the paper aside. This could mean only one thing.

He ran to the door, pulling on a jacket. His mother stood in the open doorway. "Stay here!" he said. He joined the throng of terrified people who ran toward the mine at the end of the street. They crossed the open square and stopped at the mine entrance, where a boiling black cloud of dust and smoke poured from the tunnel opening. People ran about, confused, excited.

"What happened?" Dugan asked a bystander. "Was there an explosion?"

The man turned abruptly to him. "I don't think so. I was in the grocery store over there when I heard a loud thump, like something heavy falling, like a whole hillside collapsed. I ran outside and saw this cloud coming out of the tunnel. I still don't know what happened. I'm not a miner. Those fellas over there seem to be." He pointed at a couple of dozen men running toward the billowing dust.

Dugan ran to the men who now stood at the edge of the dark cloud, wiping dust from their faces and shaking dust from handkerchiefs. "Know what happened?" said Dugan.

"Don't know for sure, but I'm guessing the top or sides of the tunnel collapsed," he said, without taking his eyes off the tunnel.

A shout went up from the crowd. A scattering of men

emerged from the billowing dust cloud, running, choking, stumbling from the cloud to the open courtyard. They wiped their faces with cloths and sleeves, coughing and spitting.

The mob pressed closer to the entrance, taking stumbling miners by an arm, helping them move away from the entrance, away from the dark cloud.

Dugan studied the miners' faces as they emerged, looking for his brother or someone he knew. He recognized a few faces, but no one he knew. Their friends mostly had the same shift as his, the afternoon schedule. Only Clay among their acquaintances had opted for the morning shift.

He frantically questioned escaping miners, blackened by soot and debris, as they emerged from the dust cloud. "Do you know Clay Adams? He's my brother. Did you see him?" Coughing, shaking heads, as they wiped their faces, stumbling away from the chaos.

"Dugan," said a soft voice.

Dugan whirled around to see a familiar face. "Finlay! Have you seen Clay?"

Finlay, once a close friend of his deceased father, laid a hand softly on Dugan's shoulder, and he knew. "Sorry, Dugan. Clay was right in the middle of the tunnel when the ceiling collapsed. It looked like the whole mountain fell. I was walking beside him back there, coming out at the end of our shift, but I fell behind when I had a coughing fit. I was back a ways, leanin' against the wall, or I woulda been in th' middle of it." He patted Dugan's shoulder. "So sorry, son."

Dugan, in shock, jaw hanging, watched the last of the survivors stumble from the dust cloud, met by family or friends, helped on their way on the street, away from the debris that still billowed from the tunnel.

Then he saw the mine owner, Christopher Throckmorton, and a few others standing in front of the office building near the mine face. He had not noticed them before in the confusion. His grief turned to anger as he strode toward them.

Dugan stopped in front of Throckmorton, leaned into his face. "The ceiling collapsed! My brother and I talked about that faulty ceiling a dozen times. A lot of others noticed the fault lines in the ceiling. We reported the weakness to you *many* times. You! Why didn't you brace it? You knew it was a danger, and you never braced it!"

Throckmorton's face was cold, without expression. He looked at the others standing with him. Billy, the owner's son, standing beside his father, spoke softly to Dugan. "This was a tragic event. We will deal with it."

"What do you mean, you will deal with it! You were negligent! You killed my brother!"

Billy put up a hand, palm outward as if to quiet Dugan. "Easy, man. I said we know this was tragic, and we will deal with it."

"Deal with it? Deal with it? That's not going to bring my brother back." He turned to Throckmorton, his face hard. He raised a clenched fist in Throckmorton's face, spoke softly. "You killed my brother, you son-of-a bitch."

The owner did not flinch. Without taking his eyes off Dugan, he turned slightly toward his son and gestured toward Dugan with a slight nod.

Billy stepped away from his father. He pulled his jacket aside, revealing the holster. "Back off," he said softly to Dugan.

Dugan frowned, braced himself, his face hard. "Don't threaten me, you monkey!"

Billy laid a hand on the pistol grip, paused, then drew and began bringing the gun up.

Dugan, grim, still angry but suddenly in control, drew his pistol quickly, whipped it up and fired. Billy was blown backward with a shot to the chest and collapsed on his back.

Throckmorton, suddenly ashen-faced, grim, stared at his son at his feet as others bent over him. Throckmorton turned slowly to Dugan. "You'll pay for this. You are a dead man."

Dugan, jaw hanging, stepped backward, turned and ran to the mass of miners behind him whose mood had changed from fear to anger as they watched the confrontation. Dugan disappeared into the mob.

———

Dugan sat with his mother at a late supper that evening. He had told her everything that happened this day, and they grieved the loss of brother and son. The family had always known about the dangers inherent in mining. The husband and father had been a miner his entire adult life. He died just two years ago in a fit of wheezing and coughing. Now the youngest son was gone, another fatality of the dangers of hard rock mining.

Dugan had already told his mother that he would have to leave town. Tonight. He would take one of their horses from the livery. She was to sell the other two and the tack to help meet expenses. He promised to send money if he found employment. If all else failed, or if she preferred, she was to pack up and go to her sister in Denver.

They looked up abruptly at the sound of loud knocking at the door. He turned to her, stood, held out a hand to restrain her movement to stand. Stay there, he mouthed. He went to the door and opened it. There stood three grim-faced men.

"Sheriff," said Dugan.

The sheriff frowned. "Dugan Miller, you're under arrest for the murder of Billy Throckmorton. Get a few things, if you like, and come with us. You ain't comin' home tonight, or tomorrow night, for that matter."

Dugan nodded to his mother who had come up behind him in the kitchen doorway. He went to his room, packed a few pieces of clothing, looked at the window, pondering. He knew, everybody in town knew, the sheriff was in the pocket of the mine owner. He wondered whether Throckmorton had enough citizens in his pocket to pack a jury. *Probably.*

He carried the small bag of clothing to the entry hall where his mother stood, misty-eyed. She hugged him and kissed his cheek. He hugged her, she touched his cheek, and he stepped outside. The sheriff took his arm, and they began to walk away, the sheriff's two companions following.

The sheriff's entourage had moved hardly a block from Dugan's house when a couple dozen men he recognized as miners stepped from the darkness of a side street and walked out slowly to stand in the sheriff's path. The sheriff and the others stopped. Dugan followed the sheriff's gaze in looking behind to see a similar number of miners slowly, quietly, walking up behind the group.

The sheriff and the others turned back to the front. "All right, Duffy, what do you have in mind?" said the sheriff to the leader of the group in front.

"Evenin', Sheriff," said Duffy. "I'll make this quick and short. You have arrested a man who shot somebody in self-defense. He shot a man who was intent on shootin' him. Ever'body knows that. I believe you know that. So we wish to see justice done by you releasing the man who you wrongly arrested. What d'you say?"

"I'd say you're interfering with a law officer who is doin' his duty."

"That's what I thought you'd say, Barney. So let's tell it like it is. If you don't agree to release Dugan right now of your own accord, we're taking him off your hands. Now, I don't think you're prepared to arrest the lot of us, which would shut down the mine, and we already have a deputation of like-minded people—they're not amongst us here—who are prepared to go to the governor to tell him all about your cozy relationship with Throckmorton."

The sheriff pondered, frowning, staring silently at Duffy. After a long moment, he gestured with a nod of his head to the two men with him, and they walked around the miners in front and into the side street.

The miners watched the sheriff and his men disappear into the darkness. Then they erupted in shouts, wahoos, laughter and back slappings. The mob disintegrated into twos and threes and walked away in all directions, chatting and chuckling.

Duffy and Dugan were left alone. "You best get lost, young man," said Duffy. "For a while, anyway, until we know what's comin' down in town. I'll take you to your horse that's saddled over there with filled saddlebags." He pointed into the dark side street. "I'll tell your mom what's happenin'. I'll be happy to receive any communication from you, but I don't know how you're gonna do that. Now, let's get to your horse so you can be on your way. I doubt you know what you'll be doin' or where you're goin', and I don't want to know. Whatever you're gonna do, it's better than bein' hanged, right?"

———

Throckmorton, seated at his desk, scowled at the sheriff who stood stiffly before the desk. "I want to see a warrant for that man's arrest," said Throckmorton, "and I want to see a bounty offered for him. Dead or alive. An associate in Denver has recommended a bounty hunter to me. He has a reputation, I'm told. He should arrive in town tomorrow and go straight to you. After you've given him my instruction, tell him to come see me. Is all this clear enough?"

The sheriff fidgeted, shifting his weight. A bead of perspiration rolled down his cheek. "Yes, sir, I'll take care of it."

"By 'taking care of it', I take it to mean you'll do it."

"Yessir."

"Keep me informed." Throckmorton dismissed him with a wave. He looked down at a paper on his desk.

The sheriff frowned, turned abruptly, and strode to the door. Outside, he walked stiffly in the hall, head down, mumbled softly to himself, "son of a bitch."

———

Dugan squinted at the setting sun, enjoying the cool respite from the day's heat. Leaving at night, he had forgotten his hat, just one indication of the turmoil he was in. From his camp just below the top of the ridge, he looked down the slope to the dusty road below and beyond, across the sage-covered flats to the distant range, darkening at day's end.

Where to go? He had never had to speculate on directions in the past since he had always known where he was going. Now, he had no idea where he was going. He figured he might find employment in mining in Wyoming or Idaho. He had heard about the placer mining there. So he figured he should be traveling roughly in a northwesterly direction.

On the other hand, Throckmorton or one of his underlings or cronies might figure Dugan would look for mining employment. Maybe he should avoid mining communities. If not mining, then what? He had no skills beyond mining.

He glanced at the mare he had hobbled in a patch of good grass near the narrow, tumbling stream. He checked the two trout skewered on a switch over the low fire. When he watered the horse on arriving here, he was surprised to see trout in the shallows and scooped them up with his hands. He hoped this was a forecast of good luck on this ride. He looked up at the low gray ceiling. *Hope my good luck also covers the weather. That cloud doesn't look good. Any other time I might welcome a nice spring shower, but not now.*

He checked the fish, jerked back and blew on his burned hand, shook it. He pulled the end of the stick from the sod, laid it on a flat stone. Pulling a knife from a boot scabbard, he sliced one of the fish, watched steam rise from the hot flesh. He lifted the fish to his mouth, then suddenly dropped the stick and the fish.

He stood quickly, drawing his pistol. A rider had left the road below and approached the camp on the same path he had ridden up earlier, moving slowly up the slope through the scattered sage, making no effort to conceal himself. Dugan looked around frantically for a place to hide.

"Hey, Dugan!" the rider shouted.

Dugan relaxed. He shook his head, lowered the pistol

and pushed it into the holster. He watched the smiling rider rein up and dismount.

"Jeremy, what in god's green earth are you doing here? How did you find me?"

Jeremy squatted at the fire, warmed his hands. "I see you're expecting company." He pointed at the fish. "Which one's mine?"

Dugan smiled and offered Jeremy the switch. Jeremy pulled off a fish, dropped it on the grass and shook his scorched hand. He picked up the fish gingerly, tore off a sliver of flesh and chewed on it. "My, that's good." He took another bite. "Um, um!" He finished the small fish in half a dozen bites as Dugan waited.

Jeremy sobered, wiped his hands on his trousers. Jeremy was about Dugan's age, a nice-looking fellow, wearing faded working clothes and a narrow-brimmed hat. "As for your question, you know Clay was my best friend ever. I would've torn old Throckmorton to pieces with my bare hands if I'd been there with you. When I heard you were charged and run off, I decided to do what I could."

"What do you mean, 'charged'? The son died?"

"He did. You've been charged with murder. You know that. You were arrested and freed by the friendly mob. You know that. Good thing I wasn't there. I probably would've shot the sheriff, and I would be on the run with you. What you don't know is that the sheriff, egged on by Throckmorton, has put out a warrant for your arrest and set a bounty hunter on your trail. There's a big price on your head, dead or alive. And, by the way, this particular bounty hunter has a reputation, I'm told."

Dugan cocked his head. "I'm glad you found me instead of him."

Jeremy clapped him on a shoulder. "I heard a couple

of days ago the bounty man was due to leave after breakfast. So I left the day before in the middle of the night.
That was two days ago, and he'll be hot on the trail by
now. I found you first because I left first and ran my horse
more than I walked him. She's ready for water and grass.
Maybe water now and grass later. We need to move."

Jeremy frowned. "Dugan, any child could have found
you! You're traveling on the main road and making no
effort at hiding your trail or your camp. Hell, Dugan, you
ain't just changing where you live, you're ridin' for your
life! You gotta be more careful. Anyway, that's why I
came, to help you get where you're heading, wherever that
may be."

"That's mighty good of you, old friend. But I don't
want you to put yourself in harm's way on account
of me."

"I'll decide what I do, old friend, not you." He smiled.
"For starters, let's move this camp. You stopped a hundred
yards off the road, in full view of the road! You trying to
commit suicide?"

Dugan slapped him on the back, stood and kicked dirt
on the fire. He walked around, rubbing the ground with a
boot, removing footprints. While Jeremy waited, Dugan
saddled the mare and removed hobbles.

They mounted and kicked their horses to a lope up
the slope, disappearing over the ridgetop.

———————

The next day at high noon, Dugan and Jeremy sat their
horses just below ridgeline. Dugan had been heading up
slope toward the top of the ridge, but Jeremy stopped
him. "Pay attention, Dugan. If we're riding on the ridge-

line, we'd be outlined against the sky and visible from below."

Even where they sat now below the ridgeline, scattered sage and other bushes provided little cover. Leaving the main trail below, they had ridden over an hour up the steep hillside to the landing where they sat now. They had spoken little during the ride. Stopping now to let their horses blow, they said little, only agreeing that they weren't sure where they were or where they were going. They stared silently at the main trail below.

"Hang on!" said Jeremy. He pointed at two tiny figures, horsemen, riding slowly on the trail. The riders stopped. One of the horsemen dismounted, walked a few steps into the sage and knelt. He appeared to examine the ground. Then he hurried back to the horse, mounted, and the two kicked their horses off the trail, heading toward the base of the slope where Dugan and Jeremy sat their horses above.

"They've got the trail," said Jeremy softly. He wheeled his horse, kicked her off the trail and up the slope. Dugan followed, and they vanished over the crest.

———

For the week that followed, Jeremy and Dugan rode through the backcountry, away from roads and trails, skirting ranches and farms, habitations of any sort. They sought cover and rode as much as possible through stands of spruce and aspen. Too often, they found themselves in open prairie with no cover.

Happily, Jeremy had brought his rifle, and they were able to find ample small game. Berries and fish from the occasional small stream added to their diet. They took care to camp in secluded spots where evening campfires would not be visible from a distance. Nights were torture since they had only horse blankets and a single thin blanket each.

Dusk. Dugan and Jeremy pulled up at the hitching rail of a saloon. The building was at the edge of a cluster of a dozen shops and stores that constituted the town. They had no idea where they were precisely nor the name of the town. It didn't matter. They had tired of their scant fare and sleeping on the ground. This day, they simply looked for a safe place to eat and sleep. They knew they would have to tread carefully. They didn't know whether the bounty hunter was ahead or behind them. Or here. They looked around, saw only a couple of men walking on the boardwalk across the street. The men stopped, looked at the two strangers a moment, then went on their way.

Dugan and Jeremy untied saddlebags, hefted them and went inside. Half a dozen men sat at two of the three tables. All looked up at the spectacle of two strangers walking to the bar, then returned to their cards.

At Dugan's question, the bartender confirmed that he had a room where they could spend the night. Yes, he would take care of their horses. He scowled, seemingly irritated, as if they were intruders rather than customers.

Dugan leaned over the bar and spoke softly to the bartender. "There is this one thing. Two men are following us. I...well...I was having some fun with this man's pretty wife, and he found out. He wasn't happy about that. In fact, he announced he was gonna kill me." Dugan pulled a face. "On this occasion, he was about to draw on me, but I was just a little bit faster and had my six-shooter in his face before he cleared leather.

"We walked away peacefully from that little encounter, but he yelled after me that he and his pard were gonna catch me and kill me. I guess I shoulda shot him right there, but didn't. Anyway, we're on the road till this settles down. We think we've put them off the scent, but just in case they come asking, we'd appreciate it if you could say you ain't seen this fella."

The bartender's scowl was replaced by a grin that had broadened gradually during Dugan's discourse. "Right!" He leaned across the bar and clapped Dugan hard on a shoulder. "Now! I'll get your plates. What're yuh drinkin'? You fellas eat fast as you can. I'll go outside for a smoke and watch the street. Keep an eye on the door. I'll come in quick if I see two strangers comin' our way." He chuckled. "By damn! Ain't had any good fun like this in weeks!" He almost skipped as he headed for the door, chin high.

They ate a reasonably good meal of beef, potatoes, beans, bread and surprise, berry pie for dessert. When they finished, Dugan went to the front door to let the bartender know they were done. He came in and ushered them upstairs.

At the top of the stairs, the bartender stopped at the first door. "This ain't your room, but I thought I should tell yuh. Don't be surprised if you hear a little commotion during the night from this room. This is Betsy's room. She's a cutie, real popular with the local fellas." He grinned. They walked to the next door. "This is yours." He handed Dugan the door key and left.

The room was tiny, containing only a bed, small dresser, one chair and a small divan at the sole window. "I'll take the divan," said Jeremy. He pulled the top blanket off the bed and threw it on the divan. They agreed it had been a long, tiring day. Removing boots and trousers, they were in bed snoring within minutes. Both had taken time to lay pistols beside their pillows.

————

Jeremy, fully dressed, stood beside the bed. He touched Dugan's shoulder. Dugan's eyes opened wide as he reached for his pistol. Jeremy put his hand on the pistol and a finger on his lips. "Time to get moving," he said softly. Dugan sat up, saw the faint hint of first light through the window.

Dugan threw the cover off, sat up, scratched his head vigorously, and stood. He dressed quickly and only then saw the paper on the floor at the door. He picked it up and read, frowning. He passed it to Jeremy. He read it, and his eyes opened wide. The note read: *Men chasing you ar in next room. Came in after dark. Stay in yur room. I will tell you when they ar gone.*

Dugan looked at Jeremy, scowling. He sat down slowly on the bed, eased up when the bedsprings squeaked. He touched his six-shooter. Jeremy checked his pistol in its holster, went to the window and looked down at the street in the dim light. The street was quiet and empty but for a dog padding noiselessly down the middle of the dusty road.

After a half hour, they heard a door open. They tensed. Then, a giggle and a soft, gruff male voice. Another giggle. Then a door closing and footsteps down the hall and on the stairs. Then silence. They exchanged glances, relaxed, waited.

Ten minutes later, another door opened, followed by footsteps and a muffled male voice as the men passed their door. The footsteps receded and then sounded on the stairs. Then silence. They waited.

After another ten minutes or so, a loud knocking on the door. "It's okay. They're gone." Dugan opened the door and saw the smiling bartender. "The one that seemed to be in charge is a sour old cuss. Other fella, a young fella, seemed to be nice enough. They didn't seem to like each other much, argued some. Anyway, they're gone. I had their horses waitin' for 'em, and they took off like they knew where they was goin'. Hope his wife was nicer than him." He snorted. "Your horses 're out front." Dugan patted the bartender on his back, and they went out.

———————

Dugan and Jeremy sat their horses on a faint trail in a deep gorge. Steep rocky hillsides on each side of the trail suggested no way out if confronted on the trail. "Wish I knew which way they're riding," said Dugan. He paused. "We've been moving in a rough northwestern direction for days. Wish we knew which way the damn bounty man took from town this morning. We might be following him." He frowned. "I wonder who's with him."

"Yeah, he could be right up ahead," said Jeremy. "Right there behind that big boulder up there." He pointed at the boulder, turned to Dugan, pointed an imaginary pistol at him, cocked his thumb. "Pow," softly. He smiled.

"Not funny." Dugan pondered. "What do you say we head due west? That should take us into Utah. We can turn north any time we want if we decide we've shaken them. What do you think?"

He shrugged. "Sounds good."

They reversed and rode till they emerged from the gorge. There, they left the trail, rode southward over a rough rolling plain for a few miles, then turned due west, according to their reckoning. They soon left the high mountains and rode in open sage country. No trail of any sort was in sight. They rode on hard ground when they could find it so the horses would not leave prints.

———

For days, they saw no one and began to feel safe, though they began to yearn for friendly company. And fresh vegetables. Rabbit and fish and squirrel provided some nutrition and bulk, but they were tiring of the fare. They saw pronghorn antelope among the scattered sagebrush, but only at a distance, so they could only watch as the shy animals bounded away.

Then, on this day, a day that Dugan would never forget, they sat their horses on a rising, looking down a dry sagebrush slope to a cluster of a dozen houses in a broad valley. Large gardens lay adjacent to the houses. A small herd of cattle grazed beyond the gardens.

"Looks like a meetinghouse, or a church, there at the center," said Dugan. "I'm guessing it's a Mormon town."

"Would we be welcome?" Jeremy said.

Dugan stared at the settlement, sighed heavily. "Dunno. But I'm getting tired of looking only at rocks and sagebrush and my horse's head. And you." He smiled thinly. "We're gonna lose the sun shortly, and it would be nice to find a bed or a warm barn to sleep in rather than the usual cold hard ground. Let's have a look."

"Risky."

Dugan shrugged and moved ahead. They rode down the slope and turned onto a dusty road. The road showed evidence of use, showing hoofprints and wagon wheel ruts. Nearing the houses, they saw a man standing in a neat, fenced garden. He leaned against a hoe, watching them. A middle-aged man wearing loose overalls stood outside the fence, watching them, his face blank. He wore no hat, and his hair stood out in all directions. Dugan waved to both of them.

Neither responded. They simply stared. Then, the farmer walked toward them, swinging the hoe. He stopped at the edge of the garden. "Howdy," he said.

"We're traveling in country we don't know," Dugan said. "Are we in Utah?"

"Yep. This is Vernal. We're a Mormon town, in case that means anything to you." His look was stern.

"Well, I take it to mean that it's a nice town where good people live." He smiled. "We've been on the road some time, and we're looking for someplace to spend the night, maybe someplace where we could eat as well."

The farmer stared at them a long moment. "Why are you on the road with no gear, no wagon or packhorse?"

Dugan and Jeremy exchanged a glance. "To tell the truth," Dugan said, "we're running from a crooked sheriff who is chasing us for something we didn't do. We had to get away till the townspeople can get rid of him."

"Hmm." He paused, frowning. "I understand. You probably know that Mormons have had trouble with crooked law for a long time."

"Yes, I know. Bad business."

The farmer frowned again, looked aside at the man standing behind the fence, then back at Dugan. "There's no public house or hotel in Vernal. You can stay in my barn. There's lots of loose hay, and I have blankets you can use. You'll eat with us in the house." Without waiting for a response, he shouldered the hoe, turned and walked on the road toward the house. The other man followed him, looking blankly over his shoulder at them.

Dugan looked at Jeremy who shrugged and nodded. They walked their horses after the farmer.

———

"That was the finest meal we've had in many a day, Mr. Alvord," said Dugan. He and Jeremy sat at a table with Alvord, four women and the other man they had seen at the garden. Alvord had introduced them as his three wives, a daughter and his brother. All smiled, embarrassed and looking down, except the brother who simply stared at them.

"You'll have Lucy to thank for that," said Alvord. "She's the head cook around here. She has a lot of good help as well." All of the women smiled. The women had said nothing during the meal after their hellos at introductions. Dugan could not remember which was Lucy, so he smiled at all.

"Lucy has put some blankets at the front door. You'll find a soft spot to bed down in the loose hay just inside the barn door."

Alvord stood, and Dugan and Jeremy followed. "Thank you, ladies," Dugan said, bowing stiffly. Jeremy added his thanks, smiling and nodding. The three walked to the front door where Dugan and Jeremy picked up the blankets stacked there.

Alvord held the door open for them. "Uh, you said you broke somebody's law," said Alvord. "Is somebody chasing you?"

Dugan and Jeremy exchanged a hasty glance. "As a matter of fact," said Dugan, "we've seen two men on our track who seem to be looking for us. We thought we had lost them, but they may still be hunting for us."

"Jesus works in mysterious ways." They all turned to see the brother who had walked up behind Alvord.

"Sorry?" said Dugan.

Alvord put an arm around the man's shoulders, smiling. "Don't pay no mind to Jody. He's in a world of his own." He looked aside at Jody, smiling. "Have you seen Jesus lately, Jody? You been riding out lots lately."

The man looked wide-eyed at Alvord. "Brother! I saw Jesus last week when I rode over to Barnabas's house. Last week, 'bout seven days ago. Jesus was wearin' a long white shirt. He was ridin' a little ole donkey with two disciples ridin' behind him."

Alvord smiled. "Did Jesus say anything to you?"

"No, he recognized me and smiled, but didn't say nothin'. One of the disciples asked me if I seen two men ridin' on this trail. I said I never seen nobody, but I would watch and tell 'em if I see anybody."

"Thank you, Jody," said Alvord. "Now get back in the house and help with the cleanup."

Alvord waited until Jody had withdrawn, then turned back to Dugan and Jeremy. "Change in plan? Jody's in a world of his own, but he does notice things."

Dugan and Jeremy looked at each other, sober. They hesitated. Dugan frowned. "Hmm. Jesus would be a great help at this point." He looked at Jeremy, back to Alvord. "No, no change in plan. We both need some sleep real bad."

Alvord paused, seemingly waiting for something more. "Okay. Hope you sleep okay. We eat breakfast early, soon after sunup. Eat with us, if you like, before gittin' away."

"Mighty kind of you. We'll be up at first light. Night."

They walked toward the barn. "Do you think it's them?" said Jeremy.

"Could be, but I don't think Alvord would turn us in to authority. Anyway, I was serious when I said we need sleep."

Dugan awakened at the sound of a rooster crowing. He shifted in his bed atop loose straw and pushed the blanket down. He sat up, blinked and looked toward the barn door. The door was open a sliver, only slightly illuminating the dark interior. The yard and house beyond were faintly outlined in the dim first light.

He frowned when he saw Jeremy standing behind the door, leaning forward and peeking outside. Jeremy looked abruptly back at Dugan who sat on his blanket, clearing his throat. "Shh!" said Jeremy firmly, softly, a finger at his lips.

Dugan frowned, puzzled, stood and walked toward the door. Jeremy motioned him to stay away from the door opening. Jeremy stepped back, and Dugan peeked around the door. He saw a horseman sitting his horse in the yard a short distance from the house. The horseman stared at the porch.

Another horse was tied at the hitching rail in front of the house where Alvord stood in the open doorway, his suspenders hanging loose from his pants. He was talking with a young man who gestured briefly toward the horseman in the yard. Jody, wearing a long white nightshirt, stood behind Alvord. Smiling, he waved to the mounted man who ignored him.

"Recognize the man on the porch?" said Jeremy softly.

Dugan hesitated. "He looks like...doesn't he work for Throckmorton in the office?"

"Yeah, that's what I thought."

They watched until the stranger touched his hat, walked off the porch, untied his horse and mounted. He walked the horse to the mounted man. They spoke briefly, then kicked their horses into a lope toward the road.

Dugan and Jeremy waited until the riders disappeared over a rising. They stepped through the barn door. "Mr. Alvord!" called Dugan. Alvord was still in the doorway, staring at the road where the riders vanished.

They walked toward the porch. Alvord watched them come, raising suspenders to his shoulders. Jody waved, smiling broadly. "Did that have anything to do with us?" Dugan said.

Jody looked wide-eyed at Alvord. "Brother, those were the disciples I told you about, the disciples with Jesus! I told you I saw two disciples with Jesus."

Alvord frowned. "Yes, thank you, Jody." He turned to Dugan and Jeremy. "Sorta ties together now, don't it? The fella asked if I had seen a couple of strangers comin' from the east. I said maybe I had, and maybe I hadn't. I think he took that as a 'yes'.

"He said if I see two strangers who don't belong 'round here and seem to be comin' from the east to give 'em a message. The message was to tell 'em that Throckmorton's man is not lookin' for them anymore. Does that make any sense to you?"

Dugan and Jeremy exchanged a grim glance.

Dugan turned back to Alvord. "Yessir, that does make some sense. That's all he said, he's not lookin' anymore?"

"Oh, he also said to tell 'em not to come home. That's all he said, Throckmorton's man is not looking for 'em anymore, and don't come home. Then they rode away. Don't make sense to me. Hope it does to you."

Dugan and Jeremy exchanged a glance. Dugan

frowned, looking down. "Not lookin' anymore. Don't come home," he said softly. He turned back to Alvord. "Could you tell which direction they rode away?"

"Couldn't really tell." He pointed at the trail. "Just over that rising, the trail splits, one branch going east, the other northwest."

Dugan looked aside a moment, then back to Alvord. "Thank you for all your kindness, Mr. Alvord. We'll never forget. We'll put the blankets on the porch and be on our way. Thank the ladies for us." He extended a hand to Jody. "And thank you, Jody." Jody nodded, sober, seemingly confused. They shook hands all around, and Dugan and Jeremy walked toward the barn.

"God be with you, fellas," called Alvord. They waved over their shoulders. They turned back when they heard Jody shout.

"Jesus be with you!" called Jody. "I told him you're leaving here!" He waved wildly. They smiled and returned the wave.

Inside the barn, they picked up the blankets, shook and folded them. Jeremy stopped, staring at the open barn door. "What does it mean?"

"Damned if I know. We'll find out some day. All I know is, for now, I'm heading west. You heard what he said. 'Don't come home.' You?"

"They know I'm with you. You're stuck with me."

———

Jon looked around. The six friends stared at him.

"West?" Mindy said. "Where west? We're left on the trail!" Laughter from the others sitting on cushions and couches. "You don't know where they went, Jon?"

"Nope. That's the extent of what I know about

Dugan. Nobody else in the extended family knows any more about him. I'm still looking."

"Fascinating story," said Carmelita. "Wonder what happened to the bounty hunter." This set off a spirited discussion while Stephany and M'lis refilled glasses. Jon put logs on the fire, meanwhile responding to questions mostly by repeating that he had no answers. This led to considerable speculation by the group.

All but Adam. Adam waved Stephany off when she offered to refill his cup. He stared at the windows, listening to the others, looking aside occasionally at those who commented or raised a question about the story. He had taken no part in the discussion.

Steph recalled that he had looked intently at Jon throughout his tale. "Okay, Adam, out with it." Everyone looked abruptly at Stephany. All but Adam. He still stared at the windows.

"Adam, are you still here?" said Stephany. Some scattered light nervous laughter from the group.

"Be damned," Adam said, still looking at the window. He turned slowly to Steph. "Bizarre. I don't know what's happening here. Jon told a story that I could have told, but from a different perspective. Unless I am completely mad, that bounty hunter is my ancestor."

CHAPTER 4

ADAM

Still commenting on Jon's story, everyone carried breakfast dishes to the kitchen where Stephany waved off their offers to help. "I'm not doing dishes, and neither are you. We need to hear Adam's story. Right now! Jon's tale was so interesting, I lost track of time. It's noon and lunchtime. Let's get on it, ladies! You boys check the weather."

The women prepared a simple lunch of salad, sandwiches and chips. Stephany made a fresh pot of coffee and another of hot tea. She opened a fresh bottle of red wine.

"Ready, ladies?" Stephany said. They nodded. "Call the boys in, and we'll sit." Carmelita went to the front door and spoke to Adam and Jon who were standing in the yard under a gray overcast. A few snowflakes swirled above their heads in the light breeze. The men followed Carmelita inside.

"How does it look?' Steph said.

"Still cold and blowing, still a light snow," Jon said, "but the overcast seems to be thinning."

"I just spoke to the resort desk," said Stephany.

"They're working on the road. They'll have it clear by tomorrow noon, if we don't get more snow."

"If that doesn't happen, Steph, they might not find anything but frozen bodies when they arrive." Everyone looked at Adam. "Last time I brought firewood in, that was the last of it."

Stephany frowned. "Hmm. Thought I had a good supply, but I'm not accustomed to burning in the fireplace all day and part of the night. The handyman at the resort usually comes up at least once a week to cut wood for me, but the snow prevented that." She smiled sweetly at Adam. "Uh, Adam, would you mind—"

"Yeah, I'll cut some firewood. I saw the down stuff behind the shed."

"Thanks, hon, you're a sweetie. There's an axe and a saw in the shed, just inside the door."

"I'll help," said Jon, "but I'm not missing lunch or the next story. Plenty of time before dinner. Will that do?"

"That will do nicely. Thanks, boys." She turned to the room. "Not sure whether I have mentioned it, but there's a small space heater in the closet of each of the bedrooms. You're welcome to use them, but sparingly, please. In weather like this, the solar panels are not much help, and the wind turbine doesn't supply all the power we need.

"Okay, back to business, everybody, lunch is ready. Take your seats, and place your order for drinks. Carmelita is pouring coffee, M'lis has hot tea, only green tea, sorry if you prefer something else. I'm a green tea addict, dates from my experiences in Japan."

The group looked abruptly at her. She smiled. "I'll tell you about that sometime. Next time, maybe." She smiled broadly. "Oh, there will be a *next time*. I'm already looking forward to it!" She clasped her hands and picked up the wine bottle. "Now...I'll pour wine, or you can hold off until you finish lunch." Everybody sat, asking for their preferred drink. Carmelita and M'lis poured, then found their seats.

Discussion during lunch was a mix of comment on Jon's story and spirited speculation on Stephany's forecast of another gathering. Stephany immediately quashed questions posed to Adam about his ancestor. Just wait for the story, Stephany said.

When all appeared finished with lunch, Stephany folded her napkin, placed it beside her plate and stood. "Okay, everybody, dishes and silverware to the kitchen. I'll get the dishwasher started while you get drinks and retire to the fireplace theater." All pushed chairs back, stood and carried tableware to the kitchen, filled glasses and cups and drifted back to sit before the fireplace. Stephany soon joined them. All looked expectantly at her.

"Okay, Adam, we'll give you as much time as you need, but we're on pins and needles to hear about this bounty hunter ancestor."

He frowned, looking down. "Okay, I'll tell it as I remember it. I haven't looked at this stuff in years. Whatever I can't remember, I'll make it up."

"Okay, Adam," Steph said. "I invent stuff in my fiction, too, but warn us when you tell us something that's pure imagination."

Adam smiled. "Just joking. I'll just tell what I remember."

———

"Hey, boss! There's trouble!" A man held the office door open, leaning inside. Christopher Throckmorton, the mine owner, and two office employees jumped up and ran to the door. Outside, they saw a dust cloud billowing from the mine entrance. Less than a minute later, miners covered in dust, coughing and sneezing, began stumbling from the dust cloud into the courtyard. Mine office employees rushed to the escaping miners to offer help.

Townspeople ran from shops and streets toward the mine entrance. They went as close to the entrance as the dust cloud permitted, trying to help the miners escaping from the tunnel, and asking if they had seen a family member or a friend. Everyone in the town had a relation or two or three working at the mine.

Throckmorton and office workers watched the confusion, the shouting and cries, as employees and townspeople side by side tried to help survivors, as townspeople found family members or began to despair of finding them.

Dugan ran back and forth, into and from the dust cloud, running side to side in desperation, asking if anyone had seen his brother. He stopped and talked intently with a dust-covered miner. The miner put an arm around him, bent to talk over the babble. Dugan's eyes opened wide, and he sobbed, hands on cheeks, as the miner tried to console him.

Then Dugan looked aside and saw Throckmorton. He strode to him, grief turning to anger. He stopped before the mine owner.

"The ceiling collapsed! My brother and I and lots of others told your people about the faulty ceiling a dozen times. We noticed the fault lines in the ceiling and reported the weakness to you many times. Why didn't you brace it? You knew it was a danger, and you never braced it!"

Throckmorton looked aside at the others standing with him. He nodded to Billy, his son, standing beside his father. Billy spoke softly. "Dugan, I think it is. Dugan, this was a tragic event. We'll deal with it."

"What do you mean, you'll deal with it! You were negligent! You killed my brother!"

Billy put up a hand, palm outward as if to quiet Dugan. "Easy, man. I said this was tragic, and we'll deal with it."

"Deal with it? Deal with it? That's not going to bring my brother back." He stepped up to the owner. He spoke softly. "You killed my brother, you son-of-a bitch." He raised a clenched fist in Throckmorton's face.

The owner did not flinch. He took a half step back and turned slightly toward his son. Billy stepped away from his father. He pulled his jacket aside, revealing the holster. He glared at Dugan, laid a hand on the pistol grip.

"Back off, Dugan," said Billy. "We're finished here." When Dugan did not move, Billy pulled the pistol slowly from the holster and began to bring it up.

Dugan, grim-faced, suddenly in control, drew his pistol quickly, whipped it up and fired. Billy was blown backward with a shot to the chest and collapsed on his back.

Throckmorton, suddenly ashen-faced and jaw hanging, dropped to his knees beside his prostrate son. He looked up slowly at Dugan, spoke softly. "You'll pay for this. You are a dead man."

———

"What! He escaped? What do you mean, he escaped? You arrested him!" Throckmorton was livid.

The sheriff stood before Throckmorton's desk. He shifted his weight right and left. A bead of sweat rolled down his cheek. "Yessir, me and two deputies arrested him at his house, but on the way to the jail, a crowd of miners, must've been fifty at least, stopped me and my deputies on the street and took him away. Nothing I could do against fifty angry miners. If I tried to arrest 'em, even if they agreed to go with me, it would shut down the mine. I didn't think you would want that."

Throckmorton relaxed. "Okay." He looked toward the window, back to the sheriff. "I suppose he's left town?"

"I went to his house and had the deputies look around places in town where miners hang out. We didn't find him. He's either hidin' out, or he's left town. I'm guessing he's smart enough to hightail it."

Throckmorton studied his desktop, tapping a pen on the surface. He looked up. "I want you to put out an arrest warrant and be sure it's distributed all over town and nearby towns. Offer a reward of $500 for information that leads to an arrest. I'll pay. I don't have any hope anybody who knows him will turn him in, even for $500, nor anyone who knows his grievance. We're not very popular among the local folk.

"So we won't wait for a local to turn him in. We're going to hunt him down. When I was in Denver last month for a mine owners' meeting, I heard about a bounty hunter who has been very successful in tracking down fugitives. He insists on dead or alive terms. Fine with me.

"Hire him. I'll tell you where to find him. Offer him $1,000. He gets no pay unless he brings him in, dead or alive. I'd as soon have him dead as long as we can identify him."

Three days later, the sheriff and the bounty hunter stood before Throckmorton's desk at dusk. The bounty man was a wiry fifty-year-old, with a head of carefully combed brown and gray hair, a creased face and a slight stoop. He wore a clean, wide-brimmed hat and a six-shooter in a holster hung low at his side.

Throckmorton studied the bounty hunter for a long moment. "Jake, is it? You've got quite a reputation to live up to. Heard a lot about you."

The hunter smiled. "Thank-ee, Mr. Throckmorton. I'll find yer man, and that's uh fact."

Throckmorton relaxed, inhaled deeply. "Good. I'm sending a man with you, Davie over there." He pointed to the young man standing against the wall. Davie smiled, nodded.

Jake looked and turned back to Throckmorton, frowning. "I don't need nobody to go with me."

Throckmorton looked aside, obviously annoyed. "He's not going with you to help you. I want him with you in case you need to send a message to me or if you need to ask something of me. He won't get in your way."

The hunter's frown deepened. "He'll be in the way just by bein' there. I work alone."

Throckmorton stood, angry. He pounded the desktop with a fist. "Then ignore him! If you want this job, he will be with you!" Throckmorton glared at him.

"Okay, okay." Jake raised a hand, palm outward, as if to calm Throckmorton. "Shouldn't take long to take care of a disgruntled miner." He smiled a slight, close-mouthed smile. He turned and went toward the door, spoke to Davie as he passed. "Come on, if you must. We'll talk."

Outside, they walked to the hitching rail and stopped at Jake's horse. He looked back toward the office. "How can you work for that man?" Davie shrugged. Jake untied his reins. "We'll ride tomorrow at first light. Meet me right here on a good horse. Don't bring no pack animal. You'll carry all your stuff on your mount, not much, mind you. Shouldn't be out long. We'll cover lots of ground, sometimes at a good pace. Hope you ride pretty good, or I'm gonna leave you in my dust."

"I can ride."

———

Jake walked from the hotel door, carrying his loaded saddlebags. He nodded to Davie who stood beside his horse. Davie's filled saddlebags were tied behind the saddle.

Jake went to his horse, threw the saddlebags behind the saddle, began tying them. "Hoped you wouldn't show up."

"Sorry to disappoint you."

Jake mounted. "Ride behind me. I'm ain't used to nobody bein' with me. I don't want to see you. If you don't keep up, I ain't waitin' for you." He kicked his horse to a lope. Davie quickly mounted and galloped after him.

———

They rode on a dusty road heading generally westward, marked by hoofprints and a few wagon wheel tracks. They loped, walked their horses, stopping occasionally. At each stop, Jake dismounted and walked back and forth in the roadbed while Davie studied the sage-covered sandy flats and the dark mountain ranges beyond. *Big, empty country. Hope we don't find him.* He turned back to Jake.

"What're you looking for?" said Davie.

Jake did not respond. He walked from side to side on

the road, kneeling occasionally. "I'm lookin' at hoofprints, of course. How am I goin' to find my man without following his horse?"

"Lots of people ride this road," said Davie.

Jake stood, frowned. "Yep." He knelt, digging in the loose dust with a finger.

"What are you doin'?"

Jake looked up. "You ask a lot of questions. I guess that's all right. Maybe you'll learn something. Maybe I'll make a bounty hunter outta you. Last year, I tracked a man whose horse had a horseshoe that had a chip out of it. That shoe made a distinctive print. He was easy to track."

"So?"

"So I got into a discussion with the liveryman back in town about horseshoes. He volunteered that this Dugan fella rides a horse with a shoe that has a nail that is just beginnin' to loosen. Makes a distinctive print if you look real close. Liveryman was gonna fix it, but somebody who was lookin' out for Dugan picked up the horse couple of days ago before the liveryman got to it. He even told me the road Dugan took out of town. We're on that road. And I've seen that hoofprint with the loose nail." He almost smiled. "Any more questions? Keep watchin', Davie boy. You might learn somethin'." Davie squinted, looked aside.

They continued to ride on the road, stopping occasionally for Jake to dismount and examine tracks. "Yep," he said, each time he found the loose nail print. Then he mounted and walked his horse, searching the road on both sides of the horse.

When the sun hung low above the western horizon, Jake reined up and dismounted. He went to the side of the road, bent to examine hoofprints. "Yep, left the road here." He looked up the slope to a stand of cedar. He led his horse through the sage, stopping frequently to examine the tracks. "Yep." He mounted and rode slowly up the slope, leaning over both sides of the horse, examining the ground. Davie followed.

Little more than a hundred yards from the road, Jake stopped beside a narrow stream. He dismounted, bent over the remains of a campfire and placed a hand on the ashes. He picked up a stick, stirred the ashes and saw a tiny glowing ember. He pushed fish bones beside the fire circle around with a boot.

He looked up at Davie. "Yep. They were here."

Davie dismounted. "They?"

"Yep. There were two people here. In addition to the loose nail track, there's another set of tracks. Saw the other tracks down on the road, but didn't decide that they were together till they left the road together. Unless one was following the other one. That don't seem likely. There's two piles of horse apples over there right beside each other. They camped here together. I don't figure it." He looked around. "We'll spend the night here. We're just one day behind 'em."

———

The next day was a monotonous ride. Monotonous to Davie, at least. Jake didn't seem to be bothered. Routine for bounty hunting, Davie assumed. They rode mostly on game trails and through open sage flats. Jake followed tracks, then lost them and searched in circles. Then he found tracks but with no loose shoe nail.

Following a hot, dry afternoon ride, Jake called a halt when the sun ball touched the horizon. They reined up at a small shallow pond, left by a recent rain undoubtedly, enough to refresh the horses. The men were thirsty enough to risk a drink.

They hobbled the horses in a patch of grass near the pond. Laying horse blankets near the fire, they chewed the last of the jerky Davie brought from home. Davie had said little since stopping. Now, he stared into the flames.

Jake watched him silently for minutes. His patience finally was at an end. "All right, out with it. I didn't ask you to come, but as long as you're here, you need to say somethin' from time to time so I'll know you're alive."

Davie looked aside at Jake, then back to the fire. "The more I think about this whole thing, the more I don't like it. I'm here because the boss told me to come, but I don't like it." He turned to Jake. "When Throckmorton hired you, did he or anybody else tell you exactly what happened?"

"I ain't interested in exactly what happened. I leave that to the law. If the law wants a wrongdoer caught and will pay me to catch him, I'm their man."

"So nobody described what happened?"

"You're not listening. I said I ain't interested. All I need to know is that the man broke the law, he ran away, and I'm being paid to bring him in."

Davie bristled. "But he *didn't* break the law. I was standing right there. I saw the whole thing. He shot the boss's son in self-defense. The son drew on him, but Dugan was a faster draw, and he shot him. In self-defense. Doesn't that make a difference?"

Jake stared at him, shook his head. "You sound like you been drinkin' too much, son, but since there's no drink around, you just been thinkin' too much. I ain't interested. All I'm interested in is gittin' paid for doin' my job."

"What if you find him, and he resists, and you shoot him dead, and you later find out he was innocent?"

Jake smiled. "You got a lot of "ifs" in there, Davie boy."

Davie shook his head slowly, looked back into the fire. "I need a whiskey."

———

Next morning, at first light, they had hardly left camp when Jake found hoofprints that led toward a trail below. He dismounted, kneeled and examined the prints. He looked up at Davie, smiling. "Yep." He mounted, and they rode down the slope to the main trail below in a sage flat. They turned left and rode into a wide canyon. The trail was bordered by steep cliffs on both sides that rose sharply from the sage-covered floor. Jake rode slowly, leaning right and left, examining the tracks.

Jake reined up, dismounted. He knelt, examined the tracks and walked off the trail into the sage. "Yep. Left the trail here." He looked across the sage flat to the steep range a hundred yards away.

"Hello," he said more to himself than Davie. He looked up toward the crest of the range on their left.

"What do you see?" said Davie.

"It's either sheep or deer. Or people." He reached into a saddlebag and pulled out a binocular. He trained the glass on the hill, mumbled to himself. "Two riders. I wager it's our man and whoever joined him." He reined off the trail and kicked his horse to a gallop toward the hill. Davie followed closely.

The two figures on the height disappeared over the ridgeline.

———

The climb to the top of the escarpment was fruitless. They saw no horsemen nor any evidence of horsemen. The stony top revealed no tracks. They rode along the peaks a few miles on a game trail, then descended on a narrow steep trail to the road below where Jake hoped to pick up the trail. He was disappointed. The road here was covered with inches of dust that lifted and swirled in the light breeze. No tracks of any kind were visible.

They continued riding, searching each side for tracks leaving the road. They saw only one set that did not show the loose nail. As the sun began to disappear at the western horizon, they approached a cluster of weathered buildings that they supposed would pass as a town.

"What do you say we try to find a bed for the night?" said Davie.

Jake, slumped in his saddle, inhaled deeply. "That's the first thing you've said on this ride that makes sense, Davie boy." He squinted. "Don't see any sign of a hotel. Saloon up ahead might have rooms. Should have drink and food for sure. We'll have a look."

They rode slowly at twilight down the dusty street lined with weathered shops. A scattered half dozen men and a couple of women stood motionless on the board-walks, silently watching them.

They reined up at the saloon, dismounted and tied reins to the hitching rail. Davie stretched, stamped his feet vigorously. "Not used to this kind of riding every day."

"I didn't ask you to come, you'll remember. Didn't want you to come."

"Yeah, yeah, I know. There's nothing either of us can do about it now. We answer to the same man, and we both know that he doesn't take well to people questioning anything he decides to do."

"Hmm. Yeah. And I don't take to a body who don't listen to me when I got something to offer."

They untied saddlebags, shouldered them and went inside the saloon. They looked around. There were a few men at each of the five tables, cards in hand. Three men leaned against the bar, chatting among themselves and with the bartender. Everyone in the saloon stopped what they were doing and stared silently at newcomers they did not recognize.

"No wonder there's so few people outside," said Davie softly. "They're all in here."

The bartender, motionless, stared at Jake and Davie. He ignored the cowboy who was holding his glass toward him. The bartender moved down the bar when Jake and Davie walked his way.

"Gentlemen?" said the frowning bartender. They both ordered whiskey. The bartender poured and pushed the glasses toward them. He remained, holding the bottle, studying them.

"Haven't seen you boys around. Passing through? Where you headed?"

Davie looked aside at Jake who stared into his glass. After a long pause, Jake looked up. "Passing through."

"Can I maybe help you with some directions? Anything?"

Jake took a long swallow, looked up at the bartender. "Actually, there is something. We're...uh, looking for a couple of friends who were riding this way, and we're trying to catch up with 'em. I wonder if you've seen a couple of strangers last few days riding through, fellas you don't know, coming from the east."

The bartender smiled, then frowned. "Hmm. Now,

let's see.' He looked up, then looked from Davie to Jake. "No, I don't think so, don't remember any strangers comin' in for quite some time from any direction. Sorry, no, haven't seen no strangers, 'cept you." He smiled.

"Hmm." Jake stared into his glass, looked up. "Possible to get something to eat?"

"Sure." He pointed at a table. "Have a seat over there, and I'll bring plates." Jake picked up his glass and walked to the table. Davie followed, glass in hand.

The bartender promptly brought plates of beef, potatoes, beans and biscuits. Jake pointed to his empty glass. The bartender looked at Davie who shook his head. He returned a minute later, deposited a full glass before Jake, picked up the empty and returned to the bar.

Jake took a long swallow from the glass and forked a chunk of beef to his mouth. "Save the biscuits," he said, without looking up, "we're gettin' away at first light."

When they had finished eating, Jake signaled to the bartender who walked over. "Didn't see a hotel in town. You got a room we can take for the night?"

"Uh, well, we don't have rooms for overnights. Sorry about that."

Jake looked at the stairs at the back of the room. "Don't you have rooms up there? Most saloons I've frequented have rooms upstairs."

"Yeah, well, I s'pose you know those are the ladies' rooms."

"You got enough ladies to fill all the rooms? I only see one dressed-up lady here." He gestured toward the attractive woman, mid-thirties probably, who stood behind a table where three men bent over their cards. She stared at them, at Davie it seemed, a hint of a smile on her lips. Davie returned her stare.

Jake saw the exchange. "Forget it," he said to Davie.

He turned back to the bartender, his face hard. "You sure you don't have a room?"

The bartender winced. "Uh, actually, we do have a room empty at the moment. I s'pose we could let you have it for a night."

"We'll take it," said Jake. "I'm bone tired."

The bartender looked over the room, waved to the woman at the card table. She stepped away from the table, he walked to her, and they talked. He pointed at the stair, leaned toward her, looking up the stair and back at Jake and Davie. She looked at the two men, frowning. Then she nodded, walked to the stair and went up, looking back over her shoulder at the men, smiling at Davie.

The bartender went back to Jake and Davie. "Betsy's gonna see if the room is ready for takers. Give her a few minutes. Girl who had that room, Annie, sweet little thing, she's been gone almost a month now. She was pretty neat, kept the room nice. Shouldn't take Betsy long to check it out."

"We passed a livery coming in town," Jake said. "Can you have the horses taken over and brought back here early? We'll be leaving at sun up."

"I'll take care of it. Now, if you'll come over to the bar, we'll settle the bill. You may be on your way tomorrow before I come in. You'll understand that I work late, and I ain't an early riser."

Jake hoisted his saddlebag and followed the bartender to the bar. While they were bent over the bar talking, Betsy came down the stairs and waved to the bartender.

The bartender offered a key to Jake. "Third room. Room's ready. Take this and lock the door after you git settled. Some drunk cowboy might forget that Annie is no longer with us and try to come callin'." He grinned. "By the way, you might hear noises from the room next to you. It's Betsy's room, and she might be workin' late. You understand." He grinned again.

Jake and Davie walked toward the stair. Betsy, standing at the bottom of the stair, leaned toward Davie as they passed and said something softly in his ear. She leaned back and smiled. Davie smiled, pulled a face.

Jake frowned. "I told you to forget it!" They both were startled when Betsy was pulled violently aside.

A scruffy cowboy held her arm tightly. He weaved slightly, spoke firmly to her. "You ain't going with him! You're goin' with me. Remember?" She winced and gently tried to push his hand from her arm.

Jake frowned a moment, looking down, then looked up in the cowboy's face. He spoke softly. "I get the impression this lady don't want to go with you. Let her go."

The cowboy weaved, frowned and leaned toward Jake. "Who th' hell are you? You never been here before and you don't know I get this whore anytime I want her. And she ain't no lady."

Jake had listened with growing irritation as his face hardened. Finally, he whipped out his six-shooter and pointed it at the cowboy's face. "I won't say this but once, you drunk son of a bitch. Take your hands off this woman, or I'm gonna put another hole in that skull of yours."

The cowboy's face fell, his mouth open. A trio of cardplayers at the table nearby jumped up and stepped back from the table, arms raised over holsters, but a quick glance from Jake and a gentle wave of the pistol in their direction convinced them to sit down.

The cowboy released Betsy and stumbled backward. He walked slowly to a table in a dark corner, looking back over his shoulder at Jake.

"Thanks," said Betsy softly, rubbing her arm where the cowboy had gripped her. "Now I'll probably have to shoot him." She glanced at the cowboy who glared at her and Jake from his table. She leaned toward Jake. "Unless you want to do it for me," she said softly. She smiled. "Never mind. I can handle him."

Jake nodded, pointed up the stair to Davie, and they walked up.

The bartender watched Jake and Davie climb the stair. When they disappeared down the hall, he rushed to the end of the bar, bent and pulled a sheet of paper and pencil from a shelf under the bar top. He licked his lips, bent over the paper, and wrote.

Inside their room, Davie found a blanket in the cupboard and said he would take the couch. Jake sat down heavily on the bed, stared at the wall.

"You surprised me," said Davie. "What was that all about?"

He said nothing, staring at the wall. After a long moment, still staring at the wall, he spoke softly. "I hate saloons. And people who go to saloons. You see, I was raised in a saloon. My mother worked there, just like Betsy. She had a room in the storage, out back of the saloon. I don't hardly remember it and have only the vaguest memory of her. She died when I was three or four, and I was put in an orphanage in Denver. I lived in that orphanage till I was fourteen when I ran away. Worked at odd jobs in towns and on ranches. Worked for a bounty hunter and became a bounty hunter." He shook his head. "Didn't mean to tell you all that. Never told it to nobody."

He leaned down, pulled off his boots. "I'm going to bed. Dog-tired." He raised the quilts, climbed into the bed and pulled the quilts over his head.

Jake, fully dressed, stood over Davie, still asleep on the couch. Jake nudged him on the shoulder, put a finger to his lips when Davie sat up abruptly. Davie looked around, confused, looked through the open window, saw shapes outside in the dim first light. The soft breeze lightly disturbed the filmy curtain.

Jake picked up the trousers draped on the chair back and handed them to Davie. He made a lifting motion, signaling to get up. He put the finger to his lips again. Davie nodded and dressed hurriedly.

Jake stood at the door, his hand on the knob. He adjusted the saddlebags on his shoulder. He looked back at Davie, his look a question. Davie nodded, quickly picked up his saddlebags and draped them on a shoulder. Jake twisted the key in the lock and slowly opened the door. They walked quietly in the hall and down the stairs. At the bottom, an old man who was sweeping, nodded to them and returned to his sweeping. The two went outside.

First light and the bartender was as good as his word. Their horses were tied to the saloon hitching rail. They tied saddlebags behind saddles, mounted and walked their horses in the empty street.

"What th' hell's goin' on?" said Davie.

Jake looked at the road ahead. "Those walls are thin. I heard coughing during the night and somebody talking in the room next to ours. Sounded like two people, and I wager both were men."

Davie leaned toward Jake. "Do you think—"

"Maybe. But trying to take them at the saloon could be a problem. We'll take 'em on the road. They won't be going back the way they came. They'll be goin' through the town on the other side, to the west, same way we're goin'. We'll be waitin' for 'em."

———

Jake stood behind a boulder that looked down a rocky sage-covered slope to the trail below. Davie squatted behind the boulder, staring blankly at the ground. Their horses were tied in a thick stand of pines nearby, so well hidden that Davie couldn't see them. The mounts occasionally stirred, stamping the hard ground.

An hour passed. Jake leaned against the boulder, alternately watching the trail below and glancing at Davie who was stretched out behind the boulder.

Two hours. Davie leaned against the boulder, staring at the upslope. Jake still stood beside the boulder. He bent over, flexing his back. He straightened, looked at the back trail and the sagebrush flat beyond through his binocular. He studied the distant dark range beyond the flat. Nothing.

He looked at the trail ahead, westward. He straightened.

"See something?" said Davie.

"Single rider. Coming this way. What the hell's he doing, riding out there by hisself?" He lowered the binocular, turned to Davie. "I'm going down. If our men got ahead of us somehow, maybe he saw them. Even if he hasn't, he can tell us about the country ahead. Might help." He went to his horse.

"I'll go down with you, in case you get in trouble." Davie smiled. He thought Jake would object, but when he didn't, he went to his horse.

They rode slowly down the hillside at an angle to meet the stranger. Davie waved to the stranger, signaling, he hoped, their friendly intent. The stranger, middle-aged, reined up when he saw the two horsemen approaching. The stranger wore loose, baggy overalls and no hat. His long hair flew in all directions.

"Good day," the stranger said. "Have you seen Jesus?"

Jake closed his eyes, lowered his head, frowning. "Jesus," he said softly.

Davie smiled. "Haven't seen Jesus but saw a pretty sunrise a while ago. Jesus must be somewhere about."

"That's right! Jesus must be about! I saw him this morning riding his little old donkey!"

"That's enough," said Jake. "Since you didn't see Jesus, did you see two strangers on the trail, two men you ain't seen before?"

"Yes! I don't know you or him!" He pointed at Davie.

Davie snorted. Jake closed his eyes, shook his head, opened his eyes. "Did you see any *other* two strangers on the trail?"

"No. Nobody."

"Except Jesus," said Davie, smiling.

"Yes!" The man pointed at Davie. "Do you want me to tell you about Jesus?"

"All right, that's enough." Jake reined off the trail and pointed toward their camp. "If this lunatic can be believed, they are not ahead of us. We'll go back up and wait." He kicked his horse back to the path that led to their camp. Davie followed. He looked back to the stranger and waved. The stranger waved wildly to him, sitting his horse, watching.

———

Jake lowered the glass, rubbed his eyes and turned to see Davie, who sat cross-legged, leaning his back against a large boulder, staring up the hillside. Their horses were hobbled nearby in a patch of dry grass.

"I don't see 'em," Jake said, "thought we'd have 'em by now."

"Good," Davie said, still staring up the hillside. "Maybe they've shook us. That's good."

Jake frowned. "You know, you're beginning to annoy me. You think too much, and you talk too much." He looked below a long moment, then turned back to Davie. "You know why you're annoying me?"

Davie turned toward him. "No, but I bet you're gonna tell me why."

"Because now I'm beginning to think about it, and that bothers me."

Davie stood. "Well, well, I begin to suspect—"

Jake frowned, holding up a hand, palm in Davie's face. "Don't suspect nothin' and don't git cute." He looked below and up at the horizon. "I've just been thinking about what you said, that you saw what happened back there, you saw him defending hisself when he fired. I like to hear about somebody who won't be bullied and fights back.

"And, what the' hell, I thought about some of my jobs in the past when there seemed to be some doubt, in some people's minds, whether the man I was chasing was guilty as charged. I have always tried to convince myself that I wasn't responsible for deciding whether the man was guilty, that when I got the hunter job, it was all a closed book. The man broke the law and deserved to be caught and punished. That's what I always thought. But you're not the first to suggest that the man I was chasing didn't deserve to get caught."

He sat down heavily beside Davie, leaned against the boulder. He exhaled, staring into the treetops.

Davie looked aside at him. "Dugan?"

Jake still stared into the branches and canopy of the tall pines. He closed his eyes, remained still so long Jeremy thought he might be sleeping.

"Jake?"

Jake opened his eyes. "I'm goin' home," softly, staring at his boots.

Davie started, frowned, looked aside at him. "What? You're going home? Really? Now? Where's home?"

Jake, still leaning on the boulder, stared at the distant range. He turned slowly toward Davie. "California," he said softly. "Nevada City. Texas before that. Fort Worth. I was a cowboy on somebody else's place. Back in 1850 I heard about the mountains of gold in California and went out there with a bunch of like-minded lunatics the next year. Worked the streams long enough to decide that I wasn't gonna get rich at that. I heard the news about Colorado gold, came here and hired on as a miner. Didn't take to that and got caught up in bounty hunting which I thought was a lot easier and made more money than grubbing in somebody else's mine. That's another story I ain't gonna tell you."

He leaned forward and stood, grunting with the effort. He smiled thinly. "I'm goin' home. Right now. How 'bout that? I'm leavin' it to you to report back to old Throckmorton. I don't envy you. I'll be long gone on the road to California by the time you see him."

Jake looked up, eyes closed, inhaled deeply. He opened his eyes and smiled. "You know, I haven't felt this good about anything for a real long time."

He leaned over and slapped Davie hard on the back. "Davie, my boy, I'm going to leave you right here and head west before I have any second thoughts. I've got enough cash in the saddlebags to get me to Nevada City and maybe buy a few cows when I get there. Yeah, I think I'm gonna be a cowman. I expect I'll like cows better than most people I ever knew. How's that for a switch in jobs?"

"Jake, I think this is probably the smartest decision you ever made. As for Throckmorton, I'm going to avoid him. I don't need to go back to Black Hawk. I have no family there, and it should be no problem to find a job somewhere else, far enough away that nobody knows me."

Jake untied his reins and mounted with a tired grunt. "I'd like to see old Throckmorton's face when he realizes that nobody in this whole mess will see Black Hawk again. Take care of yourself, Davie boy, you're a good man." He leaned down and slapped Davie on the back. "If you git tired of wanderin', come see me. California. Nevada City. Maybe I'll give you a job." He chuckled and set off at a walk down the slope.

Davie, frowning, fidgeting, watched him go.

"Jake! Wait up!" said Davie. Jake pulled up and looked back.

"Did you mean it when you said you might offer me a job?"

Jake smiled. "Sure did. I don't know anybody where I'm going. And—now don't let this go to your head—I decided we could work together just fine."

"Give me a couple of minutes. I'm going with you."

Jake smiled again, hooked a leg over the saddle horn. "Good on you. Glad to have you. Take your time."

Davie untied his reins, mounted and rode to Jake. Jake leaned over, smiling, slapped Davie on a shoulder. "California, here we come!" They rode to the sandy road below and turned westward. Jake looked at Davie, smiled. "Be damned," he said.

"Before we leave this country," said Davie, "I would like to find Dugan. He still thinks a bounty hunter is after him. If we don't tell him he's safe, he'll be running the rest of his life. We need to tell him."

Jake frowned, looking at the road ahead. "I s'pose you're right, but we haven't found him so far."

"Just a few more days. I've got a feeling, now that the search is for a different reason."

Jake looked over, smiled thinly. "Wish I had your outlook." He spurred his horse. "Let's git on it!"

———

They rode in a land of plains and peaks for three days. They passed scattered cattle ranches, a few wagons and horseback riders on the roads. Davie questioned anyone who would stop and listen. No one had seen two men that matched his description. Mid-morning on the fourth day, they had just about decided to give up and admit that Dugan and his companion had outwitted them and left the country.

Minutes after deciding to give it up, they saw a cluster of a dozen houses in an arid valley of sage and cactus with a small church in the center. Gardens lay alongside houses. A few cows grazed on scant grass beyond the gardens. They saw a man standing on the porch of the first house and rode to him. The man was drying his hands with a cloth, his suspenders hanging loose over his trousers. He watched the two riders coming.

Jake reined up in the yard while Davie rode to the porch and dismounted. "Morning," said Davie. The man nodded, staring intently at the stranger. Davie said he had a message for a couple of men he knew but had lost touch with. They might have ridden this way just a few days ago, he said, and he wondered whether the farmer might have seen them.

No, the farmer hadn't seen two strangers passing through in months. Yes, he would be willing to give the strangers a message, if they should appear. Davie's message was short and simple: tell them the man who was chasing them is no longer looking for them. And tell them they should not come home.

"That's all? said the farmer.

"That's all," said Davie, "they'll understand." Davie thanked him, mounted and rode to Jake.

Jake slapped Davie on the back, shouted a loud wahoo and spurred his horse up the incline. Davie kicked his mare to a gallop after him.

Adam looked around at the others, seated on couches and cushions before the fire. "And that's the end of my story."

"That is so bizarre," said Stephany. "Not only that the stories are intertwined, but that the two of you are here together." She turned to Jon. "You never talked about this with Adam?"

"We had no idea of the connection before right now."

"You know nothing of Jake in Nevada City, in California?"

"Nothing. Seems he disappeared, like he never reached Nevada City. I'm hoping he did. I'm still looking."

"Bizarre," said Stephany. "These stories seem to be about real people who become ghosts." She stood. "Somebody stoke the fire while I check the weather." She went to the front door and outside. Only a moment later, she came back inside, rubbing her arms, shivering. "Freezing! No more snow in sight, but there's no sign of a thaw or snowplow either."

She looked around the room. "I'm ready for another story to warm me up," Steph said. "Who's next?"

"Yeah, me too," M'lis said. "Should we wait till after dinner?"

"Good idea!" said Stephany. "I don't want to go off on any journey on an empty stomach. Set the table, boys, while the girls find something edible to put on it." All went about their assigned duties.

CHAPTER 5

DONNA

Conversation during dinner was relaxed but with subdued excitement. They were all caught up in the ancestor stories, commenting and asking questions. Most had gone out on the porch before sitting down, then came back inside, shivering and confirming that the weather gods were still in a foul mood. Large drifting snowflakes fell silently, the only sounds coming from the rustling and clicking of bare branches in the light breeze.

"It's interesting that so many of the ancestors in these stories are headed for California," said Stephany. "I suppose that's understandable since they are ancestors of the bunch around this table. The gold rush seems to have been the greatest attraction."

Carmelita put down her fork, frowning. "On that point, I'd always heard that Californios, Mexicans, were discriminated against in the mines, but I didn't know the same was true for others, like Jews and Chinese and other foreigners like Australian and French." She looked at Mindy. "I think you said that white Americans sort of decided that the placers were reserved for white Americans."

"That's my understanding," said Mindy. "The largest numbers came from the East."

Donna shifted in her chair, staring at her empty plate. She looked up. "Okay," she said rather loudly. Everyone looked at her. "It's true enough that great numbers came to the mines from the East. That includes the *Far* East. China. Thousands came to California in mid-century from China. Some settled in San Francisco, some built the railroads, and a great number went to the California gold country." She pursed her lips, staring at her plate.

After a long silent moment: "Donna?" said Stephany.

Donna looked up. "Okay. I suppose it's my turn. My mother was fascinated with a particular ancestor. She said knowing about her would help me know who I am. We researched her together. I'm named for her."

Xiangxi leaned on the rail of the steamship, her face cooled by the light breeze. She looked over the side at the placid sea that stretched to the horizon. All in her view was water, and so it had been for over a week. She closed her eyes, slowly shaking her head. A crewman had told her that morning that they would not reach California for at least two more weeks.

She looked around at the clusters of people, almost all Chinese, standing at the rail and seated on the deck, huddled together under blankets against walls, under overhangs, their meager belongings in small cases and sacks beside them. Some were no older than her own parents who had wanted to make this voyage but were persuaded their frailty made the voyage impossible. But *you* must go, they said to her. Get rich and take care of us in our old age.

She looked up at the smokestacks, belching gray smoke in heavy spirals. She turned and stared at the horizon, the breeze cooling her face, remembering.

———————

Xiangxi left her parents, fleeing their poverty-stricken village in Guangdong Province, at the age of eighteen. That was seven years ago. She had refused to marry the fifty-five-year-old man who had bargained with her parents for her hand. The union would have promised security for them in their old age, but Xiangxi would not have it. She promised to help in some fashion, but not by marriage to a man she had not even met.

She went to the British enclave of Hong Kong where she found work in a vegetable market. She sent small amounts of money regularly to her parents. At the market, she befriended a young English soldier who found a position for her on the army base. She was a bright girl, learned English quickly and soon became an interpreter. The English had so much difficulty pronouncing her Chinese name that Wally, her soldier friend, named her Donna, which in Chinese means "pretty". Wally soon became her sweetheart, and they married.

Six months after their marriage, Wally was killed in civil unrest, a prelude to the outbreak of the Taiping Rebellion. The tragic war against the central government was instigated by a Chinese Christian zealot who claimed to be the son of God Jehovah and the younger brother of Jesus Christ. Twenty to thirty million people would be slaughtered in the ensuing holy war.

Donna was shattered at her husband's death. Her

parents pled with her to return to the village. She refused and continued to work at the army base and continued sending small amounts of money regularly to her parents.

Then came the event that would change her life. News of the gold discovery in California that was transmitted to the world arrived in the Pearl River Delta of Guangdong Province on the southeast China coast. Donna's parents decided to join other excited villagers who began planning to make the voyage to golden California. This was their opportunity to escape their poverty forever.

Alas, the villagers planning the journey refused to accept Donna's parents into the group. "You are too frail," they said, "you will hold us back." The parents were distraught. They turned to Donna, insisting that she, their only child, go in their place. She would become rich and care for them in their old age. So they said.

Donna was devastated. She had learned to live with the loss of her husband and was content with her life in Hong Kong. She did not want to go to California but felt obligated by tradition to obey her parents. She was invited by the group from her parents' village to join them for the journey to California, but she declined. She would travel alone. She believed her life was at an end.

———

Arriving in San Francisco at dusk, passengers crowded the gangway and slowly stumbled single file to the dock, carrying their meager belongings in small cases and sacks. Some were met by Chinese who greeted them, smiling and bowing, a few embraces, and led them away, chattering and laughing. The remainder stood on the dock, bewildered, looking about, huddled together in small groups, talking softly, uncertainty becoming fear.

Standing alone, Donna pondered, staring into the growing darkness and the flickering lights that were beginning to appear. In her anxiety and lack of enthusiasm, she had thought little of this moment. She had no plan and little money, having spent most of her savings on the cost of the ship passage. But what to do now?

She was startled when two white men, middle-aged, well-dressed and groomed, approached her. "Hello," said one in English. "Do you speak English, Spanish?" He smiled, looking her over.

She frowned, uncertain how to respond. "English." She did not smile.

"Can we help you in any way? Is someone meeting you?" Her mind raced. She said nothing. "Come with us. We'll find you a place. You must be tired. You need to lie down." He grinned.

She hesitated only a moment. "Yes, friends are coming. Maybe you have seen them. One of them is very big, tall."

The men looked at each other and looked nervously around the dock. They mumbled to each other and regained their composure. The speaker smiled. "I don't think nobody is meetin' you, pretty lady. Now, you just come with us, and we'll introduce you to the U.S. of A. and San Francisco." He reached for her arm, grinning. Suddenly, his eyes opened wide, and his jaw dropped. He stepped backward, his arms wide.

"Don't mess with me, arsehole!" She held up a cocked pistol pointing at his face. Her hand shook slightly, her eyes blinking rapidly.

"Whoa there, woman! Be careful with that thang." He backed away, his arms outstretched. "We're leaving. Be careful." With that, he turned around, collided with his companion, and they ran off the dock toward the street.

Donna lowered the pistol and bent forward, breathing heavily. She erupted in tears, hands on knees.

"Can I help you with that, little lady? You're about to shoot your foot."

She jerked around and saw the man standing at her side. She started to bring the pistol up but saw him holding his arms outstretched. She shuddered, bent forward.

"I'm trying to help. You need to decock that gun before you have an accident. You're still about to shoot your foot." She looked at the pistol. "Can I help with that?" he said. She again looked at the pistol, handed it to him. He took it and slowly released the hammer. He examined the gun. "Where in the world did you get this? Thought I'd seen all the handguns in the country." He handed the pistol to her, grip first. "Looks foreign."

She took the pistol, looked at this stranger. He was young, late twenties, she guessed, a nice-looking fellow. He was dressed in clean working clothes or traveling clothes. She picked up a bag at her feet and pushed the pistol into it. "It's English. It is...was my husband's, in Hong Kong. He showed it to me and showed me how to use it. He said he hoped some bad man would threaten him someday so he could say: "Don't mess with me, arse-hole!" She almost smiled, leaned forward, gagging and coughing.

"You okay?" She nodded. "Yeah, I thought that was what I heard. I was passing over there." He gestured with a nod toward the street. He looked around. The crowd on the dock had dwindled to a few knots of Chinese, huddled together and looking around, fearfully it seemed.

She looked aside blankly, then back to him. "I'm Kirk," he said. "Just arrived in San Francisco yesterday myself, out of Boston. I was crew on the ship and decided the minute I stepped on the dock that I was going to stay. About half the crew did the same. I'll be talking with people tomorrow about the gold country and how to get there and how to go about mining. I'm completely ignorant on all that."

He waited. "I'm Xiangxi," she said. "Or Donna. I guess I'm Donna in California. My husband named me Donna. He said Xiangxi was too hard for foreigners to pronounce." She looked aside. "I guess I'm going to the gold country, too." Her eyes clouded, a teardrop rolled down a cheek. "That was always the plan." She shook her head. "I don't know what I was thinking. I was so...so disturbed. I have no idea how to get there and what to do if I get there." She dropped to her knees, sobbing.

"Hey, hey." He bent, took her arms and helped her stand. "Let's get you someplace. You must be worn out from that sailing and the worry." He picked up the bag and sacks at her feet and took her arm. She pulled back, her face a mask of fear and exhaustion.

He smiled. "Missy, Donna, you don't need to be scared of me. I'm not gonna hurt you. I want to help you. I have a room just off the wharf. If you don't have someplace to go, come with me. The room's got a bed and lots of cushions. I'll sleep on the cushions. I can sleep on anything. Cushions, pine needles, hard rock. The bed is yours, and I'll face the wall." He smiled, raised a hand, palm out. "Promise."

She looked a long moment at his face, wiped her cheek with a sleeve. "Thank you. I will go with you." She took a bag from him, looked up, spoke sternly. "Don't forget I have the gun." She smiled thinly and pointed a finger at his face. Her face clouded, and she looked aside. "Sorry."

"Yes, ma'am. I'll sure remember. I've seen you in action." He smiled, took her arm and supported her as they walked on the dockside street. She shuddered and leaned against him when she saw a small group of Chinese huddled together in the dark entrance to a building, their bags at their feet. She recognized them from the ship.

———————

"That's the best meal I've had in a month." She looked up from her empty plate. They had walked from the wharf down the road of hard-packed sod to a small café he had discovered that morning. She decided that the plate of beef, potatoes and beans was most welcome. And apple pie for dessert!

He sipped his coffee, leaned toward her. "Tell me about yourself. And why you came all the way from Hong Kong by yourself." He leaned back abruptly and raised a hand. "Uh, sorry, if you don't want to talk about yourself to this stranger, it's okay."

She half smiled. "I don't mind." She told him about herself, her growing up in rural poverty, leaving her disappointed parents for Hong Kong, her marriage and the loss of her husband. She marveled to herself that she had so fully described her life to this man she met only a few hours ago.

"Now you know me," she said. "What about you?"

He leaned back. "Nothing much to tell. Grew up in the East, eastern United States, that is, Pennsylvania, and been a sailor since I was twelve. I heard about the gold discovery and booked on the first ship for California I could find that needed crew. And here I am. That's the whole short story of my life. Pretty boring."

"You never married?"

He leaned back, looked up, then back to her. "Nope.

Never was in port long enough to get attached, and ships don't take lady crew." He smiled.

While listening to him, she had glanced aside and past him. Five of the other six tables were occupied by two or more men, each who divided their attention between their plates and her.

She leaned toward Kirk, spoke softly. "Why is everyone staring at me?"

He smiled. "Didn't men stare at you in Hong Kong?"

She frowned. "Well, yes, not so much when I was with my husband, but when I was alone. Not so much from Chinese men, but lots from English. The English men seemed to think that every young woman by herself was available or a prostitute. Sorry."

He laughed lightly. "Not so different here." He leaned forward. "Pretty lady, you are an oddity here. Look around when we go outside. You won't see a solitary woman on the street, certainly not a young, pretty woman. A young woman walking by herself, especially after dark, is assumed to be available for a price. It seems even more so in the gold country. Some fellows I talked with in a tavern last night who had been to the gold country said they saw not a single unattached woman there. There were a few Indian women who they said were abused badly by miners. They saw a few Chinese women, but they were old, no young women, and they were with a group. If you go to the gold country—you said that's what you had in mind—you're going to have to be very, very careful. You'd best keep that pistol available. Loaded."

She looked down at the coffee cup she held. "Oh, my. I didn't think about all that. I don't know what I was thinking. I don't know how I am going to the gold country or what I'll do if I get there. I guess I thought there were groups you could join to go there."

"No." He frowned, sipped from his cup, looking through the open door to the darkened street, shadowy figures passing. "No," he said again.

He looked back at her, leaned forward. "How about this? Go with me. We'll travel together, we'll work together. We'll be partners. We'll share in profits, fifty-fifty. You'll be safe. You'll have the pistol for protection, and you'll have me."

Her eyes opened wide as she listened to him. Her hands went to her cheeks. He put his hands on the table, palms up. She slowly reached and put her hands in his. "You will be good to me?" she said softly.

"Yes, ma'am. I will indeed." He smiled. "You can shoot me if I'm not good to you." She smiled thinly. He leaned back. "Now it's time for bed. I'm still on Boston time." He stood, hesitated when she did not follow. He leaned forward, said softly, "I'll face the wall."

Kirk and Donna stood at the rail of the steamboat, *New World*, cruising in midstream on the Sacramento River, bound for the town of Sacramento, the largest settlement in the central valley. They exchanged waves with horse-back riders on the streamside trail and with passengers and crew of a steamboat and occasional sailboats cruising downstream toward the bay.

This morning Kirk and Donna had gone back to the same café where they had eaten supper the previous evening. He questioned anyone on the street and in the café who would talk with him about preparations for the gold country. All who voiced an opinion agreed that anyone planning to head for the placers should buy what they needed at Sutter's Fort in Sacramento rather than San Francisco.

————

Landing in Sacramento, Kirk and Donna hefted their few possessions and walked toward the fort, an imposing four-sided structure built of logs and adobe, protected by cannon in corner bastions and holes in the parapets for riflemen.

Founded in 1839 by the Swiss immigrant, John Sutter, the fort was the largest agricultural enterprise in the central valley until the gold discovery in 1848 transformed it rapidly into the principal outfitter for the diggings. Shops and structures inside the walls that had provided goods and support for agriculture now sold tools and implements to support placer mining.

Approaching the fort, Kirk saw the livery nearby and motioned toward it. "We'll need riding horses and a pack horse," he said. "Do you ride?" She shook her head, her lips pursed. "Doesn't matter. We'll get you a nice little mare with good manners, and you'll do fine." She frowned. "The pack horse will carry our personal stuff and mining goods."

At the livery, they piled their bags beside the corral, and he went to the shop where he saw the liveryman standing in the doorway. She leaned against the corral poles, her chin on an arm, looking at the horses inside. She didn't see the two scruffy characters walk up behind her. The men were dressed rough with untended beards. They grinned at each other.

Kirk walked from the shop and stopped beside Donna. He nodded to the two men.

"Headin' to the diggings, I suppose?" said one.

"Yep," said Kirk, "soon as we get the stuff we need."

The men grinned, eyeing Donna. "I see you already got what you need. Brought your own little doxie with you, did yah?"

Kirk turned slowly to the speaker. He was not amused. "She's no doxie, and this conversation's finished."

The man put up his hands, palms forward. "No problem. Tell you what, I'll give yuh five ounces for her." He pulled a small sack from a pocket and offered it to Kirk. The other man, grinning, stepped toward Donna.

Kirk stared at the men. "You don't seem to hear well. I said the conversation's done." He saw the other man reaching for Donna. "Don't touch her," firmly, softly.

"Okay, okay." The speaker raised his hands again. "I see yuh like 'er, so I'll make it worth your while. Twenty ounces." He grinned, smug.

Kirk frowned. "You're really trying my patience. I've got no time for this. Now, get lost, both of you!"

The man pulled his hand back and stepped toward Kirk. "You don't talk that way to me, sumbitch, I'll—"

Kirk punched him hard in the belly, and he staggered backward. He recovered, and both men lunged toward Kirk.

"Don't mess with us, arseholes!" Both men stopped abruptly, jerked around toward Donna, staring into the muzzle of the pistol aimed at their faces. They stepped back, arms extended.

One of the men turned to Kirk. "Is she serious?"

"Cock it, Donna," he said softly, staring at the men. She pulled the hammer back slowly with her thumb. The men recoiled at the click.

Terrified, the two spun around and ran toward the fort, looking back wild-eyed over their shoulders. One runner stumbled and fell, struggled up and ran after his companion who had not slowed for him.

Donna looked at Kirk, an embarrassed smile playing about her lips.

He smiled. "Did I say back there that you will be safe with me? I'm gonna feel real safe with *you* looking after *me*."

_____

Kirk and Donna rode on a dusty road in a flat landscape of grass and patches of colorful wildflowers, poppies, lupine and fuchsia. Stands of oak and black walnut lay well off the trail, some scattered large redbud shrubs closer by. A considerable array of hoofprints and wagon tracks marked the road, evidence of heavy traffic between Sutter's Fort and the gold country.

They rode mares bought from the livery at Sutter's Fort. He had ridden his mount around the fort corral and nodded his acceptance to the liveryman. He helped Donna mount her mare and gave her some little instruction on reining and walked her around the corral. She was a bit tense at this new experience but soon calmed and smiled thinly.

He planned at first to put the reins in her hands and ride alongside, watching her carefully. She would not have it. She balked immediately at that routine. She wanted him in complete control of her mount. For a day or two at least, she said.

On the road, Kirk held the lead of the packhorse loaded with their clothing as well as camping and mining gear bought at Sutter's. He also held the lead line attached to the halter of Donna's horse.

The liveryman had watched Donna's reaction to her

introduction to riding. He suggested the halter to Kirk. Aware of Donna's ultimatum and the liveryman's suggestion, he bought the halter and would lead the horse until Donna felt comfortable on her new mount. Then, he would exchange the halter for a bridle. The liveryman assured them that her little mare was the gentlest horse he had owned in years. Kirk figured this was a standard seller's tale since he must sell horses to many newcomers bound for the diggings who had ridden little or not at all.

At sundown, they left the road to camp nearby in an oak wood. Kirk built a fire, and they sat together on the blankets they bought at Sutter's. They munched on a delicacy they bought at a shop outside the fort walls, a treat the Californio called enchilada. They had each eaten one at the time and liked it so much they bought two for the evening. The seller said a compatriot of his recently opened a café in the diggings that sold enchiladas. Kirk and Donna agreed that they hoped to settle on a claim within walking distance of the café.

In the dusk, Kirk gathered kindling, placed some boughs on the flames and dropped the remaining beside the fire. Warming his hands over the flames, he looked down at her. "Now, missy," he said, "to bed. We have two blankets. We can each have one and hope to stay warm. Or we can share blankets and, well, stay warm. Up to you." He smiled.

She looked up at him, reached over and took his hand. "I want to be warm." He pulled blankets from the packsaddle and laid them out beside the fire. He helped her stand, took her face in his hands and kissed her.

Donna pulled the blanket down and squinted in the bright sunlight. She looked at the yellow sunrays piercing the canopies of the oak grove. She raised on an elbow, closed her eyes tightly, opened them and saw Kirk saddling her horse. Reaching under the blanket, she found her trousers and pulled them on. Buttoning her shirt, she called, "hey, Kirk, come over here." He turned, smiled and walked to her. He knelt, took her cheeks in both hands and kissed her.

"Zăoshang hăo," she said. He pulled back, frowning. She put a hand behind his head and pulled him down, kissed him. "It means 'good morning.' I'm going to teach you Chinese." She smiled.

"Good luck with that. I'm still learning English." He reached for her drooping trousers and pulled them up. She brushed his hands away and began buttoning. "I still laugh when I remember the man's surprise when you said you wanted to buy trousers," he said.

"I would never be able to step into water to find gold in that dress. I would probably be swept away and drown."

———

Kirk and Donna rode on the wide trail toward the sun that had just cleared the eastern horizon. A bridle on her mare had replaced the halter, and she held the reins expertly in her left hand, as instructed. She smiled smugly at Kirk.

Soon after leaving their campground, they fell in with a couple of riders who had waved and beckoned them to join them. They introduced themselves as Harley and Curly and now rode together, chatting about mining, weather, Sutter's Fort and nothing in particular, passing a pleasantly warm morning. The two miners had just returned from San Francisco, where they had gone to sell gold and spend the proceeds, enjoying themselves and reminding themselves what it meant to be sociable with people other than miners.

"We'll help you folks find a claim, if you'd like that," said Harley. "There's a few spots near us that have been abandoned and a few that have never been claimed. The stretch where we are is a pretty good producer."

"That would be most helpful," said Kirk. "I haven't the faintest idea about all this. In fact, after we find someplace to settle, I would appreciate it if we could watch you awhile, till we get the hang of it."

Curly smiled. "We would be flattered if you think we could teach you anything. Sure, you can watch us." He grinned, nodded toward Donna. "But only if you bring the little lady with you." She smiled.

Kirk gestured toward her with a nod of his head. "I'll bring her with me, but I'm warning you. She can take care of herself. She can take care of *me.*"

Harley guffawed. "Yeah, I'll bet she can!" He recoiled, looked aside at Donna. "Oh, sorry, that didn't come out right, sorry."

Kirk glanced at Donna who smiled thinly. "No problem," he said. He looked ahead at a dense line of trees. "Does the thick woods ahead suggest a stream?"

"That it does," said Curly. "We'll come up to our place pretty quick."

Following Curly, they left the road on a well-traveled trail shaded by a lengthy grove of huge oaks that bordered the stream. They rode on this trail about a half hour, then turned right on a path down a gentle slope to a small clearing that bordered the stream, placid, slow-moving, about twenty feet wide.

"Here we are," Harley said. They dismounted and tied reins to tree limbs. Harley and Curly removed bags from behind saddles and carried them to the brush arbor just off the beach. The structure was tightly woven and covered with a heavy canvas tarp.

"Looks cozy," said Kirk.

"We've been talking for months of building a cabin," said Harley, "but never got around to it. Maybe before winter. We'll see."

Okay," said Curly, "plenty of time to talk later. What you folks need right now is to find yourself a claim. Let's walk upstream to a couple of spots that look promising, if they ain't occupied. C'mon." He headed for the path and beckoned. The others fell in behind him.

On the trail above the camp, Curly turned to the right, upstream, and walked briskly, the others following. They passed claims where miners squatted in shallows, dipping pans into the water. They turned at Curly and Harley's shouts and waved, smiling and shouting. In spite of the trousers, some recognized a pretty woman and good-naturedly shouted to bring her down. Curly simply grinned and waved again.

After walking a half hour, Curly turned off the trail and plowed through brambles and tall weeds down a gentle slope to a sandy beach on the slow-moving stream. The others followed and stopped beside him at the beach.

"What do you think?" said Curly. "I don't see any evidence of anybody claimin' it. I pass by here every few days when I go up to the store and never saw anybody down here. Don't know why. There's paying claims all around. If you want to give it a try, we'll help you set up.

We have a corral and lean-to at our place where you can leave your animals, if you like."

Kirk looked at Donna. She simply stared back at him. He turned to Curly. "Looks good. We'll give it a try and appreciate any help you can give us getting started. How do we establish ownership? Do we have to file on it someplace?"

"Nope, just unload your packhorse and dump the stuff on the ground," said Harley. "That indicates that the spot is claimed." He looked up the path through the line of oaks above the camp at the sun that hovered above the western horizon. "Not much daylight left. You'll need to get your camp set up, and we need to have a look at our claim to see if anything's missing since we've been away. I'll drop by your place in the morning on my way to the store upstream. Come with me if you like. It's an easy walk. You have something for supper and breakfast?"

"Yes," Kirk said. "That's about all we have. We'll go with you to the store."

"Tomorrow," said Harley. He and Curly went up the path to the trail, waved and turned left, heading downstream.

Kirk looked around. He put his arm around Donna's shoulders. "Just you and me now, pretty lady,"

"Just "Donna" will do. Or Xiangxi." She smiled. "If you call me "pretty lady", people will think you're a little crazy."

"Okay, Chang-see. Let's get the tent up and a fire going. And see whether we actually have anything for supper. Good that we're going to the store tomorrow. I'm anxious to see what prices we're going to be paying there. We'll need to start collecting gold pretty fast, or we'll have to learn how to get along without eating."

———

After a light breakfast, Donna and Kirk were standing on the trail above their new claim when they saw a smiling Harley striding toward them. He waved, and without a word, stepped off, Kirk and Donna following.

They walked under a line of large oaks that shaded the trail, the green canopy rustling in the light breeze. Donna took Kirk's arm and held him close. "Pretty," she said. "I like it."

Harley waved at any miner at streamside that noticed them. Some returned the waves, others ignored them and continued panning. Two men stood beside a wooden contraption at streamside. One waved as he dumped a pail of water on the contraption. The other mumbled something to him as he shook it.

"It's called a rocker," said Harley in response to Kirk's frown. "You scoop a bucket of water from the stream and dump it on the top level of the rocker. Then you move it back and forth, just like rocking a baby. Any gold in the water will be caught behind riffles on the top level. You lose some flakes in the runoff this way, but you can process a lot more water with the rocker than you can with panning. We have a rocker. I'll show it to you." He quickened his pace.

A few minutes later, they saw the store. "Here we are," Harley said and turned off the trail. Kirk followed, then stopped when Donna did not follow. She stood on the trail, looking ahead, frowning.

"Donna?" said Kirk. "You coming?" He walked back to her. Harley stood where he had stopped, waiting.

She did not respond, still looking up the trail, squinting. "Do you hear that?"

He frowned, listening. "Sounds like a bunch of chipmunks."

"It's Chinese!" she said, "Chinese people who are excited about something. Let's go up there and see."

They started to walk off. Kirk turned to Harley. "Coming?"

Harley shook his head. "No. I'm staying away from that camp, and you better stay away. Some miners ain't happy about that camp of Chinamen. I heard talk about it before we went to San Francisco."

Donna looked puzzled. "Talk? Talk? I'm going up there. I want to see what Chinese are doing in the mining."

"Maybe we shouldn't," said Kirk. "Sounds like there could be trouble."

She stiffened. "I'm going up there. You stay if you like." She stepped off up the trail.

Kirk looked at Harley who still stood where he had stopped. Kirk shrugged and set out to catch up with Donna.

They had walked but a couple of minutes when they stopped, looking down at bedlam. The broad beach of the large claim was swarming with a multitude of Chinese scurrying about the site, harassed by a dozen white men who were shouting and waving their arms. Most of the Whites carried clubs, a few held drawn pistols. The Whites turned over rockers, threw pans and utensils about the camp, kicked at tents and fire circles. The Chinese were frantic, packing possessions into sacks, trying to stay away from their tormentors.

Donna was aghast. She walked slowly down the path toward the camp, pulling away from Kirk who tried to hold her back. At the bottom of the path, she went to a white man who had just pushed an old Chinese man.

"What's happening?" she said. "Why are you hurting them? What have they done?"

He stopped, turned to her. He was obviously surprised at this young Chinese woman who spoke good English. But she *was* Chinese. "You, git on about it." He grabbed her arm and roughly pushed her toward the mass of Chinese who were dragging sacks on the paths that led to the trail above.

"That'll do." Kirk stepped between the man and Donna. He had come down the path, unseen by either. "She's not with them. She's with me. Take your hands off her."

The man whipped around. "Who th' hell are you? Step away, mister, or you're in trouble." He tightened his grip on Donna's arm and pulled on her.

Kirk grabbed the man's arm and spun him around. "I said take your hands off her, you nitwit. Are you hard of hearing? I said she's not with them, she's with me." The man tightened his grip on her arm and raised the club he held in his other hand.

He stopped, wide-eyed, when he saw Kirk's pistol pointed at his face. The miner's eyes opened wide, and he released Donna. He looked aside to see half a dozen of his compatriots walking slowly toward them. The men held clubs, and three had pistols pointed at Kirk.

The miner who had held Donna grinned. "Well, fella, I said you was in trouble, didn't I?" Donna cowered behind Kirk.

Kirk pushed his pistol muzzle hard into the man's cheek. "You're the one that's in trouble...fella. Tell your cronies that if they fire on me, even if they hit me, I'll naturally squeeze this trigger, and you're a dead man." The miner looked aside at his friends, then back to Kirk.

"On the other hand," said Kirk, "we can settle this by

you telling your cronies to lower their weapons and walk away. You will go up to the trail with my friend and me. We'll be on our way, and you can go back down to do whatever you're doing. How's that?"

The man looked a moment longer at Kirk and cross-eyed at the muzzle of the pistol, now hardly an inch from his nose. He turned to the line of his friends and motioned sideward with a nod of his head. They slowly lowered the clubs and pistols and walked toward the Chinese, who had stopped what they were doing and silently watched. Kirk motioned with the pistol toward the path. The man moved up the slope toward the trail, Kirk and Donna following.

Now back on the trail above the camp, Kirk lowered the pistol. "Why are you doing this?" Donna said to the miner.

He leaned toward her and spoke angrily. "There's no place for Chinamen in the diggings! This place is American! If they want to open a café or a laundry, that's okay. But there's no place for Chinamen in the diggings!"

Kirk motioned down the trail with the pistol. The man backed away, turned and started down the path toward the camp. He looked back over his shoulder. "This ain't over."

Kirk and Donna walked slowly down the trail. He looked back over his shoulder more than once. Kirk recalled the evening of his arrival in San Francisco. Dining and drinking at a portside saloon, some miners in town for a respite told of life in the mines. Among the tales, they mentioned altercations between Chinese and Whites. Judging from the tales, the Chinese, trying to avoid confrontations with white miners, customarily occupied only placers that were considered worked out, claims that Whites had given up on. The Chinese moved in and worked hard. If they were successful, even moderately, they were chased and white miners returned to the spot. He decided this was probably what happened here. As they walked, Kirk told Donna something of the problems Chinese miners encountered.

She held his arm with both hands and leaned her head against it. "I don't understand," she said softly. "Why do some people hate other people just because they look different or come from some other place?"

He put an arm around her shoulders, pulled her to him and kissed her cheek. "I think people do this when they feel threatened. If the Chinese are taking gold that the Whites think belong to them, they react. And white people in general seem to think that anybody that looks different from them are not as good as they are."

He stopped, turned to her. "Did the English in Hong Kong think the Chinese there were their equals?"

She took his arm again and started walking, pulling him along. "No, I guess they didn't. I never thought much about it. When I worked in the market, I didn't see many English. When I saw any, it was usually men who smiled and wanted to talk."

"And wanted to pull you into an alley. Did any of the smiling Englishmen want to touch you here?" He lightly touched a breast.

She punched him on an arm.

"Well, did they?"

She wriggled and pulled on his arm. "Yes." She sobered, frowned. "You know, when I worked at the army base, there wasn't much of that. The soldiers saw me working. They saw that I did good work, and I think they respected me."

"Too bad the white miners don't have that same respect. Fact is, I think they are prejudiced against Chinese miners not only because they are Chinese but because they seem to be good miners.

"Here we are." He pointed at the store. They walked across the open yard, up the stairs and inside. They stopped just inside the door to look around, surprised. The store was well stocked and arranged. It displayed a considerable array of foods, from beans, potatoes, cheese, coffee and fruit, to tinned oysters and sardines. Mining implements hung from ceiling hooks, and shelves were filled with everything miners might need, from shirts, suspenders, belts and trousers to lanterns and chamber pots.

Kirk and Donna were astonished. He leaned toward her and spoke softly. "We'll come back when we have cash or gold to spend." While she wandered about the store, he selected vegetables, fruit and coffee. He could not help noticing the four shoppers, likely miners, who were visibly distracted by the presence of this pretty woman. Donna smiled thinly at a man who stood at a potato bin watching her, a single potato held motionless over the bin. He blinked and returned to counting potatoes for his sack.

After he paid the shop owner from a small leather pouch, Kirk showed Donna the almost empty pouch. He whispered to her that he would do some hunting in the next few days while she collected gold.

———

Kirk and Donna spent most of the next week at Curly and Harley's claim. They watched them panning, scooping up water and gravel at streamside, whirling it in a circular motion, pouring the water out slowly, searching the sediment for the sparkling, golden flakes. At their invitation,

Donna and Kirk gave it a try. On her third pan, Donna was perfectly thrilled to find a sparkling golden flake.

Harley demonstrated the workings of the rocker, pouring water at the top end of the wooden tray, moving the unit like a cradle and examining the sediment separated behind baffles and draining through a sieve. Donna's eyes opened wide when Curly held up a shiny flake, then another and—he grinned broadly—a pea-sized gold nugget.

"Wow," said Kirk, "that's impressive." He helped Donna stand. "We need to hustle to our place and get to work."

————

Now, Kirk and Donna eagerly set to work. They practiced panning, trousers rolled up to their knees, squatting in the shallows. Each had a small glass bottle on the sand behind them. Each shouted and grinned at the discovery of each gold flake. It became evident shortly that Donna was the most adept, or the luckiest. She soon had a thin layer of flakes in the bottom of her bottle. Beaming, she showed the bottle to Kirk.

"Wow. Fine with me. I need to work on the tent. Guy lines need tightening, and I need to dig a trench around it. Harley says we're bound to get some rain pretty soon."

She dipped her pan into the stream and swirled it around. "You said you were going hunting. We need meat."

"Tomorrow. Curly said he would show me where he shot a buck in a little valley across the stream, just over the hill. Harley is coming up to be with you while we're away. I'm still a little nervous about the lunatic we had trouble with at the Chinese camp. I asked Harley to take you to

the store where you'll be among people till we return. You
and he will leave here when Curly and I leave."

————————

Donna and Kirk had just finished their skimpy breakfast
of fried potatoes, bread and coffee when Harley and Curly
shouted a greeting as they moved down the path. Harley
was afoot, Curly was mounted, leading Kirk's saddled
mare and his packhorse. Kirk vowed silently to build a
corral and shed for their animals at his own claim.

"All set?" said Harley. He rested his hand on the stock
of his rifle in its scabbard.

"Yep," Kirk said, "really appreciate the help. I'll find
some way to return the favor."

"Oh, I won't let you forget that!" He grinned.

Kirk went to the tent, came out tightening his pistol
belt, his rifle under an elbow. He slid the rifle into the
saddle scabbard and patted the mare on the rump. He
checked the fittings on the packhorse. "All set."

Donna stood beside him. "You be careful. I never saw
so many guns in one place."

Kirk smiled. "Well, we don't intend to wrestle with
these deer." He sobered. "And I haven't forgotten the
threat from the dolt at the Chinese camp. But we'll take
care of ourselves. Okay?" He pointed at Curly, who gave
him a wave and a smile.

"All ready? Donna, you and Harley are walking to the
store. Curly and I will ride alongside till we come to the
store. Then we ride on a bit over a mile to the ford. Stay at
the store until we return. Curly tells me we should get
back by late afternoon or so. Stay at the store. Okay?
Promise?" She nodded.

———

Kirk and Curly sat their horses on the bank at the ford. The stream was wide and shallow at this point, about a foot deep, running over a rocky bottom. "Take it slow," said Curly. "The rocks are pretty slippery. I've seen horses almost fall. Some of the boys have been talking for months about laying pebbles here at the ford, but it ain't got beyond talk." He kicked his mount into a slow walk in the shallows. Kirk followed, holding the lead rope of the packhorse.

Leaving the stream, they rode on a lightly traveled trail through a dense alder thicket, then through a stand of pines. Kirk looked up at the heavy canopy, slivers of sunlight piercing the pine boughs. The trail soon turned upward, then leveled off on an open flat covered with thick buckbrush.

After a half hour's ride, Curly reined up at a line of oaks. He turned in his saddle and pointed ahead. "Just beyond this bunch of oaks is where I have taken deer a few times. They seem to hang out in this little low spot, sort of a little meadow. We'll get as close as we can." Kirk nodded.

They rode into the oak wood and stopped at the far edge of the copse. Curly dismounted, tied reins to a bush and pulled the rifle slowly from its scabbard. Kirk had followed and now stood behind him, rifle in hand. Curly motioned ahead with a nod and stepped slowly ahead on the trail.

He stopped abruptly and stooped, looking back at Kirk. He motioned downward with a hand. Kirk bent forward. Curly pointed ahead and made a lifting, curling down motion. Kirk nodded. He understood that deer were just over the thick stand of buckbrush ahead. He moved aside slightly so that Curly was not in his line of sight.

Curly moved a step ahead, rose slowly, then stood abruptly, bringing up his rifle. "There! Fire!" he said softly.

Kirk straightened quickly, bringing up his rifle, and saw half a dozen deer bolting from a small clearing toward the buckbrush beyond. Kirk and Curly fired simultaneously. Two deer stumbled, fell and tumbled.

The two hunters looked at each other, both grinning. "Ha!" said Curly. "Good thing we agreed on where to shoot." Curly had downed the buck on the left side of the bunch and Kirk one on the right. "Both young 'uns, judging from the racks, so should be good eating."

They spent the next hour dressing the kill, then loading the carcasses on the packhorse. Curly wiped his hands on his trousers. "Well, that was a morning well spent. Let's get on with it. How 'bout you and the little lady coming to our place this evening and we'll start on our buck." They walked to their horses.

"Yeah, let's git on with it." Kirk and Curly jerked around and saw three men step from the thick buckbrush. Kirk recognized the miner he had branded a lunatic at the Chinese encampment. The miner and another held pistols aimed at Kirk and Curly. "Maybe we'll go to your place and enjoy your buck *and* your little lady," the lunatic said.

The speaker's companions guffawed. "You tell 'em, Horace," said the armed companion, waving his pistol at Curly.

Horace pointed his pistol at Kirk's face. "And you, smart ass, you ain't goin' no place. Unless somebody carts your body down to the diggins for buryin'." He pointed at Curly with his free hand. "You, untie that packhorse and give the lead to Bertie there." He nodded his head toward the armed companion.

Curly looked aside quickly at Kirk, then walked to the packhorse. He went around the horse to the offside, fumbled at the saddle and reached for the lead, then stepped out abruptly, pistol drawn, and fired at Bertie. Horace reacted by swinging his pistol toward Curly, then was blown backward by Kirk's shot. Kirk had drawn rapidly while Horace was distracted.

The third assailant had retreated a step at the shootings and now stood spraddle-legged, jaw hanging and hands held high. "I ain't armed," he said, shaking.

"Good for you," said Kirk. "Now you got a chore ahead of you. You can leave these carcasses for the buzzards, or you can strap them on their horses and take them to your camp. Up to you. Now listen to me. If I hear any talk around the diggings that tells a story different from what happened here, I'm coming for you. Do you understand what I'm saying?"

He nodded.

"Do you understand? Say it!"

"Yeah, I understand."

"Okay, drop your arms and do what you decide to do." He turned to Curly and nodded. "Let's be on our way. We're finished up here." They untied reins, mounted and rode on the trail into the thicket, Curly holding the lead of the packhorse. Kirk looked back to see the miner standing over the two bodies, scratching his head.

———

Kirk stood on the grocery porch with Donna and Troy, the owner. Curly sat his horse in the yard, holding the reins and lead of Kirk's mare and the packhorse.

"Thanks for letting Donna sit with you, Troy. Appreciate it. I'll bring you a hindquarter this afternoon."

"My pleasure, and I mean pleasure," Troy said, smiling at Donna. She smiled. "She was a bit of a distraction. I could have sold her half a dozen times! One fella actually made me an offer. Twenty ounces! I think he was serious."

Kirk put an arm around her shoulders and pulled her to him. "Yeah, she's money in the bank."

"One man asked Troy if I spoke English," Donna said. "Troy said, 'yeah, better than you do, you backwoods hayseed. Uh oh,' I thought, but both of them laughed."

"Yeah, she speaks English and has to explain a word to me from time to time," Kirk said. "I'm converting her to American English." He took her arm and walked her toward the stair.

"Thank you, Troy," she said. "If I get tired of this one, I'll be back." She waved as Kirk tightened his hold on her shoulders and pulled her along. He waved his other arm over his shoulder without looking back.

In the yard, he took her cheeks in his two hands and kissed her.

"Curly's looking," she said softly, eyeing Curly over Kirk's shoulder.

Kirk smiled, still holding her cheeks. "Of course he is. And the sun is still shining, and the breeze is still blowing, and the flowers over there still smell nice." He kissed her again. "And all's right with the world." They walked down the stair.

She turned to him. "What does that mean, *all's right with the world*?"

He frowned. "It means...that's a tough one. Gotta think about it." They reached Curly who handed Kirk his reins, and Donna and Curly exchanged smiles and a wave. Kirk mounted, Donna stepped up into a stirrup, and he pulled her up behind the saddle. Curly reined toward the trail, and Kirk followed.

Encircling his waist with her arms, she leaned forward and spoke into his ear. "Can you tell me now?"

"I'll answer and tell you lots of other things, soon as I lie down. I think better when I'm lying down."

She squeezed her arms around his waist and pressed her cheek on his back.

———

Curly and Harley's instruction and Kirk and Donna's frequent visits to their benefactors' claim paid off. They soon excelled at panning while agreeing that they did not intend to build a rocker. Donna declared the rocker was no fun, and they were doing fine at panning.

"Anyway," she said one day, standing in the shallows, holding her pan at her side and staring at the line of oaks across the stream, "we're not going to be here forever."

Kirk, who had been cutting firewood beside their tent, stood upright, frowning. "Now, this is interesting. What do you have in mind, missy?"

She turned, smiled. "I don't know. Just thinking out loud." She looked at the stream, a gentle current from light rains upstream, the line of oaks and maples across the water, leaves rustling softly in the gentle breeze. She looked back at him. "I don't know. I love it here, but sometimes I wonder if there's something else that might be more...more...compelling? Satisfying? Something that says something about our future?" She slumped, smiled. "I'm not making sense, am I? Sometimes, I wake up and remember dreams about another time and another place. All nonsense, I suppose." She turned back to the stream, bent and dipped her pan in the water.

Kirk stood a moment, watching her. He leaned the axe on the stack of wood and went to her. He encircled her shoulders and rested his cheek on the top of her head. "You always make sense, sweetheart. You're smarter than I am, and I'll always listen to you. You keep on dreaming and tell me about them. I'll listen." She turned, took his cheeks in her hands and kissed him.

———

Donna held Kirk's hand, pulling him as she walked briskly on the streamside trail. They walked on a path they had never seen. Past the store, past the Chinese claim, northward. Early this morning, before leaving their bed, she rolled over beside him and said she wanted to see some country they had never seen.

He agreed that was a good idea, but worried at leaving the claim unattended. He worried about their gold. They spent some flakes now and then at Troy's store, but they had filled a dozen bottles with flakes and nuggets which he had buried inside the tent at the edge, near the stack of clothing. Most miners buried their accumulated gold on the claim, but the stashes generally were away from the tent or cabin. He had not heard lately about any thefts, but still asked the twins if they would check on the camp two or three times while they were away.

The riverbank trail where they walked was mostly divided into recognizable claims, all furnished with a dwelling of some sort, generally a tent or rough cabin. There were a few wickiups, an oval frame of tree limbs covered with grass or whatever brush was available. He had improved their own tent by covering it with brush woven tightly and covered with a canvas top, tied down securely. Thus far, it had proven tight and waterproof.

They stopped in early afternoon for lunch, sitting in a sunny meadow of lush green grass just off the trail. Splashes of color marked the meadow, blue Columbine and lupine, orange California Poppies, Purple Coneflower.

Holding her sandwich of bread and sliced beef, she inhaled deeply, sighed. "So pretty, so much color," she said, "and nobody is here."

He smiled thinly. "The only color the old boys on the stream like at the moment is gold. Maybe in another life, it will be different. But at the moment, they are single-minded." He stood. "Let's be off. I want to reach a place I've been told about before dark." He reached for her and took her hand, helped her stand. They went to the trail and turned upstream.

———

"What do you think?" Kirk said. They stood at dusk on the trail, looking at a trim frame building the size of a small house, unlike anything he had seen since leaving Sacramento. It was set on a small island but ten feet or so from the shore. A narrow footbridge led from the trail to the island. The channel under the footbridge was shallow and clear, showing a bottom of small pebbles. A few oak trees on the island shaded the house.

He felt a few drops of rain on his face and looked up, turning up his collar.

She beamed. "Oh, it's so pretty. Is it somebody's home?"

"Well, that and a guest house. Let's have a look." He took her hand, and they walked across the footbridge. A sign beside the door read simply: *Eat Stay Enjoy the View*.

"I hope we can get something to eat and spend the night." He knocked.

The door opened immediately. A smiling matron wearing a clean white apron stood there. She opened the door wide. "Come on in!" They stepped into what appeared to be a small café. Two men seated at a table in the corner watched them enter. One waved with a fork, both looked Donna over carefully, then bent over their plates. The other two tables were unoccupied.

"What can I do for you?" she said. "I've got dinner and a room for the night for you!" she said, smiling.

"Exactly what we want," said Kirk.

She pointed at the table under the window that looked out to the stream. "Sit over there, and I'll get your plates. Coffee?" Kirk nodded, not at all bothered that he would drink both cups.

They had hardly sat when the woman returned from the kitchen with the two coffees, then back to the kitchen for their plates. She set the filled plates down, bent and looked through the window. "You got here just in time. Looks like we're gonna get some weather." They looked out the window at the rain, pelting the window and gently roiling the stream. "Your room is ready when you are." She pointed. "Through that hall door and first room on the right." She smiled and went to the kitchen door.

———

Kirk jerked awake to a loud knocking on the bedroom door. He pushed the covers down and rolled out of bed. The dark room was only faintly illuminated by the dim morning light from the windows. He heard the heavy rain drumming on the roof and windows.

Donna blinked, frowned. She reached down and

pulled the blankets to her chin. "Hey, you woke me up. It's still night." She snuggled under covers and closed her eyes.

"Something's up." He pulled up his pants, raised the suspenders to his shoulders and buttoned the pants as he strode to the door. "You need to get dressed fast." He opened the door and saw the café owner. She was wide-eyed, her hands clasped at her chin.

"Sorry to wake you up, but I think we need to get to the shore. The stream is rising like it's never done before." Kirk followed her through the dining room toward the outside door, nodded to the two fully dressed men who sat at a table pulling on shoes. Two candles on tables dimly illuminated the room.

She opened the door, stepped out on the small porch and drew back. Rain fell in heavy sheets, almost obscuring the soft early morning light. The stream between the bank and island, which yesterday had been a six-inch deep clear flow over pebbles, now was a deep rushing torrent that had risen to barely a foot below the level of the café door. The footbridge had vanished. Across the flow, a half dozen men stood on the darkened trail looking anxiously at the house.

"You gotta get back over here!" shouted a man from the trail. "You're almost floating!"

Kirk stepped out. Donna, now dressed, pulled the woman back into the room. Kirk pondered. "Can you find a heavy rope!" he shouted to the men. Three men bolted, running in different directions on the trail. In less than a minute, a man ran back carrying a load of stout rope. "Coil it, hold the end and throw me the coil!" Kirk shouted.

The man dropped the rope, coiled it hurriedly, picked up the coil, braced himself and threw the rope. Kirk leaned out over the torrent and reached for the rope end, but the coil was heavy, and it fell into the stream. The man on shore let out a stream of obscenities, and with the help of a bystander, pulled the rope quickly to the shore. He recoiled the rope, now wet and heavier. The two men hefted the coil together, swung it back and forth and threw it. The end of the coil fell at Kirk's feet, and he grabbed it. He pulled the rope and wrapped the end around a tall oak beside the corner of the house and tied it securely. The rope now stretched across the channel.

He waved to the men on shore. "Tie the rope to a tree, and we'll come across, one at a time." He looked up, squinted at the rain that fell in sheets, soaking him and streaming down his face.

Kirk turned back to the doorway where all had gathered. "Volunteer? Who's first?"

One of the two men standing in the doorway pushed outside. "I'll go." He moved in front of Kirk, put a hand on the rope, shook it, testing it. Stony-faced, he looked across to the bank and down at the water, now a torrent flowing almost level with the island surface. "I'm coming!"

He stepped slowly from the bank into the torrent. He shouted as the rope lowered and slanted downstream with the flow, and he sank to his waist. He recovered, moving hand over hand, as the men on the bank shouted encouragement.

Then, hands grabbed him and helped him step from the water to the bank. Shouts and pats on the back from the onlookers. Everyone looked to the island.

"Good man, Johnny!" shouted the man's grinning companion from the café doorway. "I'm next," he said and went from the door to the rope. Kirk patted him on the back. He gripped the rope with one hand, waved to the watchers on the bank with the other hand and stepped into the flow. He reached for the rope after the wave but was hit hard by the current and only his fingertips touched the rope.

He lost his hold and was swept away. He immediately submerged, surfaced, shouted, arms flailing, then went under as all on the island and the shore watched in horror. They waited for him to surface, but all they saw was the roiling, rushing torrent. He was gone.

Everyone was in shock, silent, frozen. Kirk looked down. He was standing in water. In the turmoil, they had not noticed the rising water level. The surface of the island was under a few inches, and a thin sheet of water now flowed through the door into the café, over the shoes of Donna and the café owner who stared at her feet, mouth open.

"Folks?" Kirk said.

"I'm going," said the woman. "I'd rather die trying to save myself than die stupidly, doing nothing. I'll go." Donna hugged her. She walked through the shallow water to the rope. She bent her head, eyes closed, muttered a silent prayer. She opened them. "Right! Let's get on with it."

She waved to the men on the shore. "Horace! I'm coming!" The man waved and shouted something unintelligible in the blowing rain. She turned to Kirk. "That's my husband. Horace. If I go in the water, don't let him come in for me." Kirk nodded. "I'm Betty. Wished we had talked more. You're two nice people." She smiled thinly.

She stepped in front of him, gripped the rope with both hands and stepped into the current. She was so light, she stayed mostly on the surface, and went hand over hand, steady, strong, without hesitation, and was soon pulled from the water by strong hands. Horace hugged her tightly, rain or tears streaming down his cheeks.

Donna stood beside Kirk. Water flowed a foot deep through the door into the café. "Donna. You can do it. You're the strongest person in the bunch."

She hugged him, kissed his cheek, went to the rope. "I'll wait for you." She tried to smile but couldn't. She put a hand on the rope, gripped it, then the other hand. She stepped into the flow and was swept horizontally in the strong current.

Kirk gasped. "Hold tight, Donna, hold tight!" She moved hand over hand smoothly, without hesitation, as if she did this every day. *If there's somebody up there, help her!*

Then she was there. The men on the bank pulled her from the water and helped her move up the bank. She waved to Kirk. He smiled thinly in reply.

My turn. Wish I had learned to swim. Sailors should know how to swim. He inhaled deeply. *My turn.* He took the rope in a hand, tightened his hold.

Whoa. The tree behind him on which the rope was coiled shuddered. He jerked around at a crunching sound and saw the entire house lift slightly, slide gently sideways a few inches and settle. He jumped aside when the tree that held the rope leaned toward the back of the house, steadied, then leaned more and fell into the stream, tree roots thrusting upward. During the fall, the rope pulled taut and snapped, the broken end singing over his head as he ducked. He gasped as the house lifted, shifted a foot downstream and settled.

He looked back to the shore at the shouts from the men there. One held a coil of rope and shouted. "Here comes a lighter coil! You're gonna have to catch this one! Okay? Ready?"

Kirk now stood in a stiff current up to his knees. "Throw it!" he said.

The speaker braced himself and threw the coil. The end fell in the water a few feet from Kirk. The man on the bank frantically pulled the rope in, recoiling it. Another man joined him, they swung the coil back and forth and threw it. The end of the thrown coil fell in the water a few feet upstream from Kirk, and he grabbed it as it flowed toward him.

He grasped the coil with both hands and pulled it from the water. The strong current almost pulled him from the island. He shouted: "When I step off, I'll be swept down with the current till I reach the bank! Send somebody down to catch me when I hit the bank!"

"Okay! Got it!" from the men on the bank. "Hang tight on that rope!" A man on the bank withdrew and set out down the bank in a run.

Kirk waved. He jerked aside when the house creaked, lifted and was swept away intact, bobbing and rolling in the swift current.

He waved to the bank, saw Donna—*my love, my sweetheart*—then stepped into the flow. He was immediately caught in the strong current and swept downstream. Donna screamed.

He rolled over and over in the current, submerging, reappearing, gasping, shouting, the current moving him downstream and toward the bank.

Then the rope was slack, floating on the surface, extending, then waving, finally touching the bank and tangling in shrubs and debris. Donna and the men on the shore ran down the trail, went down the bank into the shallows, frantically searching through shrubs, pulling and pushing limbs, digging through debris, searching.

They could not go deeper into the stream to search because of the depth and current.

The searchers finally stopped, looked at each other, shook heads. Donna climbed back up to the trail. She stood, swaying, hands on cheeks, sobbing. She collapsed to her knees, shaking, rocking back and forth. The men who had searched and others, gawkers and passersby, touched her on a shoulder, offered consolation. Sorry for your loss. What can I do? Head bowed, she nodded in response.

Two men who had been among those at the landing that helped with the ropes stopped behind her and offered to walk her to her claim. She nodded, and one helped her stand. She set out down the trail, her mind blank, simply putting one foot in front of the other, nothing more.

They rounded a turning in the trail, and the men behind her stopped abruptly, gasping. She had been walking head down and turned to look at them. The men stared, open-mouthed. One pointed.

And there he was. Kirk stood in the middle of the trail, looking at her. His soaked clothes hung on him, and his wild hair was filled with plant debris.

Her legs gave way, and she dropped to her knees, swaying aside until one of the men supported her. She struggled up, ran to Kirk, colliding with him, and he struggled to keep from falling. She threw her arms around him as he embraced her and held her close.

Donna and Kirk sat with Harley and Curly at their fire. By chance, Harley and Curly had met them on the trail, listened to their story and told them to come to their camp for settling and supper. No discussion on the matter. Curly had stopped at Donna and Kirk's claim for dry clothes for both. Now, clothes changed and supper finished, they sat at dusk with coffee at the fire.

"It was the logjam that did it all," said Kirk. "The woman at the café said this high water was strange. They'd had big rains many times but never had water so deep. Well, the reason was the logjam downstream that caused the backup. It was just like a dam that created a sort of lake.

"But it was that logjam that saved my life. I can't swim, you know." He smiled at Donna. She punched him on an arm, harder than usual, and he flinched. "I had just about given up the ghost when I washed up on a log in the jam. After I got my breath, I climbed up on it, then crawled across the jam to the bank." He tightened his hold on Donna's shoulders. "And saw my sweet woman on the trail. I thought I was in heaven." She squeezed his arm and rested her head on his shoulder.

They stared into the flames a long silent moment. "Now what?" said Curly.

Kirk stared blankly a long moment at Curly. "Curly, now why would you say that, 'now what?'"

Curly hesitated, seemingly formulating an answer. "Well, it's been my experience that somebody who has had an experience such as you just had, something that threatened your very life, you begin to think deeply about the future, what's coming up for you."

"Curly, you are a prophet." He looked at Donna. "My little woman here and I have been thinking lately about what comes next. We have enjoyed our time here, but we don't plan to spend the rest of our lives standing in water up to our knees. What we haven't thought much about is where do we go from here? We want to stay in California, but not sure what we'll be doing."

Curly and Harley looked up simultaneously from the flames to look at each other, frowning. After a silent interval, Curly and Harley both nodded. "That's an interesting observation," said Harley, "since Curly and I have been mulling over the same question. But we think we have an answer. We've also been satisfied with our time on the river. We've enjoyed the country and filled up a bunch of bottles with gold, but we figured now's the time to spend it on something we both find real satisfying."

"And?" said Kirk.

"We decided to do what we always planned to do before we got the California gold bug. Ranching. We were cowboys in north Texas, you know, and always said someday we would work our own cattle rather than somebody else's. Now, we have the means to do it. Cattle ain't as cheap as they were before the U.S. of A. took over California, but they're still cheap, I'm told.

"If you're serious about leaving the placers and don't know where you're going, how 'bout joining us? We like you folks. We can form a partnership, buy land in NorthernCalifornia and a herd of cattle. We have enough capital to tide us over till we start selling beef. There's thousands of Americans pouring over the passes to California, and they got to eat." He paused. "How 'bout it?"

Kirk turned to Donna. After a moment: "How 'bout it?"

She smiled. "Yes!"

Donna smiled at the group who stared at her, waiting. "That's it," she said.

"Wow, I was prepped for a really sad ending when

Kirk was lost in the river," said Mindy. Murmurs from the group.

"Did they do it?" said Carmelita. "Did they build a ranch?"

"I have a few documents that put them in Northern California near the Oregon border," said Donna. "I'm still looking. Now I'm encouraged to look harder."

"Interesting that you and Mindy both had ancestors in the California Gold Rush. Wouldn't it be something if you found that they met each other in the diggings?"

"Let's keep in touch, Donna," Mindy said. "I can just picture these two couples sitting around a campfire, sharing experiences. I get goose pimples." She smiled, shuddering.

CHAPTER 6

MELISSA

The ladies were content to be up before the men and busied themselves in the kitchen. They were almost finished when Jon and Adam appeared from the hall.

"How can we help?" said Adam.

"Good timing," Stephany said. "Breakfast is ready."

"The table's not ready," said Mindy. "Set the table."

"We can do that, ladies," Jon said. They opened the dishwasher, took out dishes and utensils and set the table.

Conversation at breakfast was relaxed, the weather and smiling memories of university giving way to pointed comments about the stories they had heard. Interestingly, each time the present day appeared in conversation, it was passed off quickly.

Breakfast was finished, cushions arranged on couches and the floor before the fireplace, cups refilled with coffee or tea. All eyes were on Stephany. She had not announced the storyteller for the day.

"M'lis is taking us on a journey." All turned to M'lis

who sat on a floor cushion near the fireplace. "Where are we headed?" said Stephany.

M'lis looked at her, solemn, silent.

"M'lis, are you okay?" said Steph.

M'lis shook her head. "Sorry. Actually, I've been working on this during evenings the past few months, as if I were preparing for this moment. Isn't that...bizarre? Your word, Steph. Every time I work on it, I don't know whether to shout for joy or cry." She put hands to her face and rubbed vigorously.

"If this is going to be painful, hon, don't do it," Stephany said.

M'lis looked at her, sober, dropped her hands to her lap. "No, I want to do it. You see, it's about who I am. I'm a direct descendant of a slave and her master's son. Most black people have only a vague idea of where they come from. I have names and dates."

———

Sam waved to three friends who stood across the street on a sunny spring afternoon in 1877 in Oxford, Mississippi. The friends waved, one called a greeting, then returned to their chatting, bending forward and laughing, gesturing. Suddenly, they sobered, eyes wide, and scattered in three directions, running, looking back.

Sam saw the lawman approaching. The white officer stopped when the three disappeared into side streets. He looked at the fleeing Blacks, tapped the short club he held in a palm, turned, and walked back the way he had come, chin lifted and whistling. Sam's friends knew, as Sam knew, that black people standing around idly in public were considered vagrants and could be imprisoned.

The Black Codes, enacted in all the southern states soon after war's end, acknowledged that Blacks were free, but described what black people could do and what they could not do. Among the listing of what they could not do, they couldn't loiter. If you're free, so went the reasoning, you should be working. The definition of work for black people virtually created slavery in other forms, forcing them to remain on the land as workers for their ex-masters at little or no pay or as tenant farmers, an arrangement in which the tenant was mired in a debt that increased every year.

Sam was a tenant farmer for the man who had been his master. At fifty-two years old, he remembered too well his life as a slave. At war's end, he became a tenant farmer for his ex-master and slipped deeper into debt every year. The manipulations of plantation owners to keep their tenants in debt were well known. Further, if Blacks were fined for even petty offenses they could not afford to pay, Whites could pay the fines, and the offenders were forced to work for the Whites, thus acquiring cheap labor.

Life was precarious for Blacks, whatever their occupation. Ex-masters resented Blacks who now thought their condition as free men gave them rights. Ex-Confederate soldiers who had not fared well in the postwar era blamed the freedmen for their condition. They stole from them, physically abused them, and in extreme cases, killed them. The law was not overzealous in pursuing the guilty Whites.

There were a few bright prospects that followed emancipation. Early in the Reconstruction era, it appeared that freedmen would receive land of their own. This was a most appealing prospect. Freedmen had worked on the land as chattels. Now, they wanted to stay on the land, but as landowners, not laborers or tenants. The prospect of landowning Blacks and the accompanying self-reliance alarmed Whites, who responded with legal restrictions and formation of the Ku Klux Klan. Finally, the Black Codes forbade the selling or leasing of land to Blacks.

———

"I don't see any hope for us here," said Sam. He leaned on a post on the back porch of a house in a black neighborhood. His wife, Annie, sat on a porch step at his feet. Ceci, their eight-year-old granddaughter, sat beside her, her head in Annie's lap. Annie absentmindedly stroked Ceci's hair. Her mother, Annie's daughter, died tragically giving Ceci birth.

Half a dozen black men sat on chairs and steps. They looked out at the neat rows of a small vegetable garden. "All we want is what white people have," Sam said, "the right to a better life. But they won't have it. They feel threatened by free Blacks. They see us as an enemy."

Jeremiah, sitting on a step, looked up at Sam who silently stared at the garden. After a long moment, Jeremiah pointed at Sam. "I can almost see that mind churnin'. You got somethin' in mind, Sam. I can feel it. Out with it."

Sam frowned, still staring at the garden. "I think we need to move. What we need is someplace where we can live free of white overseers of all sorts."

"You got a place in mind?" said Jeremiah. "I ain't interested in Liberia or any of them other places Whites want to send us to." Others mumbled agreement. They had all followed the wave of nervous, desperate interest in emigration to African countries, chiefly Liberia. The interest passed, but not before two ships sailed to Africa with small contingents of hopeful black emigrants.

Sam frowned, shook his head. "No, not Africa."

"Where then?" said Jeremiah.

Sam looked across the garden, past the back fence to open pasture. "The Promised Land."

The men looked up abruptly at him, and several answered simultaneously: "What?"

"I prayed hard last night. I asked the Lord to help us. He replied that He would help. He said that just as He provided a Promised Land to the children of Israel, He will provide a Promised Land to us. *Where's that, Lord?* And he replied: 'Kansas.'" Murmurings and head-shakings.

Jeremiah looked up at Sam. "I been hearing a lot about Kansas lately. If the Lord says to go there, I'm ready. Mississippi is our Hell. I'm ready for Kansas." Amens all around.

It's not as if they had never heard of Kansas. For months, there had been such speculation about Kansas that it was given a name: Kansas Fever. They heard that some organization was giving plots of land to freedmen, also that they were being given wagons and plows and mules and everything else they needed to get started. All the freedmen had to do was ask for help. So said the rumors.

Ceci sat up, took Annie's arm, pulled her head down and whispered in her ear. "What's Promised Land, Grandmama?"

———

Excitement was high, and meetings were held. Black people everywhere talked about Kansas as the place of their dreams, where they could live their lives without the constant fear of domination and exploitation by Whites. In Kansas, so said the Kansas Fever, they would be free, finally and forever.

"And that's not all," said a notable Kansas trumpeter. "General William Tecumseh Sherman has said he will personally welcome us to Kansas!" This was an encouraging and baffling prospect since Sherman had been a leading general in the Union Army.

Sam was not convinced. But he was sufficiently intrigued to investigate. When he had first begun to think about the possibility of a move to Kansas, Sam looked up an Oxford friend who had talked incessantly and enthusiastically for months with anyone who would listen about his plan to leave for Kansas within days. The fellow seemed to know a lot more about Kansas than Sam, and perhaps he could help Sam reach a decision.

By the end of their conversation, Sam realized that the man did not know precisely where he was going, nor how he would travel there, what resources he would need, nor who he could appeal to during travel and on arrival. In short, Sam realized, the man knew nothing of his plan. Yet, when Sam asked for clarification and details, the man simply smiled and was undeterred. God will supply, he said, smiling. I put my faith in God. Sam had thanked him, walked away, determined that he would not test God in this fashion.

While he was pondering what to do, Sam weighed the reports of organizations and worthies who argued for and against the migration to Kansas. A leading advocate for the move was Benjamin "Pap" Singleton, sometimes called "Black Moses", who would lead his oppressed people to the Promised Land of Kansas. Singleton traveled throughout the South, praising Kansas as God's gift, the ultimate solution to the suffering of black people. Leave the South and the oppression of Whites forever, said this view. Work out your destiny in Kansas, a land of the free that had attracted the noted early abolitionist, John Brown.

Conversely, said an opposing view, listen to Frederick Douglass, a leading spokesperson against the evils of slavery, who argued that freedmen should stay in the South and work out their destinies there. As much as freedmen revered Douglass, his argument was not convincing. Hadn't he escaped slavery and gone north to shed the oppression of white Southerners?

Sam had pondered all this before he told his friends about his prayer and God's revelation of salvation in the Promised Land of Kansas.

Now Sam, standing on the porch with the circle of friends, touched Annie's shoulder, and she looked up at him, smiling. He remembered their conversation the previous evening when he told her about the Kansas plan. She had pledged her enthusiastic support.

He put a hand on the top of Ceci's head, and she looked up at him, smiling. *This is for all of us, sweetheart, but mostly for you.*

Annie had been eager for as long as she could remember to leave this place that held such sad memories. She was the offspring of a beloved mother and the master's arrogant son who had violated a dozen plantation women. Her mother had died giving birth to her second child by the master's son. The baby would have been Annie's little sister.

Annie suffered less than other slaves on the plantation, physically at least. She worked in the big house, and the mistress was kind to her. The mistress dressed her in nice clothes and taught her to read. Word around the plantation was that the mistress didn't know for sure about Annie's parentage, but she suspected. Annie's light skin was a giveaway.

Less than a week following the announcement of war's end, Sam and his compatriots, now freedmen, killed the son and threatened the master. The master, now ex-master, angrily told the lot of them to leave, get off his land! It required less than an hour for him to recant and ask them to stay. He had no choice. The conditions he imposed hardly changed the freedmen's circumstances, and they had no place to go.

Until now.

———

Dusk. Thirty-one black people, including a dozen young children, crowded around evening cooking fires. The flames cast dancing lights and shadows on the canopy of large oaks that surrounded the party.

Sam stood at the fire, warming his hands. "Folks, the worst part of our journey is over. Tomorrow, we arrive at the wharf where we'll board the steamboat. Then it's easy sailing to St. Louis. From St. Louis, we'll go by wagons to Kansas." Cheers and murmuring all around. "We're almost there," he said softly. Amens and thank-the-Lords and a few hallelujahs rose from the group.

"Good thing we're gettin' there soon," said a woman from her place at a cooking fire, stirring a vegetable stew in a large pan. "This is just about the last of the cooking supplies. If we don't get there real soon, you men gonna have to start looking for wild stuff like berries and four-leggeds." Snorts and laughter.

The group suddenly fell silent. They watched a half dozen horsemen approaching at a slow walk from the gloom. They reined up at the edge of firelight, their features dimly illuminated. Ceci looked up at Annie, then buried her face in her grandmama's shawl as Annie pulled her close.

"Where is this bunch plannin' on going?" said a horseman.

"We're going to the river," said Sam.

"Goin' fishing?" said another rider. He chuckled. Other riders laughed softly, and another giggled.

They're drunk. "We're catching the steamboat for St. Louis," said Sam.

"Oh, you're catchin' th' steamboat for St. Louis, are yuh?" said another rider. They laughed lightly.

"Yessir."

"No, you ain't catchin' a steamboat for anywhere, blackie," said the apparent leader of the group, the rider who had spoken first. "You're turnin' around right now and goin' back where you come from, th' lot of yuh!" Drunken muttering from the others.

Sam stared at the speaker.

"You understand what I'm saying? You're turnin' around. Now!" A couple of riders behind him slowly drew pistols.

"Yessir. We're turning around." Sam extended a silencing hand toward the members of his party who had muttered softly.

The leader turned to his companions. "Are we good on this?" Low murmuring, yeah, okay boss, you said it right, a few chuckles and giggles.

The leader shouted, wheeled his horse and kicked it into a gallop, followed quickly by the others, all shouting, laughing, and a loud wahoo!

Sam watched them go, shaking his head. The people watched Sam.

"Sam?" said Jeremiah.

"Let's move camp now. There's enough light. We'll find a spot well off the road." He looked around. "Everybody! Out of sight in that thick stand of oaks over there." He pointed. "No fires, and we keep quiet. Get the kids to sleep fast. Tomorrow at first light we pack up and head for the river."

———

"Here comes a boat!" Sam shouted. He stood with Annie and three men on a small wharf that locals had pointed out to him. The locals said boats sometimes would pull in if hailed. That is, they would pull in if the boat were not already filled with cargo and passengers, or if the captain had space and thought there might be cargo or paying passengers on the wharf.

Sam and the others waved their arms wildly and cheered when the steamboat turned slightly to starboard, heading toward the wharf. Sam looked back to the woods just off the shoreline where members of the party were bending over breakfast cookfires. "Annie, run back there and tell everyone to pack up fast and be ready in case this boat will take us."

She ran off the wharf toward the encampment. Ceci ran after her, holding tightly to her grandmama's long dress.

Sam remembered tales he had heard about parties having difficulty with riverboats. Just this morning he had talked with a man whose party was camped near his. They had failed boarding three boats in the past week. Two had declined his wave to come in, and the third had refused taking them aboard when they could not pay the passage fee.

Sam pondered. Probably half of his party's members, those who had been working for wages, had a small purse of cash, but he knew they would be reluctant to spend it on anything but mules and a plow and other necessities on arrival in Kansas. They had been hopeful, back in Oxford, when they heard stories about philanthropic organizations that handed out wagons and mules and plows, but they said they would believe all this good fortune when they saw it.

To Sam's surprise and delight, the boat continued its glide toward the wharf. He looked back to the camp to see people coming toward the landing, sacks on their backs or dragging. Annie struggled with two bags on her back. Ceci put a shoulder under one of the bags, stumbling, trying to help.

"Hurry! Hurry!" Sam called.

The people crowded together on the wharf just as the *City of Vicksburg* nudged the pilings. Crewmen tossed lines to the wharf and climbed over the gunwale to tie the lines to pilings. Two ship's officers stepped ashore.

"Who's in charge of this bunch?" said a frowning officer.

"I s'pose I am," said Sam.

"Where you goin'?"

"Kansas."

"You know this boat doesn't go to Kansas, I suppose. Closest we get is St. Louis in Missouri."

"Yessir, we know."

"Can the lot of you pay the boat fare? Four dollars each."

Sam expected the question. He had talked with other travelers who had been confronted with the demand. Everyone had heard the tales that government or philanthropic organizations would arrange free passage or would pay their passage. He had also heard that boat captains usually ignored the arrangements.

Sam decided that he must be creative if they were to be permitted to board. That the boat pulled in meant that there was space onboard for them.

He straightened, put on a stern face. "Some can pay, and some cannot. A few have some cash, but they will need to buy teams and plows and other stuff in Kansas. If you will give me an address where we can pay later, after we have begun to earn a living in Kansas, we will send full payment."

The two boatmen glared at Sam. A long moment passed. "Bullshit," said one. The other, presumably the senior officer, simply frowned. Sam hoped he was considering.

Sam inhaled. *Now for the rest of the story.* "Sir, I was a soldier in the Union army. I am a United States citizen and a voter, and I know my rights. If you don't take us, I will go to court and sue you and the boat company for damages." He locked eyes with the officer, hoping his shaking knees were not visible.

"Damages? What damages." He chuckled, then frowned.

"What bullshit," said the junior officer, staring hard at Sam. Sam blinked, but stood his ground, chin up.

The captain pondered a long moment, frowning, staring at Sam and the people huddled behind, their faces a question. He turned to the junior officer. "Let 'em come aboard." He turned to Sam. "I'll talk to you later."

After the officers boarded, Sam slumped, eyes closed, and inhaled. He had heard the soldier-citizen-suit story shortly before leaving Oxford, never thinking he would use it. He learned much later that the scenario was used many times by the leaders of parties trying to get special treatment on steamboat passages, and the captain, each time, had probably heard it before.

The party was directed to the stern deck, where they stacked their belongings and made their place for the voyage to St. Louis. They rationed their scant food, supplemented by offerings from a few white passengers who saw their need. To escape the frequent spring rain showers, they huddled against walls, under overhangs and in the few inside public places they were permitted to enter.

———

On a sunny afternoon, Sam and Annie sat in the shade of an overhang on the stern deck, watching the occasional boat pass, looking up at birds gliding motionless in the boat's wind current. They looked aside at Ceci, leaning against the cabin wall in the shade, bent over the book she had picked up earlier from a passageway floor. She read aloud, slowly, softly and distinctly.

"Listen to that," Sam said softly. "She reads better than I do. I'll have to get her to teach me."

Annie leaned forward slightly, looked past Ceci. She turned to Sam and spoke softly. "I think you can't see them, but there's two young crewmen around the corner of the cabin, sitting on a big rope coil, pressed against the wall. They're staring at Ceci's back, listening. I'll bet they can't read at all."

"What're you doing there! Get to work!" A crewman stood over the boys. They jumped up and scurried down the passageway, looking back over their shoulder at the crewman. He watched them a moment, then came around the corner and stood in front of Ceci. He stared at her a moment.

He softened. "So this is what's keepin' my boys from doing their work. I heard somebody reading. Was that you, little missy?"

She bent over the book, looking at her feet. "Yessir."

He frowned. "Where did you learn to read?"

She studied her shoes. "From my grandmama and my teacher at school."

"Hmm. Didn't know black kids went to school in the South." He looked at Annie and Sam, still frowning. "You her grandmama and granddaddy?"

"Yessir," said Sam.

"You taught her to read?"

"It was all Annie," said Sam. "I don't mind admitting that Ceci reads better than I do."

He softened. "I can relate to that. My two little 'uns sometimes have to read stuff for me." He straightened. "We land in a couple of hours. I understand you lot are headin' for Kansas." Sam and Annie nodded. "Good luck with that. I don't envy you." He looked down at Ceci. "You look out for your grandmama and granddaddy, hear? They're gonna need help." He smiled thinly and set off up the passageway.

Annie and Sam looked at each other. "Well, that's not encouraging," said Sam. He stood and offered a hand to Annie. "Let's pass the word to the others. We land in a couple of hours."

———

Sam and his group disembarked at St. Louis. They watched other passengers, mostly Whites, a few Blacks, walk down the gangway, waving to friends on the dock who smiled at them, hugging, laughing and walking together toward the town.

Sam's party huddled together on the pier, looking around, cases and bags of their meager belongings at their feet. They had no idea what to do now.

Ceci was the only person in the group who was able to smile. Leaning against her grandmama, she clutched tightly the book that the crewman from yesterday handed her as she stood in the line at the top of the gangway. "This is for you, little missy. My daughter left it on the boat when she was here last. She's finished with it, and I thought you should have it." He had smiled and patted the top of her head. She was so surprised she said nothing when he handed her the book. Walking down the gateway, she turned and tearfully waved to him. He smiled and returned the wave.

Sam and his party were surprised when a half dozen people walked toward them, smiling and waving. The group included Blacks and Whites, men and women.

"I suppose you folks are headed for Kansas," said a white man in the group.

"Yessir, we are," said Sam, "but we don't rightly know where we're goin' or how we're gonna get there."

The man smiled. "I understand. We're here to help. I'm Robert Wright. We're from the Blessing Way Foundation. Unless you have other plans, we recommend you go to Nicodemus. It's a town founded by black people for black people. We've helped other groups like yours go there. Does this sound like something that would interest you?"

"Yes, sir, it sounds just right for us," Sam said. The people that had collected around them nodded eagerly and added their thanks.

"Okay, first we'll find places for you to spend the night. I will return tomorrow with information on how you will travel. Once in Nicodemus, we'll put you in touch with organizations there that will help you with wagons, plows and mules. They will also help you file for homesteads." People crowded around, listening and gasping at each revelation of help.

"God bless you, sir," said Sam. "Surely, He will reward you good people for what you do for us. You are our saviors."

The Blessing Way Foundation found temporary shelter and meals for Sam's group at churches and in homes, mostly provided by local black people.

––––––

By arrangement the next morning, Wright and two others walked Sam's party to the train station. Wright handed Sam train tickets. "May God be with you and give you good harvests," Wright said. Every soul in the party, some with tears streaming down cheeks, crowded around him and his companions. The travelers thanked them, touching an arm, bowing slightly, smiling.

The freedmen hefted their bags and walked to the passenger cars. Some hesitated at the door, unsure. "Don't hold back, brothers and sisters," said Jeremiah, "we're almost to Canaan. Hallelujah!" Others responded with hallelujahs and praise-the-Lords and crowded at the car doors.

Whites, waiting to board, stood apart from the Blacks. They hesitated, looking at each other, some surprised, some seemingly fearful. The black people, seeing Whites trying to board, stepped aside, nodding and smiling. The white passengers, unsure how to respond, at first looked at each other, waiting, then nodded, some smiling, and boarded. Once the Whites were aboard, the Blacks crowded into the doorway and climbed inside the coach.

The train ride was a revelation. Some in the party sat rigid, fearful, silent, eyes clenched. Others were excited at this new experience. They watched the prairie and farm buildings stream past the window, people standing near the tracks, some waving.

The children in their coach seats were the least fearful, the least surprised at this new experience. They had not yet learned what was new and frightful. To them, it was simply fun. Ceci, seated at a window beside Annie, her face aglow with excitement, took Annie's arm. "Grandmama, I want to ride a train every day!"

———

Sam's party stepped down from the train at Topeka, the closest the tracks lay to Nicodemus. They were met immediately on leaving the train by Blessing Way people who ushered them to wagons for the journey to their destination, not far, they said, only about eighty miles. The people were constantly surprised, astounded, by the assistance they were receiving.

Sam, Annie, Ceci and three others sat in a wagon bed, surrounded by their bags. Annie stared at the flat prairie, the gentle breeze rolling the tall grass in waves to the horizon. She looked at the Blessing Way driver, leaned toward Sam and spoke in his ear. "Sam, where are the trees? There are no trees?"

Sam smiled. "Dunno. I guess the Lord decided that Kansas was supposed to be croplands, not forests. We won't have to clear trees and brambles before we plant."

———

The orange sun ball hovered over the western horizon. The six wagons pulled off the road where drivers jumped down, lowered tailgates and helped their passengers climb down. A driver spoke to the people who were stretching and pulling bags from wagons. "About an hour of daylight before sundown, folks." He pointed aside. "There's some fire pits over there you can use to fix your supper. I'll rouse you at first light tomorrow. We'll need to be on our way early."

Drivers unhitched teams and hobbled them nearby. The drivers pulled small bags from under wagon seats and went to a fire circle where they worked on their own supper.

A black man who had carried his bag to a fire circle, looked around, puzzled, and went to the group of drivers who now sat around a low fire. "Uh, I don't see any wood over there." He pointed. "What are you burning?"

A driver leaned over, picked up a small bag and handed it to the questioner. "Use this."

He took the bag, looked inside. "What is it?"

"Buffalo chips and cow chips."

"Uh. What's that?"

"Dried buffalo shit and dried cow shit. Burns pretty good. You'll get used to the smell."

"Oh." He walked toward the fire circles, looking inside the bag. He showed the chips to others who had walked to the circles carrying their bags. They soon had fires lit and sat around them, eating and chatting.

At dusk, the people were startled at the approach of a party of horsemen, about twenty, who rode slowly into the camp. They stopped at the drivers' fire. A low conversation and a few chuckles followed. The people strained to hear, but could only pick up an occasional word from the rider closest to the fire. The others were but shadows in the dim end of day, but the leader's face was illuminated by the drivers' fire.

Annie leaned over and whispered. "Sam, he's a black man. Seems to be wearing a uniform."

Sam replied softly. "Yeah. I think they are all black. Black soldiers."

The soldier who had spoken reined aside, and the troop rode away slowly toward the sunset. The white driver stood and walked toward his wagon.

Sam stood. "Black soldiers?"

The driver stopped. "Yeah, I'm right happy to have 'em around. They're good soldiers. Buffalo Soldiers, they're called. I think the Indians named them, referring to their bushy black hair, but also because they are strong and fierce, like buffalo. He said they had word there were Indians ahead. They're having a look. That's good. Indians don't want to mess with Buffalo Soldiers."

———

Arriving in Nicodemus, the Oxford party was met as promised by representatives, two Blacks and one White, of the Blessing Way Foundation. They led them to tents set up at the edge of town, where they would stay until they were settled elsewhere on their own. Then they took the men to the livery and shops where they were given teams and plows, basic farm equipment and seed, blankets and simple furniture and kitchen goods. The freedmen received the equipment and supplies and animals with eyes wide, jaws hanging, and not a few tears.

The local representatives also guided them through the process of applying for homesteads. At the Nicodemus land office, staffed by three Blacks and one White, each of the men in the party filed for 160-acre plots as near the new town as possible. The representative from the Foundation paid the filing fee for each applicant. He turned to the assembled freedmen. "And that's it. You are now landowners."

The freedmen were ecstatic! They shook each other's hands, slapped backs. Each went to the Foundation man and thanked him, some shaking his hand, others simply nodding, bowing, cheeks wet.

"Oh, what a joy and what advantage to be a real, legal, voting citizen, and now a landowner," said Sam. Nods and mumbles of agreement.

"That's not all, folks," said the black man seated at a desk, "the railroad will be here before many years, and you'll be shipping your produce back East by rail."

"Praise the Lord, and thanks to you good people for all your help," said Sam.

———

In the months following, the people from Oxford would learn that Missouri, St. Louis in particular, was becoming increasingly hostile to the influx of desperate southern Blacks. By contrast, Kansas was welcoming, applauding the Southerners' efforts to build a better life. The incoming freedmen were thankful for the good wishes but enjoyed little material help from the Kansas government. It was philanthropic organizations and resident black people who provided most support for the migrants.

A week after their arrival in Nicodemus, Sam, Annie and Ceci stood on their claim just a mile from the Nicodemus town limits. With the help of the philanthropic group, they now owned a wagon, a plow, a team of mules with all the necessary tack and the most important basics for a home. They felt blessed.

Sam bent and collected a handful of soil. "Annie," he said, "this is free land, and it belongs to us." He let the sand trickle from his hand. "Exodusters they're calling us. Just like the Israelites who escaped slavery in Egypt and went to the land the Lord provided for them. That's who we are and that's what we're doing. Kansas is our Promised Land." They knelt, bowed their heads and thanked the Lord for their deliverance and settlement on their own land.

The Oxford settlers would hear in coming months about a multitude of less fortunate sblack arrivals in Kansas. The movement of black people from southern states became a deluge as freedmen decided that Blacks had no future in the South. This sentiment spread, meetings to talk about Kansas were held, and talk of leaving the South became more open. Whites who would be affected in some way by the departure of Blacks became increasingly uneasy, then angry. Beatings and occasional lynchings were the result.

Arriving in Kansas, the freedmen were homeless, without funds, many dressed in rags. Most were oblivious of what to do next. They left their homes in the South with no sure plan on how they were going to reach Kansas or how they would proceed once they arrived there.

Philanthropic organizations, including the Blessing Way Foundation that had helped the Oxford settlers, were soon overwhelmed with the number of arrivals who needed help, and their resources were exhausted. They and local government leaders increasingly tried to persuade the recent arrivals to return home, but the black people said they had no homes to return to. They had sold or given away all their possessions they couldn't carry with them. Now, all they owned were in the sacks they carried. Out of desperation, many of the new arrivals settled in eastern Kansas towns and worked for wages, hoping and praying for the day when they could buy or homestead and own their own farms.

Complicating the arrival of southern Blacks who yearned for their own land and a new start in this Promised Land, a multitude of northern Whites also saw Kansas as a land of opportunity and migrated there. Most of these Whites had some capital and competed with black arrivals who had little or none.

The Oxford contingent heard about the poor Blacks who had arrived after them. They shook their heads at the suffering of these poor folk. They thanked the Lord for guiding the Oxford party early and safely to Nicodemus and prayed for those stranded in Missouri and eastern Kansas.

Politics early on began to play a role in the movement of freedmen from the South. Democrats charged the dominant Republicans in leadership roles in Kansas with welcoming the arrival of southern Blacks and providing financial help for political reasons. The freedmen, according to this argument, were citizens, and the men were voters. Never mind that the Kansas government gave little actual financial support to the newcomers. Vocal political support at least gave the private philanthropists moral support. In fact, established resident Blacks probably provided more support to the arriving freedmen than government or philanthropic organizations.

Many Kansas citizens, Democrat and Republican, believed that any sort of support to the migration encouraged more freedmen to come, thereby enlarging the problem. Interestingly, some support for the exodus came from southern sources. Southern governments and white citizens often encouraged the departure of the black malcontents, even to the point of providing some little financial support.

Conversely, some organizations, white, black and joint white-black bodies, sent representatives to Kansas to investigate whether a move to Kansas would be a good move for freedmen. The findings, more often than not, suggested that a majority of the late Exodusters were not faring well in Kansas.

In the months following their arrival, the Oxford settlers built soddies, a rectangular structure of hard clay blocks, usually half below ground level, with a wooden roof covered with blocks of grassy sod cut from the prairie. This was their new home. They dug wells, plowed the land and planted crops. Near each soddy, the claim had its kitchen vegetable garden. Beyond, their wheat and corn fields soon turned green, a promise of good crops.

The newly settled farmers enjoyed a wet spring and mild temperatures this first year in Kansas, and they felt doubly blessed. They were free people, they were living on land which they owned, land that promised a good return, and they were obliged to no man.

While they were proud of their soddies, each vowed to build a real house as soon as possible, a house above ground that did not leak, shed soil on their heads, and provide a hiding place for all manner of insects and varmints. Until then, they were content they even owned a dwelling. The house would be constructed after they were making a profit from their farms.

The Exodusters' white neighbors did not share in their joy. The neighbors, mostly cattlemen, saw the influx of settlers who planted the land with vegetable and field crops as interference with their use of the land as open range for cattle grazing. And the new settlers were Black.

Sam heard a rumor in Nicodemus that some

cattlemen just north and west of the freedmen's farms had decided they would let their cattle make their point. He was not surprised when one morning he saw a scattered herd approaching his wheat and corn fields. As he watched, the cows slowly moved into the fields, grazing on the fresh green sprouts.

Sam and two other farmers shouted to the three mounted cattlemen, appealing to them to control their cattle, then angrily demanding that they move the cattle. When the riders simply sat their horses and ignored their pleas, the farmers whipped the cattle with ropes and boughs, trying to drive them from their fields.

"Easy, fellas, don't you hurt them cows," said a cowboy. He wasn't smiling. Sam noticed the cowboys wore pistols at their belts.

"They're on our farms!" said Sam. "They're eating our crops! We have homesteads! We own the land!"

The riders looked at each other, grinning. "These cows cain't read," said one. "All they know is this is where they been grazing since they were little bitty calves. They think it's their land."

"Okay, boys, pull 'em back." The cowboys looked up to see the new arrival. They frowned and grumbled a bit but kicked their horses toward the cattle and began moving them slowly from the cultivated field, their horses adding to the trampling of crops.

"Thanks, mister," said Sam. "You must be the boss. Can you tell them to keep the cows out of our fields?"

"These cows graze on open range. Your crops are on what has been open range from the beginning of time. I can't station my men on the prairie to keep my cows from your fields. The only way you're gonna keep my cows from your crops is to build fences."

Sam frowned, straightened. The land office man told

him to expect this confrontation and how to respond to it. "I can't afford to build fences. And I don't have to. *You* have to. When we filed for this homestead, they told us about the Kansas fence law. It says the owner of the stock has to prevent his stock from going onto private property and damaging crops. And if the stock does damage crops, the owner of the cows has to pay damages to the farmer." Sam and the others stared defiantly at the cattleman.

The cattleman frowned. He looked down at them. "So you've read the fence law. One of the worst laws in history. And it simply doesn't work. If the farmer puts up a fence, it encloses a few dozen acres. Can I be expected to put up a fence hundreds of miles long to enclose the open range?" He looked down, shook his head. "Won't work. Not gonna happen."

A cowboy behind him waved his fist at Sam. "We don't need a bunch of blackies movin' into our country. Go back where you come from!"

The boss turned in his saddle. "That'll do, Eddy. Get on with it." He turned back to Sam, as the cowboy angrily whipped his horse around. The boss pondered, staring at Sam. "Let's work on this together. I'll tell my boys to try to keep the stock off your farms. You do the same. We're both gonna have to build fences someday. Let's work together and try to delay that till we can afford it. Will that work?"

Sam smiled. The others relaxed. "That'll work. I hope we can be good neighbors. You talk to your cattlemen neighbors, and I'll talk to my farmer neighbors." The boss waved, wheeled his horse and kicked him into a lope.

Sam exhaled and looked at the others who smiled.

"Didn't know about that fence law," said Jeremiah.

"You know now," said Sam, "pass the word around. Maybe we can get along with the cattle owners."

Jeremiah frowned, shaking his head. "You think so? You think they'll be able to keep their cattle off our land? You think they'll even try?"

"Probably not. They don't like us, and they don't want us here."

———

"Have you heard about what's happening in Kansas schools?" said Toby. The couples who owned the four adjoining homesteads sat on chairs and log ends before a warming fire in the adobe fireplace at Sam's soddy. The fire illuminated their faces and upper bodies and the scattering of furniture that faced the fire. Half a dozen young children on the floor behind the adults played in near darkness with an assortment of rag and corn husk dolls and marbles on the hard-packed sod floor. Ceci was among the oldest and clearly was in charge.

A fire as bright as this one was a luxury. When they first settled, they found dried buffalo dung on the prairie that burned with a low blue glow, but the buffalo chips were mostly gone now. Lately, they trekked to pastures where cow patties could be collected and spread in the soddy yard to dry. When they wanted flames and illumination, like this evening, they added scarce twigs and brush and even dry grass to the fire.

Annie looked back at the children, smiling thinly. She and Sam had wanted more babies, but all she had borne were Ceci's mother and two miscarriages. She hoped that her protective nature had not restricted Ceci. She also admitted that she loved other people's children and sometimes treated them as if they were her own.

Sam and these good friends had been fortunate when they filed for homesteads. The four claims were adjacent, and the families often met to talk about crops and prospects of all sorts. It was an easy walk between the four 160-acre farmsteads.

"No, haven't heard about what's happening in the schools, but you're gonna tell us," said Sam, smiling.

"There's talk of separating white and black kids into separate schools. Yeah! Here we thought becoming free people and real citizens and voters meant that we're equal in everything, but now they're saying our kids may have to be in separate schools."

"I don't want to be in separate schools," Ceci said. The group turned to look at this child who wanted to be a part of the big folks' discussion. Ceci had perked up when the grown-ups had begun talking about schools. Now, she was raised on her knees, facing the group. "I sit with Robin and Frankie, and we play together at recess. I like them. I don't mind 'em bein' white."

The group smiled, some chuckled. Isiah leaned toward the fire, extended his hands, warming them. "Sure hadn't heard about separate schools in Kansas. My two little 'uns say the same thang Ceci said. They say they sit with white kids at school and play with them outside. They say they like 'em and the white kids seem to like them. Sure never heard that in Oxford." He turned to Toby. "Did they say they're gonna do it or just talking about it?"

"Talking, I think. They said they've already separated the schools in Topeka. If that's the way it is in the capital, they said it's probably gonna happen everywhere. The school people say the black schools will be just as good as the white schools."

"Do you believe that?" said Toby.

"Nah, if they thought black kids deserve as good as white kids, they wouldn't separate them, would they? I thought we was going to be through with that sort of thing when we moved to Kansas." Mumbled agreement from the others, staring into the fire.

"Well, it ain't gonna happen in Nicodemus. We got only four white kids in the whole school, and nobody is going to build a separate school for four kids. Especially when the folks who makes these decisions in Nicodemus is all *black*. Anyway, we wouldn't want to make the white kids feel like they wasn't wanted." He chuckled.

"That ain't all of it," said Jeremiah. "Old boy on the homestead beyond me, Freddie, I think, said he heard from a merchant here from Topeka that some of the little towns in eastern Kansas were telling black people they cain't bury people in the town cemetery. Blacks are gonna have to build their own cemetery, he said."

Sam shook his head. "Sounds like everything we thought we had left in Oxford is catching up to us."

The people lapsed silent, staring at the flames, watching the children at play. "There's this other thing," said Abraham, leaning back and gesturing with his pipe. "So many freedmen are settling in the Kansas towns that even people who have been helping Blacks are now worrying that there's too many of us. Some of these people are saying that the problem of too many black people will be solved by helping move them out to *west* Kansas. And that's scary. That country is called desert. Dry and sandy. Not enough rain and the soil ain't good."

"That's true," Sam said. "I give thanks to the Lord in my prayers every night that we came to Kansas when we did. Last time I was in town, the land man said the country for miles around has been filed on. We don't have the problems in Nicodemus that most Kansas towns have since we're mostly black folks here, but lots of things happening in Kansas now is pretty scary."

"Yeah. And sad," said Toby, pointing his pipe at Sam. "Sam, you called Kansas 'the Promised Land.' Remember? Well, it has been for us, but not for most of the black people coming in now.

"They just keep on coming. You'd think the word would filter back down south that things up here ain't as good as they've been led to believe." He pushed a hand in his pants pocket and pulled out a crumpled paper. "Look at this flyer I found on the street in Nicodemus last time I was in town." He passed the paper to Annie. Everyone knew Annie could read.

Annie smoothed the paper. "The paper is named 'Sunny Kansas: Land of John Brown'. It promises to everybody $500, forty acres and a mule. It says 'Apples as big as grapefruit.'" She frowned. "Don't know where that's coming from. It shows the names of the Presbyterian Church and the Freedmen's Aid Association. I s'pose these are the people who put out the flyer."

"Sounds wonderful," said Toby. "Imagine how poor people in the South feel when they read stuff like that. I wish it was all good news for our people, but it ain't. I heard some really terrible stories in town. Black people who thought Kansas was gonna be heaven on earth are finding it's hell instead. Lots of black people who spent all they owned getting to Kansas and didn't find land or work here want to go back home. But they can't because they have no money to pay for the trip home. Really sad. Wish I could do something."

"That's the interesting thing," said Jeremiah. "Seems there's lots of white folks back home that have finally, *finally*, come to their senses and realized how much they depended on black labor and wish they had never left. The man at the grocery in Nicodemus told me he had heard that white folks in some southern towns are even talking about offering to help black people come home from Kansas by paying their way home, and they should tell the Blacks in Kansas that if they want land, there's millions of government acres in the South that can be homesteaded. Other Whites said don't tell 'em that. We want them to come home, but we don't want 'em to get their own land. We want 'em to work for *us*. Anyway, the man at the grocery didn't know whether any of this talk ever came to anything."

"And there's this," said Toby, gesturing with his pipe. "Ever'body knows about Frederick Douglass." Most nodded at the mention of Douglass, the most outspoken and eloquent black spokesman for the rights and well-being of black people. "Douglass says black people should stay in the South. He says it's a big mistake for black people to leave the South because of hard times. Stay in the South, he says, it's your home. Work hard and demand your rights. It's a mistake to be scared off and forced out."

"Yeah, so says old Douglass sittin' at the dinner table at the White House," said Isiah. "Yeah! He's invited to dinner at the White House! The white politicians like to show that they respect black people by inviting one to sit at the table with them in polite society."

"Yeah. He's a good man and all," said Jeremiah, "but did he stay in the South and preach about the rights of black people? Naw, he left the South and lives a soft life in the North."

"There's so much being said about all this," said Toby, "it's hard to know what to believe. I heard in town that St. Louis passed a law that says that anybody who brings a, uh, a pauper into the city is gonna be fined $300. I also heard that some steamship companies have offered to carry Exodusters from St. Louis back home free of charge! How 'bout that!"

Sam frowned. "I doubt they could afford to do that for free. Probably somebody's paying 'em, probably Whites in St. Louis or Whites in the South."

The group fell silent, but for the giggles and soft, playful chatter of the children. Annie sat on the floor at Sam's side, her arm around a leg and her head leaning on the leg. He rested his hand on her shoulder.

Annie looked around, sat up straight. "I know somethin' I'll bet nobody else here knows."

"Oh yeah," said Isiah, pointing at her. "What do you know that we don't know? Let's have it, girl." He smiled a you-don't-know-anything-I-don't-know smile.

She smiled thinly, ducked her head. "Remember when we started talking about Nicodemus, we figured the town was named after Nicodemus in the Bible?"

"That's so," said Toby.

"Well, it's *not* so," she said. The others were suddenly silent at this unequivocal pronouncement.

"When Sam and me were in town last, while he talked to the liveryman, I went to the haberdasher. While we talked about sewing and stuff, I told the woman there that we are new to Kansas, and we really like Nicodemus. She just outta the blue asked me if I knew where the name came from. I said it came from the Bible. She laughed and said, 'no, it didn't.'"

"Course it did," said Abraham. "I found Nicodemus in the Bible."

"The haberdasher woman showed me a copy of an old Topeka newspaper. She said she keeps it to show to people who don't believe her when she tells about the name of the town." She looked pointedly at Abraham, then back to the group. "She pointed to a poem in the article that she said told it all. She said she can't read, but the person who gave her the newspaper read it to her. I wrote it down. Here." She offered the paper to Abraham.

He frowned, leaned back, turned aside, sober. Everyone looked at him.

She winced. "Oh, sorry. I'm sorry, Abe. Here, I'll read it." She turned so the paper was illuminated by the light from the fire and read.

> Nicodemus was a slave of African birth
> And he was bought for a bag full of gold;
> He was reckoned a part of the salt of the
>   earth,
> But he died years ago, very old.

"I've heard that poem!" said Jeremiah. "Years ago, but I never thought about it havin' anything to do with Kansas. Course, years ago, I'd never heard of Kansas!" Laughter from the group.

"Sam! Sam!" He stood in his garden, wiping his face with a bandanna, the hoe leaning on a shoulder. He looked at John Henry running toward him. John Henry had a farm two sections east.

John Henry slumped over, breathing heavily, his hands on his knees. Sam steadied him with hands on his arms. "Easy, John Henry, what's going on?"

John Henry gulped, stood upright as Sam released him. "My wife. She's okay, but ...I was over at Toby's all morning helping him with his broke plow." He gulped, swallowed. "When I got home and went inside, there was Hannah, scrunched on the floor in the corner with her hands on her face. She was cryin'. Sam, she never cries."

Sam waited.

"She'd been violated. She told me about it. Three white men barged into the soddy, asked if I was around, then proceeded to violate her. She fought 'em and got a black eye for it. Two of 'em held her while the other one did it. She said they smelled of drink.

"Will you help me? I'm gonna find 'em and kill 'em!"

"Cool down, John Henry. Let's sit." Sam took an arm and led him to the bench against the barn wall, and they sat. "I'll help. We'll not put up with that. We're gonna need help."

———

Sam, John Henry and three black neighbors rode bareback on mules on the lightly traveled road north, through open prairie toward the ranch buildings.

They rode past the corral toward the bunkhouse. Four cowboys had seen them coming and now stood in the yard. "I don't recall we invited no blackbirds to come calling," said one, frowning.

The five farmers dismounted. John Henry recognized the speaker from Hanna's description. He had long, wild hair and a fresh gash on his left cheek that was still red from Hannah's fingernail. John Henry opened the bag strapped to his waist and withdrew the pistol. He aimed it at the speaker.

The cowboy stepped back, his eyes wide, arms stretched wide. "Whoa, blackie. Be careful with that piece. It don't look like a toy."

Two other cowboys began to reach for the pistols on their belts. They stopped when they saw the pistols aimed at them by two of the farmers.

"No, it ain't no toy and I'm about to blow your head off for what you did to my wife."

"Hang on, John Henry, "said Sam, "you agreed we'll let the sheriff handle this. We'll take him to the sheriff and let the law take care of it."

John Henry held the gun steady on the cowboy's head. "The sheriff is white, and the court is white. Sam, they'll let him off."

"He's got a good point there, Sam." John Henry and Sam had seen the rancher walk up and stop beside the cowboy. "Sad to say, but he's probably right. We can at least do this." He turned to the cowboy who still held his hands wide. "Randy, did you do this?" Randy looked at the other cowboys. They looked down and at each other.

"You boys were in on this?" said the rancher.

The two looked down, back to the rancher, grim. "We was drunk, boss," said one. "It was just him. We just watched."

The rancher turned to Randy. "Randy, you don't work for me from this moment. I don't tolerate what you did. I've told you boys what I expect of you, and this behavior is not acceptable. Randy, you have one hour to get your things together and get out of the country. If I see you again, I personally will see you are turned over to the sheriff and see you charged. Now git!"

Randy blinked in disbelief. "Really? You talkin' to me or to the blackies?"

"Move. You're using up your hour."

Randy lowered his arms and glared at the rancher. He turned and walked slowly to the bunkhouse, kicking the ground at every other step.

The rancher addressed the other cowboys. "Spread the word to the other hands." They walked slowly toward the bunkhouse, looking back at the rancher and farmers.

The rancher faced the farmers, who had lowered their pistols and watched the rancher's delivery. "Will this work? Frankly, I can't see a better way to handle it. I won't say we won't have some problems, and we'll need to work them out. We're going to be neighbors, good neighbors, I hope. My name's Chapman, by the way. Sam Chapman, in fact." He smiled.

Sam smiled, extended a hand. "Nice to meet you, Mr. Chapman. Sam." They shook. Sam took the reins of his mule from a farmer.

Chapman waved to the others who had found their mules and stood waiting. "You boys take care. Good luck with the crops this spring."

Sam paused, standing by his mule, reins in his hand, staring at the mule's back. He turned back, grim. "Since we want to get along, Mr. Chapman, Sam, we should be real frank with each other. Back in Mississippi, we were 'boys', like 'do this, boy, do that, boy.' In free Kansas, we're men, not boys."

"Oh, sorry, I didn't mean it like you heard it in Mississippi. The term up here is one of endearment. Everybody here who wants to be accepted wants to be 'one of the boys'. But thanks for the explanation. I'll be sure I'm understood when I use the term."

"Thanks. We're gonna get on fine," said Sam. He and the others mounted and turned the mules toward home.

After riding quietly a half hour, they had left the ranch property behind. John Henry, riding at the back, broke the silence. "Well, that was settled pretty good. I would feel better if I had shot him, but I suppose things are better this way." Mumbles of agreement from the others, a few snorts. "Thanks for all the help...boys." Snorts and loud laughter.

The outlook for Nicodemus and the Exodusters was bright. Wet weather and moderate winters meant good crops of corn and wheat and productive vegetable gardens. Farmers were meeting expenses and making some progress toward a stable, solvent lifestyle.

Nicodemus became a lively little town of eight hundred citizens. It boasted two newspapers, some small hotels, a livery, three shops and as many churches, a bank, an ice cream parlor, and dozens of homes of townspeople around the town's outskirts.

It was all an illusion. The good times and hope declined as the weather reverted to the more usual scant rainfall and drying winds. Crop yields dropped alarmingly. Nicodemus began a slow, steady decline as people in and around the town began to suffer. The hope for the railroad to come to Nicodemus evaporated as lines bypassed the town.

Some farmers left the land and moved to towns in eastern Kansas to work for wages. Others were forced to sell equipment and turn to hand tools to work the land. To supplement income, some farmers collected buffalo bones for miles around to sell to buyers who ground the bones for fertilizer.

On an unusually warm spring day, Sam and Annie stood in the yard of their soddy, a dry breeze blowing across the sandy yard, tousling their hair and forcing Annie to hold her long dress down, her other arm around Ceci's shoulders. Ceci held a handful of Annie's dress and leaned on her. Sam put an arm around Annie's shoulders ,looked back at the soddy. "We never got that real house, did we?"

She leaned her head against his arm. "We did what we could. I've not been unhappy in our old dirt house." She looked up at him, smiled. He leaned over, kissed the top of her head.

"Abraham and Jeremiah and their families are gone. I wonder who's next." He frowned, looking up, eyes closed. He opened his eyes and turned to her. "Annie?"

"Sam?"

"I've been thinking. Maybe it's time for us to move on. I don't see a future for us here. Old timers I've talked with who have lived roundabout here a long time say this weather is usual for this country. We were lucky to have a couple of wet, mild years, but that's changing back to what they say is normal. Dry, hot, windy." He stared silently across the field of dry corn.

She looked up at him a long moment. "I wager that's not all you been thinking. Let's have it."

"I don't want to go to eastern Kansas to work in some white man's business. I don't want to go back to Oxford, or anywhere south."

"Where then?"

"West. I hear lots of talk in town about the West, especially California. I hear the population there is growing and there's lots of opportunity."

She took his arm, leaned her head against it. "For black folks?"

"I think so. I'm told California made slavery illegal in 1850 when they became a state. 1850! That says something about attitudes."

"That's thirty years ago, honey."

He squinted, stared at the dry corn. "Yeah," he said softly.

She put an arm around his waist, leaned on his arm. "I'm ready. We thought Kansas was the Promised Land. Maybe it's California instead."

"Done. We'll sell everything we own and book passage on the train. Sam Chapman, the rancher, you know, told me just last week to let him know if any of our friends decide to give up on their claim. He said he would help one of his men to buy the improvements and equipment and take over the homestead."

"That's mighty nice of him."

Sam smiled. "I figure it's just his way of expanding his ranch. I'm sure he would like to own title to land that was once open range. If he'll give us a decent price, we'll sell him everything we own that we can't carry, including the homestead."

He pulled Annie to him and rested his cheek on her head. "I guess the Lord gave up on us, Annie."

She pulled away abruptly, frowning, looked up at him. "Don't you question the Lord, Sam! We're going to California and we're going to be so happy with the move that we're going to thank the Lord for taking us there. You'll see." She took his cheeks in both hands and kissed him.

She put her hands on Ceci's cheeks. "What do you think, sweetheart? We'll go to a new country far away and meet lots of nice people."

Ceci frowned, and Annie hoped she was not going to cry. Ceci brightened. "Can we ride the train?"

"Yes! We'll ride the train all the way to California! Now let's get busy." Annie took Ceci's hand, reached over and took Sam's hand, and they headed for the soddy.

———

"Absolutely fascinating story," said Adam. "It's all new to me. I thought I knew American history, but what I know, most people as well, I think, we know about our own past generally, what we learn in school. Thenwe learn about the underlying history, particularly in the lives of people. Does that make sense?" Murmurs of agreement.

"Bittersweet ending," Stephany said. "Hope they made it to California. You never ran across any reference to them in California?"

"Nope," Melissa said, "but I'm still looking. I'm headed to the Bancroft Library first chance I get."

"Did you ever hear about what happened to Nicodemus?" said Jon. "Interesting town, sounded unique, but seems it was on its last legs."

"It was indeed," Melissa said. "So many people moved away that stores closed, the church closed, post office closed, and the population fell to a few dozen. But it didn't die. A few descendants of the original settlers stayed. Some of the buildings about to collapse were restored, low-income housing was built, and people who had some connection to the town returned to retire there.

"Then in this century the state and people interested in history decided they should preserve Nicodemus, the town and the story. The church and some buildings were repaired and restored, and the town was designated a National Historic Landmark. It became a tourist destination. I visited myself a couple of years ago for the annual Homecoming Celebration. During the town's heyday, it was called the Emancipation Celebration."

Melissa brightened. "And get this! At a coffee at the church, I met two women who said they were descendants of early Nicodemus settlers. The more we talked, the more excited we became because our stories seemed to be meshing. They were descendants of Jeremiah and Hannah! And they had heard about *my* ancestors, Sam and Annie!"

"Wow, what a coincidence," said Stephany.

"That's not all. They said that their ancestors, Jeremiah and Hannah, moved to Topeka where she and her sister live now. But, get this, they heard that Sam and Annie and Ceci went with them to Topeka where Sam and Annie and Ceci boarded the train for California!" Melissa leaned back in her chair. "How about that," she said, softly.

"Double wow," Stephanie said. "Good luck at the Bancroft."

CHAPTER 7

STEPHANY

Jon and Adam went outside to check the weather. They walked briefly on the road, chatting about the morning's story, before hustling back inside to stand before the fireplace.

The ladies brought steaming bowls of ramen, unbuttered toast and three jars of jam from the kitchen and placed them on the table. Stephany poured coffee while Mindy poured hot water for Melissa and Jon who had already placed tea bags in their cups. Everyone's preferences were known at this point.

Stephany sat in her chair at the end of the table. "Slim pickings today, folks. Hope you like ramen. We've just about cleaned out pantry and storeroom, just a few bites left for dinner, if we're still here. If we don't leave soon, somebody's got to go hunting." Conversation was lively and no one spoke of an ending since they knew storytelling wasn't finished. There would be time for endings and goodbyes later.

When lunch was finished, they poured coffee and hot tea water and found their places at the fire, settling into their accustomed spots. They waited silently for Stephany who finally left the kitchen and settled into her preferred seat on the couch.

She looked around at the silent group who all looked intently at her. "So. Here we are. It's my turn. I'm taking you on a jaunt to Texas. You may remember I grew up in Fort Worth. The Texas roots are deep. The story takes place in the Texas Panhandle, not too far west and north from Fort Worth."

———

"Doug," said Bernie, "I'm looking forward to a little action. This sittin' around on our butts is boring. How 'bout you?" The two soldiers sat in their quarters in Santa Fé, sharpening bayonets.

The pards had arrived in New Mexico only two months ago. They decided to make the trek with a wagon train, partly from youthful curiosity, but mostly to escape the continual pressure to join a military unit for service in the Civil War. They had no particular political views but opposed slavery, a contentious stance in their native Missouri.

The Civil War was not the principal concern of the federal military in New Mexico. General James Carleton, commander of Union forces in New Mexico in 1864, resolved to punish large bands of Comanche and Kiowa for their attacks on Santa Fe Trail wagon trains. Military units in New Mexico depended on the wagons for replenishment of supplies. General Carleton appointed Colonel Kit Carson to lead a New Mexico Volunteer Cavalry unit against the bands said to be gathered in their winter campground in Palo Duro Canyon in the Texas Panhandle.

Doug and Bernie had decided to join the unit for

something to do. At least, they wouldn't be fighting white people.

"I'll enjoy gettin' outside and riding in fresh air," said Doug, "but I won't enjoy the cold and dodging arrows and bullets if we see any hostiles on this assignment." He looked through the window at the scattered snowflakes swirling in the light breeze this November morning.

"I ain't worried about hostiles," he said. "We'll have enough firepower to face a whole rebel regiment, much less a handful of Indian hostiles. I hear we'll have a large supply train, a cavalry of 260 men, 75 infantry and 72 Indian scouts. And a couple of cannons. *And* Colonel Kit Carson who is the most experienced Indian fighter in the whole U.S. of A. He knows these Indians and he knows the country where we're going from when he worked for William Bent. Remember we saw Bent's Fort on the Santa Fé Trail on our ride to New Mexico?"

The two lifelong buddies, still in their early twenties, had ridden with the wagon train to Santa F on a lark, bored with their jobs as dock workers in St. Louis and tiring of the pressure to enlist in either Union or Confederate units in conflicted Missouri. Only days after arriving in Santa Fé they accepted an offer to join the Union Volunteer Cavalry unit for employment and accommodation. Located far from Civil War battlegrounds, they assumed they would see no action.

"Yeah. I've also heard that the Indians are hoppin' mad," Doug continued. "They blame the wagons and Santa Fe Trail travelers in general for killing buffalo and scaring off other game animals they depend on."

"Hmm." Bernie slowly polished the bayonet with a cloth. "Well, th' Indians just gotta stop runnin' around the countryside makin' trouble. They need to settle down and go to farming. They will someday. They just might need a little persuading." He looked up, grinning.

———————

The expedition led by Carson set out from Santa Fé in a late November snowstorm. The weather was so bad Doug began to wonder whether the decision to join the volunteer unit might not have been wise.

The storm had just begun to abate when the Volunteer column arrived in the Texas Panhandle where army scouts reported to Colonel Carson that his Ute and Jicarilla scouts had found the trail of a large Indian band. Carson ordered the drivers of the supply wagons to set up camp in a shallow arroyo where they would be protected from the cold north wind. The infantry would remain with the wagons to protect the camp. Carson now proceeded with cavalry and scouts and the two mountain howitzers and a wagon filled with cannon balls into the mostly flat prairie grassland, broken only by occasional shallow arroyos.

Carson called a halt at the shallow Canadian River. He ordered one cavalry unit to ford the stream and proceed down the north bank while he led the second cavalry unit on the south side. The cannon and wagon would follow the unit on the south side as closely as possible.

Doug and Bernie rode a few horsemen behind Carson on the south side. Bernie, grinning from ear to ear, looked aside at Doug who looked ahead, side to side, sober. Doug leaned forward when he saw two scouts, galloping hard, rein in sharply at Carson's side. He strained to hear, but their voices were carried away in the light breeze. Carson listened, nodded and raised an arm. He waved forward and kicked his horse to a gallop, the column following close behind.

"Here we go!" said Bernie, looking aside at Doug and grinning broadly. Doug did not respond.

The column topped a low rising, flowed down the slope and immediately attacked a sizable Kiowa village of dozens of lodges. Surprised by the assault, warriors rushed from lodges with bows and rifles. After firing a few shots, they frantically mounted horses and galloped from the village in different directions.

"Wahoo," shouted Bernie, "they're running!"

Soldiers fired at the departing Indians, and some began to give chase.

"Stay in the village!" Carson shouted. "Wait for my orders!" Troopers reined up, rode slowly through the village, guns trained on the few women and old men who stood before lodges.

The silence was absolute. A single gunshot sounded, and troopers watched an old man collapse in front of his lodge. A grinning soldier, looking around at his comrades, slowly lowered his rifle. The breeze gave way to a stillness as smoke from cooking fires rose vertically and dissipated.

Some troopers began dismounting. "Stay mounted!" shouted Carson. "I don't like this. Warriors do not leave their women. They——" He stopped at the sight of scores of horsemen charging into the village from all sides, whipping their horses, firing rifles and shooting arrows.

"Follow me! Follow me!" Carson shouted. He kicked his horse into a gallop on a trail leaving the village. Troopers followed, furiously kicking their horses to a gallop.

———

"Was that enough action for you?" said Doug. Bernie rocked back and forth on his knees, grim, gripping his rifle and peering over the debris protecting them.

Carson had led the command four miles from the Kiowa village to a collection of ruined structures of adobe and wood. The troopers had dismounted and crouched behind the ruined walls.

Carson was familiar with the site from his association with George Bent who had built the fort he called Adobe Walls in 1845 for collecting buffalo robes from hunters. The post at that time was repeatedly attacked by Indians who were furious at the hunters' intrusion into their hunting grounds.

Indian troubles continued to erupt at intervals. Three years after its construction, Bent and the traders decided the fort was indefensible. They blew up the post and abandoned it.

Now, history repeated itself. Comanche and Kiowa warriors had followed from the village Carson's column had attacked earlier and now galloped around the ruins, firing at the troopers. Riders leaned over the offside of their horses, shooting under the horse's neck. One of the attackers replied to Carson's bugler with his own bugle, confusing the soldiers. More and more warriors arrived until Carson estimated their number to be over a thousand. Another officer guessed three times that number.

"It's the cannon that's holding 'em off," said Doug. Barely minutes after the troopers settled into the ruins, the cannons and wagon of balls, pulled by mule teams, had rolled into the encampment. Now, each time the cannon roared, the attackers fell back, whether from the blast, real damage or simply surprise and fear, was uncertain. Whatever the reason, the thundering fire from the cannons seemed to cause the Indians to cower.

But they did not lift the siege. Eight hours passed with no change in the intensity of the attacks. Indeed, it seemed that more and more horsemen joined the Indian force. Carson, conscious of the effect of the cannon fire, worried when the store of cannon balls began to run low. Rifle ammunition also now was in short supply.

Carson ordered a retreat to the Kiowa village. Troopers fired a withering volley, then hurried to horses, mounted and followed Carson. Arriving at the village, the soldiers found the lodges empty, but for a scattering of old men and a few women. Troopers collected buffalo robes and trinkets, killed a number of old and disabled villagers and burned some lodges.

Riding slowly through the village, Doug pulled up before a lodge where a wizened gray-haired old man, a heavy robe pulled tightly around his shoulders, sat cross-legged in the entrance to a lodge, watching him. An old woman stood nearby at a cooking fire, still sending up a thin smoky spiral, staring at this solitary soldier whose rifle was still in its saddle scabbard.

Doug started at a shot behind him. He turned to see across the open village center a trooper lowering his rifle as an old man seated before his lodge slowly fell sideways and lay still. The rider slid the rifle into its scabbard and dismounted. He looked around, went to the lodge, stooped and went inside.

Doug hurriedly dismounted and went to the old man behind him. He beckoned anxiously to the old woman to come to him. He pointed at the man, then to a heavy brush thicket behind the lodge. He put both hands over the man's shoulders and made a motion that he hoped signaled that they should take him to the thicket. She hesitated, puzzled, then understood and nodded vigorously. She touched the old man's shoulder.

Each holding an arm, they lifted the old man and helped him walk around the lodge. They pushed into the stand of heavy sage shrub until the old man and woman were invisible. Doug signaled them to sit.

He stepped back, convinced the two were hidden. He turned to see the trooper across the village center step from the lodge and stop when he saw him. Doug leaned forward, both hands fumbling with the front of his pants, pretending to button them. The trooper turned around and walked back into the lodge.

Doug closed his eyes, exhaled. He held the robe the old man had dropped as he walked across the open space to the lodge entrance and looked inside. "Find anything useful?"

The trooper looked up. "Nah. I think somebody beat me to it. You find anything?"

"Only an old buffalo robe." He held out the robe the old man had dropped when he and the woman helped him to the brush cover. He had absentmindedly picked it up. "Too heavy. Take it if you like. I don't want it." The soldier hefted it, rolled it up and carried it away. *Damn. I wanted that!*

Doug went to his horse, leaned on the saddle and exhaled. He mounted and joined a half dozen soldiers who were riding slowly through the village, pausing occasionally to shoot an old or disabled villager in front of his lodge, dismounting at times to look inside a lodge. Occasionally, a soldier afoot would pull a burning stick from the fire and set the lodge afire. Doug rode with the group, watching, silent.

Soldiers noticed that Doug did not kill the old and disabled or torch the lodges. They frowned at him but said nothing. He wondered whether his reluctance would be reported to Carson. He decided he didn't care at this point. He would have nothing more to do with this expedition except to try to prevent any more killing, troops or Indians.

Carson now ordered the command to ride toward the supply train which he hoped had escaped the fighting. Undoubtedly suspecting his intent, Indians set fire to the prairie the soldiers would have to pass through. Carson called a halt when the wall of fire approached the column's path. For a moment, it appeared he would have to order a retreat. Instead, he had backfires lit which stopped the advance of the Indian fires. The army passed through the billowing smoke.

Carson's force rejoined the supply wagons that evening. Infantry there questioned the cavalrymen about the action at the village and adobe ruins. The wagons had not been assaulted by Indians. Troopers breathed a collective sigh of relief, hoping the action was completed. Carson ordered soldiers to prepare camp for the night and expect orders in the morning.

Doug and Bernie decided they needed water before they prepared for anything. Soldiers who had been camped here for days guarding the supply wagons told them about a spring in a shallow arroyo a short walk from the camp. They hobbled their horses in a patch of dry grass and walked in that direction.

They were relieved to find the small pool of cool water fed by the spring. They bent to their knees, cupped water in hands and drank. Doug closed his eyes, refreshed and satisfied.

"Uh, Doug," said Bernie softly. Doug looked at him, then followed his gaze and saw a half dozen mounted Indians riding slowly in the arroyo toward them. The Indians stopped when they were but ten feet away. The two men in the lead held rifles which they began bringing up slowly.

A woman hurriedly rode up to the man in the lead and said something rapidly to him in Kiowa. The leader looked behind her at the wizened old man slumped on the horse. The leader said something to her, and she replied, again strongly, angrily. The leader nodded to the warrior beside him, and they pushed their rifles into saddle buckets. He said something softly to the woman, then to the other warriors, and they all turned to the back trail. All but the old woman.

The old woman stared at Doug. He stood, bowed slightly to her. She hesitated a moment longer, then reined her horse around to follow the others. The old man nodded to Doug and followed her.

After the Indians had disappeared around a turning in the arroyo, Bernie, now standing, wide-eyed, looked at Doug. "Whoa," he said softly. "The way they looked at you, I didn't know whether they were going to shoot you or...hug you. What's going on?"

Doug wiped his mouth. "Maybe they were good people who wanted to see an end to the killing. There are good people everywhere if you look for them."

———

The expedition was not finished. The following morning, soldiers saw a large body of Indians on the top of a nearby hill and wondered whether they intended to attack. Carson's Indian scouts in a small wood nearby skirmished with some Comanches, but there was no general attack from the hilltop force.

Carson decided that nothing was to be gained from pursuing the operation. He ordered a return to New

Mexico. Some officers and scouts objected, complaining that they still had the upper hand with their firepower and had not sufficiently chastised the Indians for their disruption of Santa Fe Trail traffic. Colonel Carson had his way, and the command returned to Santa Fe.

The command had hardly settled into their Santa Fé quarters when the action was given a name: The Battle of Adobe Walls. Doug thought it a pompous label for an action that was more defense and retreat than battle.

The end of the Civil War led to the shuffling of military units in New Mexico and the dissolution of the New Mexico Volunteer Cavalry.

Doug and Bernie were at loose ends. "I'm stayin' on," said Bernie. "I like Santa Fé." They leaned on the bar at their favorite cantina, nursing their glasses of aguardiente.

"And Chiquita," said Doug, smiling.

"Yeah, Chiquita," said Bernie, pointing at her at the other end of the bar. She looked aside, embarrassed. She was young, pretty, probably no more than eighteen or nineteen.

Bernie pointed a finger in Doug's face. "I'm staying for Chiquita, but there's also the ranch. I like the work." He raised his glass, emptied it. "I'm gonna have my own place someday soon. Just watch me."

Since the soldiering job vanished, Bernie and Doug had found work as cowboys on a ranch just a couple of miles from Santa Fe. They spent their days working on the ranch and many evenings seated with other cowboys at a fire circle near the bunkhouse, talking about their pasts and speculating about the future. Doug and Bernie also spent many evenings at the Tomasita cantina on the edge of town.

As usual, they sat this evening at a table in a dark corner where Bernie had a good view of Chiquita as she moved between the bar and tables. Their liaison was well known, and customers only jokingly made a pass at her. She finally waved to a staring Bernie who smiled and returned the wave.

Doug held his glass of aguardiente on the table in both hands, staring at the clear liquid. He raised the glass, sipped slowly, grimacing at the burning sensation in his throat. "Yeah, me too," said Bernie. "José said he's going to start stocking red wine, so many Americans are calling for it." Doug looked aside at him, nodded. "On the other hand, your problem is not drink, it's Lucia. What happened to her? Haven't seen her around. I thought you were gettin' serious about her."

Doug looked aside at him, back to his glass. "Ah, Lucia. Maybe you haven't noticed that she doesn't work here anymore. I thought I was gettin' a little serious about her, too. And she thought so as well. That's why she told me last week that she's married."

"What!"

"Yeah. That's what I thought too. She said she didn't care much for the fella, but she said she's carrying his baby and should stay with him. She quit work the day after she told me. Haven't seen her since."

"Wow," said Bernie softly.

Doug straightened, raised his glass and emptied it. He grimaced, eyes closed tightly. He opened his eyes, set the glass carefully on the table, slapped Bernie on the back. "All of which gives me an opening to tell you what I have been pondering. I'm going buffalo hunting."

"What! You're full of surprises. What brought this on?"

"Met a fella up at the livery last week. He and his pard are in town buying supplies. They're off in a couple of days for the Texas Panhandle where they are joining a party of buffalo hunters. This likely will be in the same area where we got entangled with the Indians at Adobe Walls. He said there's a small settlement there now that's mostly involved in providing goods and support for buffalo hunting in the area."

"What about Indians?"

"Yeah, I told him about our experience there with Carson. He said he hasn't been there, but he hears that Indians in the area are pretty well beaten down and don't cause any problems for the hunters. I'll send word after I get settled. Seems travelers heading for Santa Fé occasionally detour south from the main trail to visit and buy buffalo robes."

Bernie put a hand on Doug's shoulder. "Hate to see you go. Come back if it doesn't work out."

———

Doug sat with Preston, the acknowledged leader of the bunch, on the wagon seat. Their horses were tied to the tailgate. Two men rode beside the wagon. Another wagon followed. Both wagon beds were covered with tarpaulins. The wagons were filled with provisions, a tent and bedrolls, and half a dozen new Sharps 50 caliber rifles that were the latest buffalo guns. Preston figured he would have no problem selling them to buffalo hunters in the panhandle. Doug bought one the moment Preston showed them to him in Santa Fé. He was dying to try it out.

Preston looked aside at Doug. "You never shot a buffalo?"

"Nope, never saw a buffalo before joining a wagon train from St. Louis to Santa Fé a couple of years ago. A fellow who said he was hired on to supply the train with meat invited me one night to ride out with him next day.

"We left the campground before daylight, him holding the line of a packhorse. We rode a good hour until we spotted a small bunch just about first light. I should say he spotted them since they just looked like little black spots to me. I wondered how we were going to get close enough on this flat prairie for a shot.

"Then he acts strange. He dismounts, looks up, closes his eyes, sniffs. He opens his eyes, bends over and picks up a handful of loose dirt. He tosses it up in the air and watches it. The light breeze blows the dirt. He mounts and we ride a short distance to a low rising, no more'n five feet or so above the plain. He reins up, and I follow. We dismount and tie reins to a shrub behind the rising.

"Then he really gets strange. He lays down on his back on the slope of the rising and motions me to lie down beside him. I just frowned at him. I figured I must be missing something. He patted the ground beside him. I laid down. He closed his eyes and began breathin' heavy. The guy's taking a nap, I thought. I figured what the hell and lay down. I figured it was okay since we had got up early that morning. I closed my eyes and must have gone to sleep.

"Next thing I know, he was squeezing my arm. I jerk up, and he lays a hand on my chest to restrain me. He's on his knees, a finger to his lips. He points to the top of the rising, crawls slowly up the slope, and I follow, just to the point we can see over the top.

"And there they are, about two dozen fat buffalo, grazing not a hundred yards away. He inches up a bit, pulls his rifle up, sights and fires. He quickly motions to get down. We slide backward a couple of feet.

"After no more than half a minute, we inch up again

and look. The buffalo are looking around, one is nudging the down buffalo. A few start to graze. He pulls his rifle up, sights and fires. A buffalo jerks aside, falls and tumbles. The hunter stands up. The herd bolts and runs away. I look at him, jaw hanging. He smiled. 'Two's enough. Let's get loaded.'"

"And you didn't get a chance to shoot?"

"No, he wasn't about to let me scare off the buffalo."

"Sounds like a man who knows his buffalo. You'll get your chance when we get you checked out on the new Sharps. I'm looking forward to firing it myself." He shook the lines.

They rode in silence. "Your experience with the hunter is one of the easiest ways to kill buffalo, but it ain't typical. The easiest way, of course, is to drive 'em over a cliff. We took over a dozen that way last year. Course that ain't typical either. You usually gotta get on a stand, out of sight and have someone ride upwind and get the herd moving your way. Then, you can pick off a few as they run past the stand.

"Then the hard work begins. I hate it. You got to remove the hides and load the packhorses to carry 'em to camp. I always hate that part since it means you leave the carcass. Sometimes, if we need meat, we'll cut off some chunks, but mostly the meat is left on the carcass. I always hope Indians come along and take the meat, and sometimes that happens, but usually the meat rots on the bones."

He stared at the team. "I hate that. I hate waste." He shook the lines and lapsed into silence.

After a long pause, Doug turned to him. "Don't Indians still hunt buffalo?"

"Oh, yeah, but they're having problems with white hunters out in numbers with longer guns." He frowned, paused. "I hunted with a friendly Cheyenne band once, years ago. They said I could go with them, but I had to hunt with a bow and arrow."

"Really? Did you?"

"Yeah." He chuckled. "They gave me a short lesson on how to use the bow. Then we found a small bunch of buffalo and set out to run 'em. I galloped alongside a fat cow and after a lot of fumbling, got an arrow off. I hit the belly just in front of the hind leg. The cow didn't lose a step. A buck rode close past me and shot an arrow just behind the foreleg. The damn arrow went in right up to the feathers! The cow tumbled, and I dodged away.

"When we got back to the Cheyenne camp, the bucks couldn't stop laughing. Then, three or four bucks went to the carcass and cut off all the meat. All of it. No waste here. That's the way it outta be. No waste."

———————

Arriving in the Texas Panhandle, Doug lived with a party of buffalo hunters that varied from six to twelve. Most had been hunting buffalo for years on the northern plains. They had seen the gradual diminishing of those herds and had migrated southward where the herd numbers were more abundant.

The hunters congregated at a settlement called Adobe Walls. A few years before, businessmen had built two stores near the ruins of the earlier trading post where Carson's troopers had sheltered. Another store was added along with a corral and sod saloon, a blacksmith and a sod store which purchased buffalo hides from the two to three hundred or so hunters who drifted in and out of the settlement, selling hides, buying supplies and visiting the grog shops.

Doug walked among the ruins of the old trading post where Carson's force had sheltered. He shook his head at the passage of time and events that had brought him here again. He learned within days of his arrival that the troubles that led Carson's force to the panhandle had not gone away.

In conversations in the saloon and with his hunter companions, Doug learned that local Indians were becoming increasingly agitated with the expansion of buffalo hunting by Whites in the panhandle. He remembered only too well that he had witnessed the earlier manifestation of that concern which led to the Battle of Adobe Walls. And he had learned only recently about the 1867 Medicine Lodge Treaty, a result of that earlier conflict, that reserved the region as Indian hunting grounds.

So the Indians were justified in their attempts to defend their rights to land that officially belonged to them. This led to considerable soul-searching by Doug.

As he pondered, a series of incidents foretold the possibility of conflict. Two hunters were killed at their prairie creek side camp. Two more were killed two days later at another camp. Word of the killings spread, and hunters began to congregate at the settlement for protection.

Then word reached the settlement that a party of hunters from Dodge City bound for the settlement was attacked by a band of Cheyenne who ran off their cattle and fired on the hunters. The party made it to the settlement and told their story. The inhabitants readied for an attack.

Early the next morning, Preston and others sounded the alarm. A huge force of Comanche, Kiowa and Cheyenne carrying lances and guns and heavy shields of buffalo hides laid siege to the settlement. The men and horses, wearing feathers and ornaments of silver and brass, were splashed with colors of red and ochre. Hunters guessed that the attacking force numbered seven hundred warriors.

In the initial attack by the combined Indian force, many warriors entered the village and engaged in door-to-door fighting. Others rode around the settlement, firing from the back of a galloping horse. Still others fired from a distance. The near attackers were finally beaten off and kept at a distance where the hunters had the advantage with their Sharps and other buffalo rifles.

During a lull in the fighting, Indian bands withdrew to distant positions around the settlement buildings. Doug walked over to a hunter named Dixon who earlier had given him pointers on the sights of the Sharps rifle.

"What do you think is going on out there?" Doug said, pointing at a gathering of a dozen or so mounted warriors on a low rising about a mile away.

"Mmm, good question," said Dixon. "I wonder if they are planning their next attack." He checked the sights of the Sharps, lay down slowly on the debris that formed their protective wall and sighted on the Indians on the rising. He held the aim so long that Doug thought he had decided against a shot. Or had gone to sleep.

Doug jumped at the shot. A warrior slid slowly from his horse to the ground. The other Indians on the rising circled their horses, looking down at the fallen companion.

Doug's eyes opened wide, and his jaw hung. "Wha— Did he—"

Dixon stood, staring at the rising, holding the barrel of the Sharps. "Yeah, I think so."

The siege lifted. The word circulated that the Indians were so shocked at the killing of the warrior at such a distance they knew they were beaten. They broke camp, ended the siege and disappeared.

The battle had ended, and hunters soon decided that an era also had ended. The numbers of buffalo in the panhandle had drastically decreased in recent years, and most hunters began to ponder the future. Some planned to move south and east to Texas towns where they might find work. Others decided to ride to Santa Fé where they might find a future. Doug cast his lot with this party.

———

Doug stepped through the door into the dark interior of the Coyote Cantina. This was the sixth cantina Doug had visited since arriving in Santa Fe, searching for Bernie. And here he was, leaning on the bar, bending over the glass he held, staring at the drink. Doug walked to him.

"I see this cantina has discovered wine," Doug said.

Bernie jerked around, knocked over the glass, and grabbed Doug, hugging him.

Bernie leaned back. "Be damned," he said softly. "I thought you were dead and gone to heaven by now. Or that other place." He grinned, then sobered, eyes misting. "But here you are." He paused, shaking his head slowly, then recovered. "Get your drink, and we'll sit down."

Doug called the bartender and received his glass of wine. Bernie took him by the arm and led him to a table against the back wall where they sat down.

Bernie watched Doug as he tipped his glass and tasted the wine. "Now talk."

Doug nodded. He took a sip, closed his eyes, opened them and smiled. "My, that's good wine. Okay." Doug took another sip, then proceeded to tell Bernie everything that happened to him since saying goodbye. Bernie listened without interrupting, nodding, smiling, leaning in as Doug described the action that already was being called the Second Battle of Adobe Walls.

Doug took a long swallow of wine. "And that's it. Now you. What's happened with you?"

Bernie leaned back, frowning. "Not nearly as exciting as you. Still on the ranch, which I still enjoy. I still expect to have my own place someday."

"Chiquita?"

Bernie bent over his glass, stared at the table. "Ah. Chiquita. I lost Chiquita just a few months after you left. Seems she became attached to an old fella who had a ranch up near Taos. I s'pose she was more interested in a well-endowed life than life with a penniless cowboy. I missed her at first, but decided that if that's what she wants, she would never have been satisfied with me."

Doug patted Bernie's back. "Sorry, pard. You deserve better."

They sat silent, sipping their wine. Bernie looked up. "Now what?"

"Now, that. I've been thinking a lot about that. I've decided that though I like Santa Fé, it's the past. What's the future? And where? I've been thinking a lot about California. I heard about the gold rush of the '50s, no doubt finished by now, but who knows? More to the point, I've heard a lot about California cattle. Seems that not too many years ago, cows were a dime a dozen in California. That's probably not the case today. I understand the gold rush attracted lots of people to California, and some of 'em likely have settled on the land, but it's a big country, I'm told, and cows must still be cheap. And property is cheap, I'm told.

"Now I've saved a tidy sum from the hide business,

and I'm ready for something new. How about a ranch in California?"

"Yes!" Bernie banged his fist on the table, rattling the two glasses. Bernie had listened intently to Doug, his eyes squinted and jaw clenched. "That's the best thing I've heard in years. I'm ready!"

———

Stephany leaned back, looked around. "That's it. I'm exhausted."

"Well," said Jon, "did they leave?"

"Still looking. That's where I lost him. Since both Bernie and Doug were enthusiastic about the move, I'm assuming they left. I'm still looking. I'll find him."

"Lots of these ancestors seem to be heading for California," said Melissa, three of them talking about setting up ranches. "Wonder whether any of them ever connected."

"That is a fascinating observation, M'lis. That would be most interesting. Not likely, though. It was indeed a big country and still lightly populated. But not impossible."

Stephany stood. "Now, let's see if we can find some dinner. Hope nobody is hungry."

CHAPTER 8

CARMELITA

The bunch sat around the table, nibbling on peanut butter sandwiches, a half sandwich each, and coffee and tea. Jon and Adam sipped from wineglasses.

"Sorry for the thin fare, folks," said Stephany. "We've cleaned out the cupboards and storeroom. If we don't get out of here soon, we're going to be reduced to eating pine needles and acorns, assuming the squirrels haven't cleaned out the acorns." Nervous smiles and chuckles. "Or the hunters in the bunch here can go after the squirrels." This last suggestion aroused protests and shivers.

After the table was cleared and the fire stoked, Jon and Adam went outside to the front porch. They sipped from coffee cups, looking up through thin pine foliage to a gray overcast and weak sun overhead. Cars and shrubs were still snowy hills and mounds. They poured dregs from cups and went inside.

Stephany stood in the kitchen, holding the cell phone to her ear. She nodded, said her thanks, walked into the sitting room where the others, cups in hand, watched her silently.

"Good news. You're likely going to have breakfast at the resort tomorrow. The resort office tells me they expect to have the road cleared by sunset today," Stephany said, "if the snow holds off, that is. If you really prefer, you might be able to drive down this evening, but I wouldn't advise it. Even after the snowplows finish, the road will be a bit risky till it gets some sunshine. I advise waiting till morning. The boys have laid in enough firewood to last the evening. In any event, you wouldn't want to leave before our last story.

"Carmel is going to tell us a tale that I am dying to hear." She looked aside at Carmelita, smiled. "I heard her out back last evening—she didn't know I was there—reciting a bit of the story. Yeah! I do the same thing when I'm writing and trying to straighten out an episode. Keep this in mind when you're writing. Tell it out loud, or read the manuscript out loud. Really helps."

She turned to Carmel, sitting on a cushion at the fireplace. "You're on, sweetie."

Carmelita pointed grimly at Stephany, then smiled. She looked into the fire, then turned to the group. "Some of you have told stories about your ancestors on their way to California. Well, my ancestor was already here before yours crossed the Sierra."

———

Larkin and Miguel sat in porch chairs looking out on the flower garden. A few plants showed blossoms, but it was February 1844 in Monterey, and most of the plants were in bud. The men sipped from their glasses of aguardiente. Larkin and Miguel were employer and employee, but they also were friends. As United States Consul to Mexican California, Larkin relied on Miguel to be his eyes and ears in Monterey, the provincial capital.

Larkin sipped from his glass, frowned. "All right, to business. Miguel, I told Captain Fremont that I'm sending you to him in case he wishes to send me a message. I told him you are an observer. You will not take part in any of his actions. You are simply there in case he wishes to communicate with me. Expect him to be rude and charge you with being my spy. Of course you are my spy, but he will tolerate you since I have sent you, and he needs my assistance in his mission, whatever that is."

"I hear Fremont is a single-minded man who wants his own way," said Miguel, "and does not hesitate to do whatever he wants, even when it antagonizes others."

"Yes, that is quite true." Larkin shifted in his chair, leaned forward. "Now, let me bring you up to date and show you where Fremont fits in. You know as well as I that Americans have been arriving in California in growing numbers in recent years. There are likely eight hundred or so now, settled mostly in the north and central California.

"The Americans are required to swear an oath to obey Mexican laws and apply for permission to settle. Many have done so. Many of those have married local women, become Mexican citizens and received land grants. Most Americans, however, were angered by the law and ignored it. With the prospect of war between the United States and Mexico over the status of Texas, this makes the question of what to do about the uncooperative Americans in California complicated.

"Now, to Fremont. He's a United States Army officer, you know. He led a sizable party into California, Topographical Engineers, he called them, engaged in surveying.

Actually, the party of sixty-two men was a diverse collection of a few soldiers and an assortment of scientists, hunters and sharpshooters, in short, a bunch of adventurers much like Fremont."

Larkin refreshed their glasses from the pitcher of aguardiente. He sipped and continued. "Now, even if the party's purpose was actually surveying, they now were in Mexican territory and Mexican authorities were suspicious. Fremont did little to persuade them his intentions were peaceful. Fremont doesn't like people looking over his shoulder, questioning his actions.

"He moved his camp several times, conducted raids on Miwok villages and killed some Miwoks. He commented about killing Indians personally, in the same tone that one tells about killing game. California authorities became uneasy about this US Army officer moving about California without permission and seemingly without any particular objective. At least, they were not aware of his objective. Nor was I. Nor *am* I."

Larkin took a generous swallow of aguardiente. "Fremont came to Monterey in January. He was still chaffing from his failure to get supplies and animals at Sutter's Fort. He asked me for a loan to buy supplies. I agreed and also introduced him to army Commandante José Castro and Monterey Prefect Manuel Castro. Both are my good friends. They accepted Fremont's explanation that his was a surveying party with no military intent and that he came to Monterey only to buy supplies. They accepted the explanation because they are my friends, and they trust me.

"Nevertheless, I could tell they were uneasy about him. Frankly, I was uneasy about him. I wondered about his intentions, as they surely were wondering. He says he is surveying for the United States government, but he is

now in California, Mexican territory. Surely not surveying, not with that party of adventurers.

"So why is he here? Is he now in California only to get
supplies? Or does he have something else in mind? After
he gets his supplies, does he plan to leave? I suspected
there was something else in the wind and worried.

"Commandante Castro gave Fremont permission to
buy supplies locally. He instructed Fremont to keep his
party inland, away from the coast. This last angered
Fremont. After the Californio officers left, he said in so
many words that he would do as he wished.

"So, Miguel, that's when I decided to send you to
him. Fremont is a barrel of cannon powder in danger of
exploding. You are to watch and listen. You might
befriend Kit Carson, a member of the party. Carson is a
complex character. He is not indifferent to Fremont's
intentions, and he is a confidant of Fremont, but he also is
an individual who goes his own way and is not reluctant
to talk. If you learn something I should know, find a local
you can trust and send me a message."

———

Miguel's first message was not long in coming. He
reported to Larkin that Fremont moved his camp often,
finally to a site a few miles from the San José Mission, on
the bay south of San Francisco. The mission was now
defunct and in private hands, like most of the other California missions. Miguel, thinking that Fremont might not
be familiar with the locality, pointed out to the captain
that he was now quite close to the coast.

Miguel dispatched a message to Larkin, telling about
the encounter that followed. "Fremont fumed. I really
thought he was going to hit me. He said to remember my

place, that I was an observer, not an adviser, that I was here only because Larkin had sent me, and I would nevertheless be removed if I didn't remember this. He glared at me, I suppose expecting me to apologize or bow or something. I just returned his stare. I don't know how long he will let me stay with him."

Larkin tapped the paper on his desk. *Hmm. I suspected it would come to this. It came sooner than I expected. Fremont is a vainglorious little twit. He is more concerned about his reputation than his mission, whatever that is, or his country.* Larkin still did not know what Fremont's mission was in California. He suspected that it might be more than surveying.

Two days later, Larkin received copies of an exchange of messages between Fremont and the alcalde of San José. The alcalde sent the copies. A local rancher had complained to the alcalde that some of his horses were missing. He looked everywhere for the animals, in the countryside and local ranches and finally came across Fremont's camp. He investigated and found the horses in Fremont's remuda. He claimed the animals were his and was angrily turned away by Fremont who told him he was lucky to escape a horse-whipping. The rancher reported the incident to the alcalde.

Before the alcalde could act on the rancher's complaint, Fremont moved his camp again. When Miguel tried to question Fremont during the packing up for the move, the captain just pointed a finger in his face. "Just notify Mr. Larkin we are moving and say no more." Fremont moved the force and pitched the new camp within view of ocean breakers near Santa Cruz.

Before Miguel had a chance to notify Larkin about the arrival near the coast, Fremont moved yet again, this time to a site on the Salinas River near Monterey. While

Miguel was working on a report to Larkin, he was shocked by another incident which he included in the message. Three of Fremont's drunken men had burst into a rancho at San Juan Bautista, near the new campsite. One of the drunks held a pistol to the head of the rancher while another attempted to rape his daughter. The rancher was able to wrest the gun from the drunk and drove the men away.

This was the last straw for General Castro. Within hours of receiving Miguel's message, Larkin was handed a letter from the general, notifying him that he was assembling a force to expel Fremont's party from the Monterey area. The letter added that he had sent a courier to Captain Fremont ordering him to withdraw.

Larkin braced himself for Fremont's response. The next day, Miguel arrived at a gallop at Larkin's house in Monterey. He went into the store, breathing hard, waved a paper at Talbot, Larkin's employee, who ran to the door of Larkin's office and knocked. Larkin came out, and Miguel handed him the message.

Larkin read Fremont's personal message. He lowered the paper, shook his head. "Shocking but not unexpected. Fremont says he told General Castro that he would not comply with 'the insulting order', he called it. He says he has withdrawn to Gávilan Peak, a hillside just thirty miles from Monterey. I know the place. At his orders, his men have chopped down trees and built a log fort and earthen breastworks. A pole has been put up flying the Stars and Stripes. Fremont ends the message..."if we are unjustly attacked, we will fight to extremity and refuse quarter...we will die, every one of us, under the flag of our country.'" Larkin looked up. "He says he expects his country to avenge their deaths."

Larkin shook his head. He didn't know whether to

laugh or roar in anger. *The pompous little twit is inviting a siege! Fremont, you vainglorious little twit!*

Larkin told Miguel to wait and went to his office. Seated at his desk, he took a deep breath and wrote two messages, one to Fremont and the other to General Castro. To Fremont, he explained Castro's order in the simplest terms, trying to explain the general's obligation to defend the interests of his department. To the general, he urged a more temperate approach, even a meeting between himself and Fremont to discuss the situation. Larkin shook his head at the ridiculous suggestion for a meeting and cursed Fremont under his breath for putting him in this impossible position.

He sent Miguel off at once to deliver the letter to Fremont. The message to Castro was sent the same day by courier.

General Castro was furious. He notified Larkin that he was in the process of assembling the force to expel Fremont's men, highwaymen and robbers, he called them. The party of two hundred horsemen and an Indian band departed within days and rode to Fremont's encampment at Gávilan Peak. There the horsemen were formed up in attack formation, and three cannons were trained on the American position. The confrontation that Fremont had instigated was at hand.

Miguel slipped away from the American encampment and galloped hard to Monterey, where he breathlessly told Larkin of the standoff. While he was mulling Miguel's report and agonizing on how to react, Larkin received a message from General Castro. During the night, he wrote, Fremont had quietly abandoned the Gávilan Peak position and led his force northward.

Before he could digest this information, Larkin received a message directly from Fremont. He said that he had left his position, "slowly and growlingly," before the force of "three or four hundred" men. Larkin shook his head. *I suppose Fremont wished the force were a thousand men, making the tale of his retreat more justifiable. The withdrawal must have injured your vanity something awful, Captain.*

Larkin assumed Fremont was heading for Sutter's Fort, either to conjure up a new scenario or to resupply, or both. He sent Miguel to investigate. Larkin warned Miguel to approach Fremont carefully since the captain would be nursing his wounded pride. If Fremont should turn hostile to his presence and Larkin's continued interest, he was to assure the captain that Larkin, as Consul, was obligated to keep in touch with any American force in California in case the force should need his assistance, or if any Washington authority should wish to inquire about the captain's circumstances. Larkin figured that Fremont surely would be flattered at any suggestion that Washington even knew him.

Miguel reported to Larkin from Sutter's Fort on this first day of spring 1846. Fremont had received him as Larkin had assumed. The captain chaffed at what he considered Larkin's meddling and said he would soon be outside Larkin's authority.

"As you suspected, he is resupplying at Sutter's," said Miguel in his message, "and plans to march to Oregon Territory. He did not indicate his reason for going to Oregon. All he said was he will lead his force homeward from there. As you ordered, I will stay with him until he leaves for the East, if he doesn't boot me or shoot me before then. He will be happy to see my back, and I will be happy to see his. He is not a pleasant companion. Everything Captain Fremont says and does is about Captain Fremont. Everything is secondary to himself."

"Agreed," Larkin wrote back to Miguel. "This has been an onerous task, and it will be finished soon. You have done well. I will be happy to see you back in Monterey. If you are still interested in joining my Hawaii business affairs, we'll talk about it." He included a message for Fremont, wishing him success in whatever he planned. He hoped the message would encourage Fremont to write to him, telling about his Oregon mission. He did not expect Fremont to respond.

The day after receiving Larkin's message, Fremont's band left Sutter's Fort bound for Oregon. Miguel packed up for this final ride, so he hoped, already relishing the prospect of a return to a settled life in Monterey or Hawaii.

The ride north was interrupted when American ranchers in Northern California appealed for Fremont's help in punishing Indians who they said were threatening them. Miguel and Carson watched Fremont lead his men in an attack on a village, killing a hundred Indians. Miguel reported later to Larkin that Carson called it a "perfect butchery." Miguel added that he was unsure whether Carson said it simply as a judgment or as a compliment to himself and his men.

————

Camped on the shore of Klamath Lake east of the Cascades in south-central Oregon, Fremont appeared prepared to end his western expedition. Seated at a camp-fire at dusk on the evening of their arrival, he told his men about his plan to survey a route from the Great Basin to the Oregon Trail. That done, he said, they would head eastward toward home, presumably on the Oregon Trail. His band cheered this announcement.

It was not to be so simple. After a convoluted journey from the eastern USvia Vera Cruz, Mexico City and Mazatlán disguised as an invalid merchant traveling for his health, Lieutenant Archibald Gillespie, United States Army, arrived in Monterey bringing news of imminent war between the United Sates and Mexico. Larkin described California affairs to him, including what little he knew of Fremont's expedition.

Gillespie was intrigued by Fremont's activity. He immediately rode north and found Fremont at his Cascades camp. The Lieutenant told of the approach of war and the rumors that foreign powers were showing too much interest in California. Fremont was excited and energized. He immediately changed his plan and announced to his party that they were returning to California.

Miguel feared that Fremont would arrive back in central California before he could send a message to Larkin. Perhaps he would have to leave the party at some point and ride directly to Monterey to report to Larkin.

He was relieved when a small party of Oregonians arrived at Fremont's camp, bound for California where they planned to settle. The leader of the group, who pronounced himself a patriotic American, was delighted at the prospect of delivering a message to the United States Consul in Monterey. Miguel pledged the Oregonian to secrecy and to tell Fremont nothing of his mission. The Oregonian, smiling at the prospect of a role in intrigue involving himself and the Consul, promised discretion. He would not even tell his own party in case any should have a loose tongue.

In the message to Larkin, Miguel told of Gillespie's

arrival and his conversation with Fremont and Fremont's decision to return to California. He knew nothing of Fremont's new plan, if, in fact, he had a plan beyond returning to California. Miguel believed that Fremont was convinced that war was imminent, and he wanted to be part of it. He said he could not describe the captain's state of mind, only that he was excited about the prospect of war.

Fremont said to no one in particular, staring into the campfire, that whatever happened in California was his destiny. Miguel added in the message to Larkin that he had to stifle his laughter since Fremont probably would shoot him.

After Fremont ordered his party of sixty to be prepared for a departure the next day, Miguel persuaded the Oregonian leader to leave immediately and travel as fast as possible so he could deliver his message to Larkin before Fremont's arrival. With only two more hours of daylight, the Oregonians hastily packed up and set out southward at a gallop.

No one in Fremont's camp or in the departing Oregonian party could know that hostilities between American and Mexican forces had already begun on the Rio Grande.

———————

As Fremont's party rode southward in California's Central Valley, they encountered settlers that were up in arms. Rumors of conflict with Mexico on the Rio Grande were heard repeatedly. Now, rumors circulated that Mexican authorities in California were preparing a force to expel American settlers. Settlers were banding together furiously to resist. When they learned that Fremont had returned, they looked to him for help.

Until he received undeniable confirmation that a state of war existed, Fremont was reluctant to commit his force to any sort of conflict in California. He encouraged the settlers but felt it premature to lead them.

Miguel was baffled at Fremont's stance. The captain had never before been hesitant when an opportunity to project himself into any situation offered a chance at self-aggrandizement.

Now that Miguel was in the central valley north of San Francisco, closer to Monterey and Larkin, they exchanged frequent messages. Miguel was never sure he had selected a messenger who would be trustworthy and discreet. He had no choice but to trust them.

Miguel's reports were simple accounts of Fremont's position, with only thin comment on the captain's posture or attitude. Larkin's replies were bland thanks and acknowledgments of receipt. Both feared interception of their messages by Fremont or Californio authorities.

Larkin also was exchanging occasional communications directly with Fremont. He sent copies of the messages to Miguel. Reading between the lines, Miguel agreed with Larkin that Fremont's reluctance to take part in the settlers' resistance to the authorities' actions to expel them simply meant that Fremont was biding his time. He would not ignore any sure opportunity to feed his vanity.

Miguel wrote that Fremont had commented frequently of late about Mariano Guadalupe Vallejo. A former general and Californio patriot, Vallejo was well known to favor an association of California with the United States and counted many Americans as friends, including Consul Larkin. Larkin replied to Miguel that he indeed was convinced that Vallejo would support American annexation of California.

Fremont, on the other hand, considered Vallejo a Californio leader and a dangerous man. When Miguel heard Fremont describe Vallejo thus, he assumed the captain believed so from ignorance. So he risked Fremont's ire and talked with him about Vallejo. He told him that Vallejo was favorable to the American intervention in California because he was convinced that Mexico inevitably would lose the province due to neglect and malpractice. Vallejo, Miguel said, would rather California unite with the United States rather than England or some other foreign power that lately had shown interest in California. Fremont, wrote Miguel, listened since this probably was news to him, but he said nothing. Miguel was convinced that Fremont was unmoved.

While he was composing a message to tell Larkin about his conversations with Fremont about Vallejo, he heard disturbing rumors about new developments. American settlers in the Sonoma area, where Vallejo lived, increasingly feared that Mexican authorities were going to make good on their plan to force Americans to leave California.

The belligerent settlers, now calling themselves the Osos, Bears, appealed to Fremont to lead the resistance. Fremont declined, still biding his time, and forbade any of his men from joining the Osos. Miguel guessed that Fremont had learned something from the Gávilan Peak fiasco. He dispatched the urgent message to Larkin.

Miguel left Fremont's camp and rode to Sonoma to try to learn what was amiss in the town. He fell in with a party of belligerents who were riding to Vallejo's home on the outskirts of the village. These were local American residents, not Fremont's men.

Arriving at Vallejo's home, the Osos declared him under arrest as the only Mexican authority in the area. Vallejo was polite to the ragtag force. He invited them into his house and offered them food, wine and brandy. He even offered his sword, which the now drunken rabble, apparently confused at the meaning of the offer, refused.

Unappointed leaders of the Osos pondered their next move.

Then things became complicated. A drunken element, impatient, went to the town, whether to buy or loot was uncertain. Back at Vallejo's home, others paced in the yard or lounged in the house, finishing the last of the spirits. Robert Semple, one of the few sober in the lot, drafted a document in which Vallejo surrendered the town with the understanding that the villagers and their property would not be molested. Some of the Osos were disappointed that there was no fight, no booty, no glory. Some said they should tear down Vallejo's house and ransack the town.

"I could only shake my head at their drunken stupidity," wrote Miguel later. "I was struck, though not particularly surprised, that one of the ruffians said in passing that Captain Fremont had ordered the whole affair, that is, the capture of Vallejo and the town of Sonoma. That's all I heard, and I don't know whether it was hope or fact."

At every opportunity, Miguel scribbled what he witnessed and something of his thoughts. He became particularly concerned when the belligerents rode away from Sonoma. "I rode with the Osos who were taking Vallejo somewhere. I didn't know where we were going. During the ride, one of the leaders, William Ide, repeated what somebody at Vallejo's house had said, that Fremont had ordered the action. Vallejo heard the comment and said that he was relieved that a United States Army officer had ordered the action. He said that this surely meant that he would be treated fairly. If I had heard Vallejo's comment firsthand, I would have been tempted to enlighten him on Fremont's what's-in-it-for-me attitude."

The party's destination was Fremont's camp. Seated at the campfire that evening, Miguel wrote a long letter to Larkin, describing everything that had happened in Sonoma up until this moment. He looked up from his pad at Mariano Guadalupe Vallejo, who sat on the other side of the fire, staring into the red and golden flames. So far, he was safe.

———

Next morning, Miguel stood beside his horse, head down, pretending to rummage in a saddlebag. He was listening to Vallejo and Fremont, sitting on a down log near the hobbled horses. He saw Vallejo's surprise when Fremont said that he, Vallejo, was not his prisoner. The captain denied any part in the raid on Sonoma and Vallejo's capture. Still, Fremont said he absolutely agreed with the complaints of the Americans in the Sacramento Valley, that they were being harassed and threatened by California authorities.

Vallejo soon was relieved when he and the other Sonoma prisoners were removed to Sutter's Fort.

———

It would be some weeks before Larkin and Miguel would know the outcome of Vallejo's confinement. Sutter was kind to Vallejo and the other prisoners, including providing medical attention. Little more than a month after their arrival, he ordered their release.

By this time, Larkin was convinced that the die was cast in the Americanization of California. An acquaintance at Sutter's told Larkin he had heard about a letter that Fremont had recently written, styling himself the "Military Commander of US Forces in California".

Later, reunited in Monterey and sitting in the consulate garden, Larkin told Miguel about the letter. They laughed so hard, they both spilled their aguardiente.

Miguel and Larkin discussed the conclusion of the Sonoma affair. The leaders had written a manifesto which established a republican government and declared that all Californios who surrendered their arms would not be disturbed. The Osos decided they needed a banner and came up with a flag picturing a crude fat bear, a five-pointed star and the words, "California Republic". The flag flew a few weeks over the Sonoma plaza, then was replaced by the Stars and Stripes as the revolution in Sonoma merged with and was replaced by the invasion of California by the United States Army and Navy.

Miguel was staying at Larkin's place when Fremont led his entourage into Monterey. Miguel and Larkin stood on the Consul's front porch and watched the party ride by. Fremont was dressed in a blousy shirt and leggings and wore a felt hat. He was escorted by five Delaware Indians who were his bodyguard. At least, they were described so when Miguel saw the Delawares in Fremont's Oregon camp. The rest of the party were a scruffy lot, rifle-wielding backwoodsmen who Fremont had forever tried to pass off as soldiers and scientists. Each was attired in a long, loose coat of deerskin and trousers of skins. They drove a herd of loose horses and a team pulling a brass field cannon.

Walking at the head of the motley column—strutting, Larkin said—Fremont glanced aside briefly at them, clearly made eye contact, made no sign of recognition and turned back to the front.

Larkin shook his head. He looked aside, spoke softly to Miguel. "I suppose he will find his uniform before he reports to his army superior. If he still acknowledges any to be his superior."

"That's not the end of the story, but it's the end of my story," Carmelita said. She sat on a large cushion at the fireplace. "Now you know Miguel as well as I do. I suppose most of you have read something of Fremont, but I hope you've learned a bit about him that you might not have known before. I sure learned a lot when I began researching my ancestor."

"Whoo," said Jon. "I always thought Fremont was one of the good guys."

"It depends on viewpoint, doesn't it?" Stephany said. "We don't *really* know what happened in the past. Read different accounts and you have different perceptions. For Fremont and the transition from Mexican California to an American California, read Hubert Howe Bancroft, still the most comprehensive historian of the period. And read Mariano Guadalupe Vallejo himself, the leading Californio historian. They actually agree more than they disagree, but you see what I mean. And read a comprehensive biography of Larkin by Hague and Langum."

"Or read Stephany," Carmelita said. "You've written good fiction about the period, Steph. I'd rather read Stephany's fiction than those guys' histories. More interesting. And you must do a lot of research for your fiction, Steph. You don't make it all up."

"Thanks for the compliment. You should write some

reviews of my books on Amazon." She smiled, pointing at Carmel. "I invent my stories—it's fiction, after all— but I try to stay close to the facts, *my* perception of the facts. Course, I alter bits and pieces when it suits the story."

She turned to Carmelita. "Anything more you can tell us about 'the little twit'? I love Larkin's name for him. Fremont didn't disappear. I've seen a lot of reference to him in my research."

"Oh no, he doesn't disappear. It's just the end of my ancestor's association with him. Miguel continued to work for Larkin. Larkin eventually sent him to Hawaii to oversee his ranching and timber businesses there.

"Fremont, on the other hand, remained in the public eye for years. Since Miguel had been so closely associated with him, officially, certainly not in a friendly way, I became fascinated with Fremont and followed his story in the record. It's interesting how such a person can make such a mark. Do you know, it wasn't long before he denied that Larkin was Polk's secret agent? Yeah, he claimed that *he* was Polk's secret agent!" Murmuring and chuckles.

"Wow," Adam said. "The guy sounds like he had a loose screw. It's surprising that his contemporaries did not suspect."

"Apparently, he was convincing. Fremont led American troops in California against Mexican and Californio forces. He served a time as military governor of California, but fell out with General Kearny, the commander of American forces in California, who ordered him to step down. Fremont refused—of course, he refused! He was arrested and sent back East where he was tried for treason and insubordination. He was actually convicted for insubordination. Polk pardoned him, but Fremont's vanity was injured, and he resigned from any public office he seemed to have held.

"Then what happened to him? He went back to California, became rich in the gold rush and was elected a United States Senator. Finally, he became a presidential candidate! How's that for a vain little twit?"

"Oh, my," said Jon, shaking his head, "vanity and injured pride can be strong incentives for pursuing any sort of objective. Even the presidency."

Chuckles and nods from the group.

CHAPTER 9

FAMILY

All the friends opted to spend the night at the cabin and be off this morning. They grumbled good-naturedly that they weren't accustomed to leaving accommodation without breakfast. Stephany apologized for not serving breakfast and assured them they would survive till they reached the resort café. Packed bags and cases stood beside the outside door.

Stephany stood beside the table, studying the assortment of friends, sitting and standing before the fireplace. "Folks, we have a few minutes before you take off to say what we want to say and ask the questions we want to ask. Roads should be clear, and I know how anxious you are to be on your way. I've made a pot of coffee for any who might be interested. If you're anything like me, you can't function before the first cup. There's also hot water and tea bags. Serve yourself."

Adam walked to the kitchen, poured a cup of coffee. He sipped. "Wonder what the weather is doing," he said. "Let's have a look."

Stephanie and Adam walked to the front door and

went out to the porch. A bright sun cast shadows in the yard. "Looks promising," Adam said. Snow had melted from the tops of cars. Fences and shrubs had emerged from their snow cover. They heard the distant growl of a snowplow down the hill.

They went inside and saw the others at the fireplace, holding mugs of coffee and tea, chatting about Fremont and snow and ancestors. She poured coffee for herself and joined the others at the fireplace. Jon said something to Adam, and they walked to the front door and went outside.

"Snow is melting," said Stephany, "and we heard a snowplow on the hill, I suppose putting the finishing touches on the road. Anybody have a final bit of wisdom to leave with us before you get away? By the way, it's interesting how some of these stories meshed, so many ancestors heading to California, a couple having an association with Larkin. It would be so interesting if we knew whether any of these ancestors met in California."

"Steph, I want to thank you for putting this gathering together," Donna said. "It has been most interesting. And stimulating!" Enthusiastic comments rose from the group. "Here's to Steph." She raised her coffee cup, and others followed, raising their cups and offering their compliments, thanks and huzzahs.

"Yes," Mindy said. "My interest in my gold rush ancestor has revived, and I'm determined to track her down. The Bancroft Library at UC Berkeley is a good source, by the way. I'm sure you've known that forever, Steph, but I didn't until the past year. I was surprised to find a reference to my Willis ancestor."

Stephany blinked, frowned. She turned abruptly. "What?"

"What what?"

"What did you say, the last name of your ancestor?"

"Willis."

Stephany recoiled. "But...but that's bizarre."

"Why bizarre?"

"My ancestor's last name was Willis."

"That *is* bizarre, interesting," Mindy said. She jumped at the sudden sound of porcelain shattering behind her. Everyone turned abruptly to look at Melissa who stood before the fireplace, the fragments of the cup at her feet. She stared, open-mouthed, at the pieces.

"What's wrong?" Stephany said.

Melissa looked up at Stephany. "My ancestor's name. You probably know that slaves usually were named after their masters. My ancestor's master's name, and his son's... was Willis."

At that moment, the front door closed, and Jon and Adam walked in. They stopped when they saw the women staring intently at them.

Jon frowned. "What's up?"

"Jon," said Stephany, frowning, "what's the last name of your ancestor?"

"My ancestor?" He frowned, looking down. "Hmm, let me think. Should know it." He looked up.

"Willis?" said Stephany, softly.

"Willis? Yeah, yeah, that's right! How did you know?"

Everyone turned to Adam, who looked back and forth among the others who stared intently at him. "You people are weird," he said.

"Adam?"

"Hmm." He looked down, frowning. "Don't remember. I've found it on ancestry.com. Hang on." He pulled his cell phone from a pocket, touched keys, stared at the screen, touched more keys, paused. He looked up, wide-eyed, jaw hanging. He spoke softly. "Willis."

Stephany slumped heavily on a chair. "I don't understand. How can this be? Can we be...related? All of us?

"Ah." Stephany looked at Carmelita who sat on the couch at the fireplace, staring into the flames. "I was about to decide that some cosmic force had made all of us related. But then there's Carmelita and Donna. So we'll have to assume that it's just a really, really, well, bizarre coincidence that five of us have ancestors with the same last name. She looked at Carmelita who did not appear to be listening, still staring at the flames.

"Carmel? You okay?" said Stephany.

Carmelita slowly looked up at Stephany. "My ancestor, Miguel Hurtado, married the daughter of a friend of Thomas Larkin. Her name was...Marion Willis."

Stephany put her hands on her cheeks. "Oh, my, my, my, my. This is really, really, *really*, well, bizarre. Can't think of a more descriptive word." She looked around at the group who were all in a state of shock.

The group, in unison, turned to stare at Donna. She stood at the fireplace, apart from the group. Her hands were on her cheeks, her eyes wide.

"Donna," said Stephany.

She spoke softly. "I don't know much beyond what I told, just...something. Kirk and Donna married and lived in Northern California, not sure where, on a ranch, I think. They had a daughter who married a local man's son. The son's name...his last name...was Willis."

Every member of the group was stunned. They looked at each other blankly.

"Where do we go from here?" said Carmelita. "We can't just go home and let this rest. There's no forgetting this."

Stephany stared at the flames, frowning. She looked up. "No, quite right," she said. "We will all go home, but we will not let it rest. Everyone, please, get back to work on this ancestor and keep in touch. I'm going to fill your inboxes with emails. I'll set up another gathering in spring.

"At that meeting, we'll each report on everything new we have discovered about our ancestors. Also at that meeting, I expect to construct a large family chart, showing where it all comes together...cuz."

A Look At:

A Harlan Hague Western Collection: Volume One

History isn't just written—it's lived.

Step into the untamed West, where survival is never guaranteed, and the pursuit of freedom comes at a cost. Award-winning author Harlan Hague brings the past to life in this masterfully crafted collection of Western historical fiction, blending adventure, romance, and raw frontier grit. From perilous wagon crossings and lawless boomtowns to sweeping cattle drives and forbidden love, each story is steeped in the triumphs and tragedies of those who dared to chase a new life in an unforgiving land.

Meet fearless pioneers, restless wanderers, and star-crossed lovers as they carve their destinies across the vast frontier. Whether it's a man outrunning his past, a woman forging a new future, or a scholar uncovering lost truths, their journeys will transport you to a time when honor was won at the end of a gun, and history was written in dust and blood.

This collection includes *Trails West, This New Country, Road to California, Now I Lay Me Down to Sleep, Leaving Ah-wah-nee,* and *Along Came Jenny*.

AVAILABLE NOW

ABOUT THE AUTHOR

Harlan Hague, Ph.D., is a native Texan who has lived in Japan and England. His travels have taken him to about eighty countries and dependencies and a circumnavigation of the globe, thereby proving the earth is round.

Hague is a prize-winning historian and biographer and award-winning novelist. History specialties are exploration and trails, California's Mexican era, American Indians and the environment. While a professor of history, he wrote history and biography and articles that were published in scholarly journals. Turning to fiction, he writes mostly historical westerns with love stories. One Western includes a time travel twist. Two novels are set largely in Japan and a novella in Belize. Some titles have been translated into a number of other languages. In addition to history, biography and fiction, he once wrote travel articles that were published in newspapers around the country, and he has written a bit of fantasy. His screenplays are making the rounds.

For more information about what he has done and what he is doing, visit his website at harlanhague.us. Hague lives in the San Francisco Bay Area.